Advance Praise for

Jack with a Twist

"Vibrantly written and visual. A funny, smart, true-to-life novel about being your own woman. Loved it!"
—Melissa Senate, author of *See Jane Date* and *Questions to Ask Before Marrying*

"Another fun-filled page-turner from Brenda. Every bit as sparkling as the champagne that the bride-to-be's mother is so fond of…."
—Carole Matthews, international bestselling author of *For Better, For Worse*

"The most delightfully hilarious wedding novel I've ever read; you'll either want to try on bridesmaids' dresses immediately or run screaming from your nearest bridal shop…. A hilarious look at the not-so-holy side of holy matrimony."
—Kristin Harmel, the Daily Buzz's Lit Chick, author of *The Art of French Kissing*

Praise for

Scot on the Rocks

"[A] rollicking debut… A breezy romantic comedy with plenty of laughs."
—*Booklist*

"Brenda Janowitz's debut novel is dynamite. The entire cast of characters is genuine and uncontrived. Her heroine is sassy, smart and fun, but also a bit naive… This is a book you would like to tell everybody about because you just can't say enough about it."
—*Coffee Time Romance*

"A quick and entertaining read. The main character's theatrical, high-energy personality comes through loud and clear, but it is Janowitz's secondary characters that develop and grow smoothly, rounding out the plot. Readers will enjoy the scheming, shopping and well-used irony that make up this New York tale."
—*Romantic Times BOOKreviews*

"A wonderfully funny, smart and engaging love story, and the narrator's voice and vulnerability make her extremely likable. I found myself routing for Brooke no matter how sometimes silly her decisions…This is a perfect book for the beach or a plane ride, or, really, any time you want a fun and funny escape. I will never look at a man in a kilt the same way again."
—Jennifer Oko, author of *Gloss* and *Lying Together*

"I absolutely loved the sense of humor and sense of surprise in this novel. There were several moments where I laughed out loud."
—Jill Smolinski, author of *Next Thing on My List* and *Flip Flopped*

"[A] laugh-out-loud debut novel."
—Kristin Harmel, author of *The Blonde Theory*

"I enjoyed *Scot on the Rocks* predominantly because of Brooke's voice. She's sweet and very funny and I really enjoyed her asides to the reader. As a character, she'll stick in my mind…"
—*Trashionista*

"Hilarious and entertaining…a believable tale of love, madness and hope."
—*Fresh Fiction*

Jack with a Twist

(Engaging your adversary and other things they don't teach you in law school)

Brenda Janowitz

"Janow

JACK WITH A TWIST

A Red Dress Ink novel

ISBN-13: 978-0-373-89555-7
ISBN-10: 0-373-89555-0

www.RedDressInk.com

Printed in U.S.A.

For Doug, the man of my dreams.

You were worth the wait.

LEGAL DISCLAIMER

This book in no way depicts any actual events or actual people. Yes, the book is about a woman planning her wedding to the man of her dreams, and Brenda Janowitz did, in fact, plan her wedding to the man of her dreams, but this book is totally not about that.

Especially as pertains to the character of Brooke Miller's mother. Please note that Miriam Miller is in no way related to, similar to, or based on Brenda's mother, Sherry Janowitz. Sherry Janowitz is a wonderful and perfect human being. She is in no way flawed like the maternal character depicted in this book. And while we're on the topic, the character of Barry Miller is in no way related to Brenda's father, Bernard Janowitz. (Although, if you want to know the truth, he isn't nearly as uppity about it as his wife. And both Barry and Bernard *are* devilishly handsome, but the similarity ends there.) Further to the point, just because the character of Brooke Miller is an only child, this in no way should be taken to mean that Brenda Janowitz does not love and adore her brother, Sammy Janowitz, sister-in-law, Stephanie Janowitz, and nephew, Noah Janowitz. And while we're on the topic, the Luxenberg family is not the Solomon family. They're just not. You'll see what we're talking about when you read the book. Which is not at all based on reality.

It's just fiction, people! Geez. Doncha hate it when people get all lawyerly about stuff?

Prologue

And they lived happily ever after….

Maybe I should have asked my mother for some clarification on that. Exactly *what happens* after they ride off into the sunset together? Do they park the white horse at Bloomingdale's and go register for wedding presents? Do their families argue about whose castle will host the wedding? When the families disagree on something, does someone end up in the moat?

Why didn't twelve-year-old me think to ask for clarification on that one?

Today should have been the happiest day of my life. Well, not the happiest—the day Jack proposed to me, *that* was the happiest day of my life—but today should certainly be *one of* the happiest days of my life. After all, I love shopping, I love that I'm getting married to Jack, and so, *therefore,* I should love wedding dress shopping. What could be better than combining these two fabulous things, à la the discovery of the Reese's Peanut Butter Cup? Well, maybe combining shoe shopping with my excitement about getting married would be better, but you get the general point I'm trying to make.

The point is, I should love wedding dress shopping. But, I don't. So far, it has been a haze of obnoxious and fake salespeople, unwanted commentary on my weight from my mother, and a wave of general dissatisfaction on my part. And that's just today.

"Are you planning on losing any weight before your wedding?" the salesperson asks me.

"Um, yes?" I say, careful to position my body just so, away from the three-sided mirror, which has the effect of thrusting my cellulite directly into the line of vision of my mother, who is standing outside the dressing room in yet another mother-of-the-bride dress. The salesperson zips me up, and I turn around to face my mom.

"Oh, my God, Brooke," my best friend, Vanessa, says, "you look so beautiful I think I'm going to cry!" Vanessa is not the type to cry—in the eight years since I've known her I can count the times I've seen her cry on one hand—so if she says she's about to cry, this dress must be really good.

"I hate it," my mother says, "take it off." And then, to the salesperson, "Do you have anything with capped sleeves? Something to hide the fleshiness on her arms." She whispers the word *fleshiness* as if, even though I'm standing but two feet away from her, I cannot actually hear her.

"I can hear you," I say, reaching for the glass of champagne my mother is holding for me, the one given to me when we first arrived at the store. That was back when wedding dress shopping was all air kisses and warm congratulations. Now that our salesperson has agreed with my mother when she called me fat, I could really use something a bit stronger, but I'll settle for the bubbly.

"Empty calories," my mother sings, moving the glass away

from me and taking a sip. "I'm just trying to find a dress that would make the most of your figure, BB." I guess I don't have to mention here that my fifty-two-year-old mother, a petite size six, with a crown of honey-blond hair, looks better in her dress than I do in mine.

"Marilyn Monroe was a size twelve in her heyday," I say to no one in particular. "And no one ever called *her* fat. I'm only a size ten."

"Marilyn was a bit fleshy, dear," my mother says, admiring herself in the mirror. If I didn't have to work and could take tennis lessons three times a week like my mother, maybe I would be a size six, too. Although, if I had that much free time, I like to think that instead of tennis lessons and mah-jongg, I'd fill my time with charity work and more important Angelina Jolie-esque type activities. And shopping.

What? You have to get new outfits for all those big important dinners at the UN, don't you?

"Your figure is perfect," Vanessa says. Vanessa *has* to say this because she's my best friend. It's in some sort of friendship handbook or something. Come to think of it, I think it may also be in the Code of the Girl Scouts. I'll have to look that up sometime. But, either way, she has to say that.

She especially has to say that I look skinny to me because she's tall and thin and is a dead ringer for Halle Berry and I'm short and not thin and not a dead ringer for anyone. Yes, Vanessa is tall and thin and gorgeous and she is *still* my best friend. I really think that says a lot about my character, don't you think?

"Vanessa's right," my mom says, now clearly tipsy from downing my entire glass of champagne in two gulps. "All of these dresses are made for skinny, anorexic girls. We Miller girls have curves. Let's get out of here."

"Let's have a bite to eat before we go to our next appointment," I say to my mother as I take the empty champagne glass from her hand.

"May I ask where you're going next?" the salesperson asks as my mother and I retreat to our dressing rooms to change back into our own clothing.

"Monique deVouvray," Vanessa says and I can practically hear, from inside my dressing room, the salesperson's mouth dropping to the ground. I look up and see Vanessa trying to pretend that she doesn't notice, as if she goes to the most exclusive dress designer in the world every day, but I can see the edges of her mouth fighting back a tiny smile. Reason number 432 why Vanessa is such a great friend—she hates this mean salesperson as much as I do for asking me if I was planning to lose weight all morning, while my mother, the size six, fit into every dress in the showroom perfectly. (Salesperson: "What a figure! Did you use to dance?" Me: "I took ballet and tap until I was twelve." Salesperson: "I meant your mother." My mother: "Well, I do love to cha-cha!")

"Yes, our appointment at Monique's," my mother says with a slight French accent, trying to stand up without teetering over. "We really must go."

My mother was so excited when we got an appointment with Monique deVouvray, wedding dress designer to the stars, that she bragged about it for three weeks at her weekly mah-jongg game, which was funny since she was mispronouncing Monique's last name for the first two of them.

"My mother will kill us if we're late for Monique," Vanessa says, leading the charge out of the dressing room.

"Your mother *knows* Monique?" the salesperson asks, doing her best to furrow a Botoxed brow.

"Yes, she does," Vanessa says, her right arm linked in my left as she guides me quickly to the elevator. "Thanks so much for everything. Bye!"

As we hit the button for the elevator, I can hear my mother whispering to the salesperson that Vanessa's mom used to model with Monique. My mother dashes into the elevator just as the doors are about to close (I was willing to leave her up there, it was Vanessa who pushed the door-open button), and in moments, we are down at the car.

Vanessa's dad lent us his car and driver for the day so that we could hop around town to our various appointments. The three of us pile into the backseat of Vanessa's father's huge Mercedes (affectionately dubbed the "Nazi-mobile" by my mother) and head uptown.

"We need to get you a bite to eat before stopping at Monique's," I say to my mother. "We don't want you throwing up all over the couture."

"There are a million little delis up Third Avenue," Vanessa offers.

"Let's go to Tasty D instead," my mom slurs. "A moment on the lips, a lifetime on the hips!"

She's been saying that my whole life.

"Tommy," I say to the driver, "would you please pull over here?" I run out of the car and hop into Dunkin' Donuts, returning with a massive cruller, a delicacy that I know my mother cannot refuse.

"Well," my mother says, "I suppose I could have just one tiny bite."

Vanessa rolls her eyes.

By the time we pull up to Monique's exquisite Upper East Side brownstone, my mother has downed the cruller…and also a stale cup of coffee that Tommy still had up front since this morning.

The brownstone looks exactly like the type of place where Monique deVouvray and her glamorous French businessman husband, Jean Luc—a couple who've been fodder for the tabloids since before Lindsay and Britney were even born—would live. To call it a brownstone doesn't even really do it justice. It's a huge brick house right across the street from Central Park. The ground floor is divided by a gated portico, and if you peek in (never mind those pesky security cameras), you can see straight back to the lap pool. On the left side of the portico is a two-car garage and on the right is a white brick stairway leading to the front entranceway—a huge mahogany double door with a big brass knocker, monogrammed with Monique and Jean Luc's initials. Basically, the entrance to their single-family home is nicer than the one in the more-than-we-can-really-afford co-op building where Jack and I live. Actually, the entrance is really nicer than ninety-eight percent of the buildings I've ever seen in New York City. And that's including Gracie Mansion.

As we walk up, I can hear clicking over my shoulder. I turn around to see a photographer hiding behind a parked car across the street. Only his lens peeks out from the hood of the car. A tiny smile creeps onto my lips. Now that I'm going to the person who designs wedding dresses for movie stars, maybe *I'll* start being mistaken for a movie star! Vanessa sees me sucking in my stomach for the camera and says: "No need to get ready for your close-up, Brooke, they're not here for us. The paparazzi is always staking this place out, just waiting for something to happen."

And it often does. In 1979, Mick Jagger took off all of his clothing in the middle of a cocktail party at Monique and Jean Luc's brownstone and jumped right into the lap pool. This probably wouldn't have made news but for the fact that as he jumped, he dragged Monique with him. Who was wearing a white dress with very little underneath. (*Playboy* reportedly offered her one million dollars to pose nude after the "white dress" pictures became public, explaining to her that everyone's already seen it all. Monique, to hear *People* magazine tell it, was unamused.) In 1985, Brat Packer Bobby Highe was caught in a compromising position in one of the guest bathrooms with Monique's niece. Who was fourteen at the time. He somehow got out of the criminal charges, but later told *Vanity Fair* that it wasn't fair—French women were so beguiling that he really had no choice. (Which, strangely, later became the advertising slogan for Monique's signature perfume when it came out the following year.) In 1998, it was Monique's husband who was front-page news—hosting a very bizarre "business" meeting in their kitchen with various condiments being used and passed around, but no actual food in sight. And on a summer evening back in 2003, you couldn't get within a ten block radius of the entire Upper East Side since Monique and Jean Luc were hosting an engagement party for Jennifer Lopez and Ben Affleck. The New York Police Department had to block off the entire eastern side of Central Park since photographers and tourists all up and down Fifth Avenue blocked traffic by standing smack dab in the middle of the street.

But I assume that nothing like that will be happening today. Even so, it's not a bad idea to suck in my gut.

"How do you know they're not looking to take pictures of us?" I ask, turning my head slightly so that the pap can get my best angle—left side of my face.

"They're not," she says. I can feel her eyes burning into the side of my head.

"Yes, but how do you *know?*" I say, careful not to move, so that I don't mess up the shot.

"I just know," Vanessa says, "okay?"

I begrudgingly nod back at her, but I can see her standing a little straighter, no doubt for the benefit of our invisible paparazzo friend.

On the first floor of Monique's brownstone, we are greeted by a doorman, which is strange for a private single-family residence. Even in New York City, only large apartment buildings usually have doormen. But then Vanessa explains the set-up to me: Monique's studio is on the second floor and she lives with her husband on the top three floors. (Vanessa doesn't say a word about the lap pool, but I know what I saw.) I should mention here that it is absolutely impossible to get an appointment with Monique—she only designs for movie stars and diplomats and really, really, *really* rich people, so she doesn't have an open showroom that you can just walk into off the street. (That and the fact that the *Post*'s Column Five gossip mavens are always looking to catch her or her husband in the act of something.) We only got our appointment because of Vanessa's mom, Millie—she and Monique lost touch for a while after modeling together in the sixties, but had recently become friendly again when Millie needed a dress for a reception at the Metropolitan Museum of Art's Costume Institute.

"You must be Vanessa," Monique says as we enter her studio, pulling Vanessa in for a hug. "You're just as beautiful as your mother. She tells me that you are a big important lawyer?"

"Well, I don't know how big and important I am," Vanessa says, "but I *am* a lawyer. And so's our bride. We actually used to work together at Gilson, Hecht before Brooke abandoned me."

"You still have Jack working with you there," I say, smiling at my self-indulgent mention of my fiancé's name.

"Ah, Brooke, our bride," Monique says.

She kisses me on both cheeks and I introduce Monique to my mother.

"Enchanté," my mother says and curtsies. Maybe we should have stopped off at McDonald's—the woman is clearly still drunk. I look over to Vanessa for some assistance with my mother, but she has meandered over to look at a framed copy of an old *Vogue* cover with both Monique and her mother on it. The contrast between Millie's dark skin and Monique's pale complexion is striking, and I watch Vanessa examine every square inch of the photograph. Millie, who I see frequently at her downtown art gallery, is every bit as gorgeous today as she was then, if not more so.

So is Monique. Who is now seated on a love seat with my mother. Who is drinking yet another glass of champagne.

"A celebration, no?" Monique says in her thick French accent, handing me my own glass. She wears black cigarette pants and a pristine white button-down shirt with its sleeves rolled up. On her feet, she wears simple black Chanel ballet slippers. Vanessa is wearing the same pair today in tan. Monique's hair is pulled into a tight bun, pinned back in exactly the same way that Vanessa's mom wears hers.

"Absolutely," I say, taking the glass, and trying to push my mother's drink as far away from her as possible without actually tipping it over the edge of the coffee table.

"So, Brooke," Monique says, "Tell me a little bit about yourself. I want to know everything. Tell me about what you like, what you don't like. Everything."

"She wants something with sleeves," my mother says, reaching across the bowl of candy that Monique has placed on the table, in a play for her champagne glass. Hasn't that woman learned her lesson?

"Mom," I say, trying to appear happy to be here with my skinny lush of a mother.

Monique intervenes: "Let us do this," she says, "Mother, you will look at mother-of-the-bride dresses while I go with daughter to look at some dresses for her. Yes?"

"Well, I don't want to steal my baby's thunder," my mother says as Monique guides her to a rack of beautiful dresses. Monique only does couture, so every dress is put together entirely by hand, with extensive beadwork and exquisite seams and workmanship. She has a few samples on hand for my mother to study and, like a baby with something shiny in her hands, my mother is mesmerized. We leave her at the rack.

Monique and I walk over to another area of the showroom where she has a number of muslin garments in different styles.

"First," she says, "we put you in just a few things to see what styles you like best. What works best. Yes?"

"Yes," I say.

"Is there a style that you know you want for sure?"

"I'm pretty open."

"Very good," Monique says, "Then we try. Off you go."

I go into the dressing room with Vanessa and she zips me into the first dress, an A-line with a sweetheart neckline.

"So, are you okay with all this today?" I ask Vanessa.

"Of course," she says, smiling as she smooths out the dress for me, "I'm having a blast. Why wouldn't I?"

"Because," I say, looking at myself in the mirror. "Well, you know. I just don't want today to bring up any bad memories for you or anything."

"I'm okay," Vanessa says, still smiling, "I'm just happy for you." I turn to face her and I notice that she's still wearing her wedding ring. I wonder if she was wearing it all day and I just didn't notice it, or if she put it on in the car so that she won't have to face any questions about her impending divorce from an acquaintance of her mother.

"So, what do you think?" I ask, as Monique comes into the fitting room.

"Beautiful," she says as she picks up an enormous sketch-pad and starts to draw. "How do you feel?"

"Pretty good," I say.

"This next," she says, gesturing with her pencil. Next up: a spaghetti-strap bodice with a huge ball gown skirt.

We go in to dress, and I turn to face Vanessa as she zips me up. "Do you want to talk about it at all?"

"No," she says. "But I have an appointment next week to meet my divorce lawyer for the first time. I was thinking that maybe if you weren't busy...."

"Of course," I say, "I'll be there. But, am I coming as your lawyer or your friend?"

"Friend," Vanessa says with a smile and I smile back at her.

"Now that we don't work at the same law firm anymore, I *could* represent you, if you want," I offer.

"You're a commercial litigator," Vanessa points out, "so if

I want to start a copyright action, you'll be the first person I call. For this, though, you can just come as my friend."

"Done. So?" I ask, twirling around like a little girl trying on her mother's dress. "Do you like this one?"

"Too princessy," Vanessa says, as I walk out of the fitting room for Monique to take a peek.

"Beautiful," Monique says again as she looks up from her sketch pad. "How do you feel in it?" She says the same thing for each of the six other muslins I try on for fit.

After the scoop neck with a straight skirt, Monique has me change and come back to the love seat. First, she tells Vanessa and I about how she makes each individual wedding dress. To demonstrate her point, she takes out some of the dresses she is working on to give us a sense of her workmanship. Each one is more beautiful than the next—miles of lace, tons of tulle and acres of silk—I'm almost afraid to touch the pristine white fabric. One dress in particular catches my eye. It's got a deep V down the front, ending in a gorgeous crystal brooch, with a flared trumpet skirt. The detail is absolutely impeccable. As Vanessa and I ooh and aah over it, my eye catches a tiny ink stain at the base of the dress. I look at Vanessa to see if she notices it, too, but she's already on to a cowl neck with an A-line skirt.

I'm completely paralyzed—what should I do? Should I dare tell *the* Monique deVouvray that there is actually something wrong with one of her gowns? One of her masterpieces? Someone's dream dress? What if this woman's wedding is this weekend and there's no time to fix the dress? I don't want to be responsible for ruining someone's dream!

Worse yet, Monique could have a you-break-it, you-buy-it policy. And let's face it, if my mother thought I looked fleshy in a simple gown, I'm quite certain she won't approve of all of the flesh that would be on display in this number.

Okay, this is fine. Be cool, be confident, and act like you didn't even notice this little mistake. Just move on to the next dress. I covertly check my hands for blue ink.

"Brooke, I see you've noticed my blue good luck ribbon!" Monique calls out.

"I didn't touch anything!" I say. I was never quite good at playing it cool.

"Flip over the fabric," she says, walking over to me. "It is a tradition that when you are making a wedding dress for someone by hand you sew in a blue ribbon for good luck. I do that for each of my dresses. So, now let us see the sketches I have drawn up. Just to give you idea of what I will do for you."

Monique has created six fabulous sketches for me—each one incorporates different details that I mentioned as being my favorites and the styles that flatter me most.

The second I see it, I know. I just know. The sketch jumps off the page and practically speaks to me. Although it's a rough black-and-white drawing, I can practically see my face in the scribble where a head should be.

The bodice has an off-the-shoulder sweetheart neckline fitted tight to the body with bones inside the thick silk. It has capped sleeves that flow naturally from the neckline and give the dress an air of romance. The bottom of the dress is an elegant A-line, not too princessy—just the right amount. The final perfect detail is a beautiful silk ribbon that ties around the waist. It is elegant and understated and everything I could possibly hope for in a wedding dress.

"That's it," Vanessa says, pointing at the sketch.

"I know," I say, turning toward her and smiling.

"Ta da!" my mother says as she comes out of the dressing room in one of Monique's gowns. I am immediately concerned about this for two reasons: the first is that Monique did not tell my mother to *try on* any of the sample dresses. Rather, she merely brought her to a rack and told her to start looking. The second is that it's not a mother-of-the-bride dress at all. It is one of Monique's wedding dresses.

"Did Monique give her more champagne?" I whisper to Vanessa. Vanessa laughs out loud and then quickly covers her mouth with her hand.

Now, if I were Monique, I would have screamed, "Take that dress off right this instant, you drunken deranged idiot!" But, Monique is far too classy for such things. Instead, she says, "Ah, yes, Ms. Miller, what a gorgeous figure. You look good in everything I create. Let me help you out of that and we can discuss your mother-of-the-bride dress."

My cell phone rings as Monique and my mother are walking back to the fitting room. I look at my caller ID and see that it's my fiancé, Jack.

"Jackie," I say. Just seeing his number come up on my caller ID makes me smile uncontrollably.

"Brookie," he says. "How's it going?"

"Fabulous," I say, fantasizing about how perfect we are going to look together on our wedding day. Even if Jack showed up in a paper bag, he'd look great—all shaggy brown hair and gorgeous baby blue eyes—but I'm sure that he'll wear an actual tuxedo. A brown paper bag wouldn't really match my couture.

"That good?" he asks. "So, I guess your mother is behaving herself?"

"Well, no," I say, glancing over at my mother who is now dancing by herself to the soft jazz Monique has playing, spinning in tiny circles like a little girl at her own birthday party. "But, it doesn't matter. Jack, I found it."

"Found what?" he asks.

"The one," I say, barely believing it as the words come out of my mouth.

"I thought *I* was the one?" he asks. "Don't tell me that you found another guy to marry?" He pauses dramatically. "Well, even if you did, you found him at a bridal boutique, so I'm sure I can take him."

"No, I mean—" I say. "Okay, yes, you are *the one,* you know that. I didn't mean that."

"What *did* you mean?" he says and I can practically see his devilish little smile through the phone lines.

"I mean, I found it! I found the perfect wedding dress."

Column Five

Sightings...

WHAT "monster" Hollywood star was seen walking into Monique deVouvray's Upper East Side townhouse yesterday? She's vowed, after her two failed marriages, never to walk down the aisle again, but could this visit to the most exclusive wedding dress designer in the world mean that she's finally tying the knot with her longtime boyfriend and "model" father of her child?

2

Since Jack and I have been engaged, we've been living in delicious sin in a two-bedroom apartment in Gramercy Park. Okay, okay, we've actually been living in sin since *before* we got engaged, but you get the general point I'm trying to make. The point is that things are fabulous, even if we did jump the gun on the whole moving-in thing just a bit. But if anyone asks you, just tell them that we were engaged before we moved in together. *Especially* my grandmother. She is eighty-two years old and a very traditional Jewish woman from Poland who most certainly would not understand living with someone to whom you are not married. In her day, a nice Jewish girl would never live with someone without the benefit of clergy. Unless you were hiding out from the Nazis, in which case it would then be perfectly all right to cohabit for a period of time. And maybe even make out a little bit. I'm not sure about that one. But to be officially, legally living in sin? Well, that's a big no-no.

Which is why she has no idea that Jack and I actually live together. I almost got busted at our last holiday dinner—after a few too many glasses of Manischewitz kosher wine (yes, I know, tastes like grape juice, but still amazingly effective in getting you tipsy), she cornered me and wanted to know all about my fiancé. She started with the easy questions, like where did he grow up? (A suburb outside of Philly.) How many siblings does he have? (Three sisters.) What does his father do for a living? (Federal judge for the Third Circuit.) Then, she asked a seemingly innocuous question that completely threw me for a loop: "Where in the city does Jack live?" When I carefully told her that he lived in Gramercy, she was delighted. She said: "How lovely! Do the two of you live close to each other?" So I did what any girl in my position would do. I cheerily responded, "Yes!" Which really isn't lying, if you think about it. We *do* live close to each other. Very very *very* close. All I actually did was to leave out the part about *how* close we live to each other. I just couldn't bring myself to actually tell her about the we-sleep-in-the-same-bed part.

Oh, please! As if you'd be running to tell your eighty-two-year-old grandmother that you were living in sin.

But a life of sin has been working out for Jack and me just fine.

"So, there's talk of this big new case coming in to the

firm," Jack says to me on Saturday morning. We're seated at our breakfast bar with mugs of hot coffee and the newspapers sprawled out.

I know. A lazy Saturday morning with your fiancé, a hot cup of coffee and *The New York Times.* Heaven.

"That's great, honey!" I say, taking a bite of my toasted sesame bagel. "Which partner is bringing it in?"

"Mel, I think," he says and I nod in agreement. "Which is perfect since he loves my work." I nod again, since I know that if Mel is, in fact, the senior partner bringing the new case in to the firm, Jack's got a great chance of being assigned to it and taking the lead on it.

I should explain: Jack and I met when we worked together at my old law firm, Gilson, Hecht and Trattner, which is why I know all of the partners there and how things work in general. I've since left big-firm life for a smaller law practice, but Jack is still at Gilson, Hecht, where he recently became a partner.

"This could be really huge for me, Brooke," Jack says and I look up from my coffee at him. He moves a stray curl of my shoulder-length auburn hair back behind my ear with a finger.

"You've already made partner, Jack," I say, putting my hand on his cheek. His face is rough to my touch since he hasn't yet shaved this morning. He looks so sexy when he's got that slight trace of a shadow. "Everyone loves you and thinks you're amazing. You've proven yourself at the firm. That's why they made you a partner in the first place. Don't you get to sit back and breathe at this point?"

"Brooke, I really need this," he says, "there are over three hundred associates at Gilson, Hecht and over one hundred partners—I just need that one big case to come my way to establish me as a force to be reckoned with in the firm. Rumor has it that this case may even involve a celebrity, so there would be media recognition, too."

"Ooh, celebs," I coo. "I hope it's J. Lo."

"She doesn't like to be called that anymore," Jack says, "and I'm being really serious here. I want to take my career to the next level. Soon we're going to be thinking about children and I want to be able to support them in the lifestyle to which you've become accustomed."

I smile and take that as a cue to glance down at my diamond engagement ring—not only is it beautiful, but it's especially meaningful to me, since it's the ring that Jack's grandfather gave to Jack's grandmother when he proposed all those years ago. They were married for sixty-two years, so a ring like that's got to be lucky, right?

The Asscher cut of the center stone is deep and thoughtful. You could get lost for days just staring down at it, deep into its center. Which has been happening to me with increasing frequency since Jack gave it to me.

Whenever I look at my ring, I can't help but think about how happy I am to have found Jack. That mythical "one." To be settling down with the man that I love. Now that we're engaged, I feel so secure. Before the ring, you live in constant fear that your guy will just come home one day and tell you that he doesn't love you anymore or that it's not you, it's him, or that he met someone else, or some other such nonsense.

That's probably because that's happened to me in real life more times than I'm willing to admit, but I'm sure that I'm not the only woman alive who's ever felt that way. Let's face it, if you've survived being single in your mid to late twenties in New York City, you're bound to have had your heart totally trampled one or two times.

Or forty-seven, but who's counting?

Truth be told, the last serious relationship I was in before I got together with Jack was with a guy who came home one day and out of the blue told me that he didn't love me anymore, that it wasn't me, it was him, and as a kicker, that he'd also met someone else. (And a bunch of other nonsense.) But I don't have to worry about that with Jack.

I don't think.

Do I have to worry about that with Jack?

"Are you even listening to me?" Jack asks, positioning his face close to mine.

"Of course I am, honey!" I say, looking up with a smile. What was he saying just then?

"You were just staring at your ring," Jack says, matter-of-factly.

"I was not," I say, smiling a little wider, "now tell me about the case."

"I really don't know any details about it," he says, "No one does. It's just a rumor right now. Firm-wide speculation that Mel's bringing in a big case and that he'll want one of the junior partners to take the lead on it, thus solidifying that junior partner's status in the firm for the rest of his or her life. Nothing that special."

"Well," I say, edging closer to him, "you're going to get the case and you'll be amazing. And I'll be the loving, doting fiancée who is here to help you every step of the way."

"*If* I even get it," he says, looking down.

"*When* you get it, you mean. You know what we need here?" I ask Jack, walking toward the living-room closet.

"What?" he asks, running his hand through his shaggy brown hair.

"To tell the future," I say, and at the precise moment that I say it, I find just what I need—a gag gift that Vanessa bought for Jack and me right when we got engaged: a Magic 8 Ball.

"That's not a real Magic 8 Ball," Jack says, as I pull the gag gift out of the closet, "That's a gag gift. It's a special *Love* Magic 8 Ball. It's pink, for God's sake. I don't think that those can actually tell the future."

"Well, you broke the real one," I say, remembering the original Magic 8 Ball that Jack, Vanessa and I used to consult all the time when we worked at Gilson, Hecht together as associates. We'd pull it out anytime we had a tough decision to make—whether it be a legal cause of action, an e-mail being sent to opposing counsel, or what to order in for dinner that night, that magical sphere always had the answers for us.

"The real Magic 8 Ball was mine to begin with," Jack says, walking over to me, "and anyway, I only broke it because I was mad at you, if I recall correctly."

"You broke it because you were mad at me? How very Stanley Kowalski of you," I say with a chuckle. When you're six feet tall and rail-thin like Jack, you can't really pull off the tough-guy thing very well. It actually turns out to be sort of cute, which, if you really think about it, is *so not* the intended effect.

"Brooke!" Jack screams from his gut, as if he were screaming "Stella!" at the foot of a long staircase. He calls out "Brooke!" again, this time falling down to his knees and ripping his pajama top apart for good measure. "Brooke! Brooke!"

I suppose that I don't need to mention here that Jack was a drama geek back in college? So much so that he actually wanted to become an actor after he graduated. Two years of waiting tables (and the fear of God put into him, courtesy of his father, the United States Circuit Court judge for the Third Circuit) kicked him of the thespian habit, though. However, he does still enjoy the random dramatic flair from time to time.

"I'm sure whatever it was, it wasn't really my fault," I say. It's important to train your man early into thinking that nothing is ever *really* your fault. I learned that little tidbit from Vanessa. Which is really good advice. And just because she's presently going through a divorce doesn't necessarily make her opinions on marriage null and void, I don't think.

"Magic 8 Ball," I say, shaking the pink globe around. "Will Jack get the big new case coming into the firm?"

"It's not a real Magic 8 Ball," Jack says, swiping it away from my grasp, "it says right here that it is a Love Magic 8 Ball, so it can really only tell the future of your love life."

"Humor me anyway. What does it say?" I ask.

Jack turns it over to read the response: "It says, You may get lucky."

"See?" I say, "it *does* work! You're going to get lucky! The case is as good as yours! Fame and riches await!"

"No," he says, sidling up to me, "It's a Love Magic 8 Ball, so I think it means that I'm going to *get lucky*." And with that, he throws me onto the couch and showers me with kisses.

"Lucky, indeed," I say and sink into his kiss. This sort of thing never happened back at the firm with the old Magic 8 Ball.

Back then, Vanessa, Jack and I were the Three Musketeers. Since Vanessa and I were the same class year, we seldom worked together—it was usually just Jack and me. Jack was the senior associate on all of our cases, with me as the junior associate for five years running, but nothing ever happened between us during that time. Okay, okay, a few things happened during that time—a massive flirtation and a handful of unbelievable, monumental kisses (the kind they write love songs about)—but in an effort to keep our jobs, we didn't really pursue things.

The story of how we finally got together is really terribly romantic—after being the best of friends for years, he came with me as a fake date to my ex-boyfriend's wedding and we fell completely, madly, desperately in love right that very evening! Well, actually, it wasn't quite that simple, since that evening ended with us getting into a huge fight and not speaking for three weeks afterwards, but *after* those three weeks, we fell completely, madly, desperately in love. But it just sounds more romantic to make it seem like it all happened that same night.

(Note to self: must read and approve all wedding speeches and make sure there is no mention of any fighting and only a focus on falling completely, madly, desperately in love….)

What? Any good bride worth her taffeta maintains creative control of the wedding speeches.

3

Back when I was single, I would do crazy things like bring fake dates to my ex's weddings and obsess endlessly about shopping and how much I hated work. But, in my new incarnation as a mature engaged woman, I find myself acting like a mentor to some of the younger women in my new law firm, Smith, Goldberg and Reede. I offer them sage advice about love, relationships and making the time for a career while having a life. We talk about the serious issues facing young women in the world today and we, like, totally love our jobs.

"Ohmigod, I cannot believe you are having Monique deVouvray design your wedding dress for you," Esther Rhee, my favorite second-year associate says to me. "*The* Monique deVouvray!"

"I know, right?" I say, leaning back in my office chair. The offices at SGR are all equipped with enormous, ergonomically correct chairs that have the ability to lean back almost a foot. Which, ironically, is probably not so good for your back.

"Did you get to meet her husband?" Esther asks. "They're in the gossip pages all the time together and he is almost as gorgeous as she is."

"I didn't get to meet him," I say.

"Actually," Esther reconsiders, "he's more gorgeous than she is. Did you see them at the premiere for the new Robert DeNiro film? He was so dreamy."

"Jean Luc does sort of have that Clive Owen thing going on, doesn't he?" I say.

"No," she corrects, "Clive Owen sort of has that Jean Luc Renault thing going on."

"True," I say, doing a quick Google search on Monique and her husband, resulting in approximately one million hits. I find the picture of them at the DeNiro premiere and turn my computer screen around to show Esther.

"They are so fabulous. You can only eat salad with balsamic vinegar, grilled chicken and grilled salmon until the wedding," Esther says, leaning onto my desk.

"I know," I say gravely, turning my computer screen back to center and then flipping my chair back to a seated position.

"Because you wouldn't want to offend Monique—can I call her Monique?—by getting fat and then not fitting into the dress she made especially for you," she says. Has Esther been talking to my mother? If she calls my arms fleshy, I'm kicking her out of my office right now. "Maybe if everything goes well with Monique—I can call her that, now, right?—designing your dress for you, maybe there's a chance that she'll design mine for me!"

"You're not even engaged yet, Esther."

"I know, but I like to plan ahead," she says. "*And* I had a very promising blind date last week."

"Has he called yet?" I ask, eyes widening. I love a good blind date story. Especially now that I'm engaged and don't have to go on them anymore.

"Well, no," she says, putting her head down into the set of documents she carried into my office. "But it's only been a week and two days. So, he's probably just really busy with work."

"Definitely," I say, trying to think of what Vanessa used to say to me after a promising blind date failed to call me.

We sit in silence for a moment before we are interrupted by Rosalyn Ford, one of the partners at the firm.

"I'm so glad the two of you are together," she says, leaning against the door frame of my office. "Were you two just working on our case?"

"Yes," I say, nodding. "We were."

"Of course," Esther says, holding up her stack of documents and waving them around as proof.

"Well, stop everything you're doing," Rosalyn says, her booming voice as loud as ever, "because they're about to cave."

"I thought that this case was going straight to trial?" I asked, furrowing my brow as if I really, really cared about the case. It was a joke I shared with Vanessa. As a lawyer, you are frequently in situations where partners dramatically pause while they're talking to you, just waiting for your reaction. It's not until well into your first year that you learn to master the various expressions you are expected to give back: the "I'm so horrified that opposing counsel would do that" face, the "I'm so excited to work on this lame-ass case with you" face, and the classic "you are so funny and clever in the way that you handled that judge/witness/child under the age of five!" face. Here, I was using the old "I am so interested in this case that I'm hanging on your every word" face and I could see over my desk that Esther was doing the same.

I've taught her so well.

"Well, it's not," Rosalyn says, her face lighting up as she gets ready to tell us the rest. "Opposing counsel called me and wants to meet me this afternoon. They're about to cave, I just know it."

"Congratulations," I say. "You've worked so hard on this case."

"Go get 'em!" Esther says, balling her hand up in a fist and raising her arm just like Rosie the Riveter. We all smile as Rosalyn leaves my office.

"Thank God," Esther says once Rosalyn is out of earshot, throwing her pile of documents down onto the floor of my office, "I totally did not want to have to read all of these documents."

"Ms. Miller," my assistant says, her velvety voice smooth even over my intercom, "Ms. deVouvray is here to see you. May I send her in?"

"Monique deVouvray?" I say, stalling for time.

"Yes," my assistant confirms.

"Um," I say, "Don't send her in. I'll come out and get her."

"She's here?" Esther asks, eyes popping out of her head like in a Bugs Bunny cartoon.

"Apparently," I say, getting up from my desk.

"You can't let Monique deVouvray come in here," Esther says, standing up and blocking my path to the door. "She is an icon of style, beauty and grace. This place is neither stylish nor beautiful nor graceful. If she sees it, she may not want to design your wedding dress for you anymore!"

"You're right," I say, grabbing boxes of documents and trying to stuff them into the drawers of my credenza.

"And then *my* chances with her will be gone!" she says.

"A little help here," I say, pointing over at the corner, where there's a huge stack of fake Levi's that I'm using as evidence in a trade dress infringement case I've been working on.

"The documents and boxes are the least of your problems. Start with the desk," Esther says to me, taking her right arm and sweeping all of the junk that was sitting on my desk into a drawer. The effect is striking—for the first time since I began working at SGR, you can actually see the deep cherry-red wood of my desk. My in and out trays sit quietly on the right corner of my desk, with my computer on the left. For a lawyer's office, it looks pretty darn elegant and refined.

I could have sworn that I had also had a half-finished cup of coffee on my desk, but when I open the drawer where Esther's thrown my things, I can't find it. There's just a huge pile of junk.

"I'd better go get her," I say as Esther shakes her head furiously, clutching her documents to her chest. I know that she is thinking the same thing that I am: I am so lucky to have a wedding dress designer who is so dedicated to creating the perfect wedding dress for me that she even visits me at work!

I guess this is why her dresses are so expensive.

"Well, this is a surprise!" I say with a smile as I approach the set of couches where Monique is sitting. SGR's offices are very understated and I hoped that to Monique, they seem elegant and refined, and not boring.

"Ah, *bon jour,* Brooke," Monique says as she kisses me on both cheeks.

We settle in to my office and I notice that Monique has in her hands an antique handkerchief with subtle embroidery. See, now this is the sort of accessory I should be adding to my wardrobe. Now that I am a newly engaged mature woman, I, too, should be running around midtown holding antique hankies like a socialite. Although I guess socialites don't work in law offices in midtown. But, nevertheless, I must remember to check with my mother to see if my grandmother has any old handkerchiefs lying around from her childhood. Before she fled Poland, that is.

"I suppose you are wondering why I am here," Monique says, raising the handkerchief to her left eye and dabbing lightly.

"Well, yes," I say, "I know that you wanted to get to know me a bit better, but—"

"It's Jean Luc," Monique says, cutting me off, her eyes

welling up with tears. I wonder why the mention of her fabulous husband would make her cry. Those don't exactly look like tears of joy.... I reach for a tissue, but then remember that Esther's dumped the entire contents of my desk into a drawer, so I grab a deli napkin out of my purse instead. "Things are not working out," Monique blurts out.

And with this, she begins to cry. Delicately. Lightly. Like a lady, barely making a sound. I'm marveling at the fact that she can cry in such a feminine manner. When I cry, it sounds like a foghorn and my nose begins running like a sieve. It must be because she's French.

"Oh, Monique," I say, as I open the drawer to look for some real tissues to offer the poor woman—clearly, deli napkins are not going to cut it here. As I open the drawer, I feel something extremely hot drip onto my legs.

"I don't really handle divorce," I explain, "I'm more of a commercial litigator, but I can certainly help you find someone great who can help you."

"I'm sorry, Brooke," Monique says as I locate the tissues and pass a few to her. "It's not that I want a divorce.... It's not the marriage. Yes, the marriage isn't going too well, either, but I think that the problem is that we work together, live together, do everything together. That's why I'm here. I'm looking to dissolve the business partnership I have with my husband."

"Monique, I'm so sorry," I say, as the coffee continues to drip onto my leg. I subtly try to find the offending cup, but can't figure out how to do so without appearing like I'm not listening to Monique.

"You did say that you specialize in commercial litigation, yes?" she says.

"Yes," I say, taking a few tissues from the drawer and draping them over my legs, which are beginning to sting.

"I thought that maybe by coming to you we could keep this out of the press?" she says, dabbing her eyes with her handkerchief. "That's why I thought it would be wise to come here." I wonder why she hasn't gone to Vanessa at Gilson, Hecht, seeing as she is friends with her mother, but I decide not to press my luck. Especially since the piping-hot coffee is beginning to hurt my legs. Is that the smell of burning flesh?

As Monique fills me in on the background of her business with her husband, I try to take notes even though all I can think is: *That blue good luck ribbon that she sews into every dress must not really work.*

Twenty minutes later, we wrap up our meeting and I've officially secured my first client. I hope that when I stand up from my desk, Monique won't notice the huge puddle of coffee that has gathered in my lap and is now dripping all the way down to my ankles.

"I cannot thank you enough, Brooke," Monique says as we walk out of my office, me brushing off my skirt and dripping brown liquid all over the carpet, "and of course, your discretion in this matter is very much appreciated."

"Think nothing of it," I say, hoping she doesn't draw me in for a hug. The ivory-colored pants she's wearing are no match for my coffee-infused skirt. And it would be a shame to lose a potential client over a dry-cleaning emergency.

"Thank you," she says.

"There is just one more thing, Monique," I say, as I walk her to the elevator banks. I'm rubbing my legs together to evaporate the coffee that's dripping down them, my hand placed over the spot on my skirt where it's all spilled, "and, I mean, this is just strictly business. I mean, this is something that the partners would want to know, you know, inasmuch as it may relate to your case."

"But, of course, Brooke," Monique says, "whatever you need to know."

"You're still going to design my wedding dress, right?"

"And the best part is," I tell Noah Goldberg, one of the founding members of the firm and the "G" in the SGR, "she's still designing my dress!"

"Well, she can't design your dress if you're representing her," Noah says with a laugh.

She can't? Why can't she? Should I have consulted the rules of ethics before I came into this meeting? Surely there's some provision about associates and their wedding dresses? "But, I am thrilled for you. Your first case!"

My wedding dress, is all I can think. *I love that dress more than anything in the world. More than the French love Jerry Lewis. More than the Germans love David Hasselhoff.* I manage to eke out: "My first case!"

"I'm really excited for you, Brooke," Noah says, "you remind me of myself when I got my first big case." It's never a good sign when a partner, founding or otherwise, tells you that you remind him of him. That can only mean one thing—you're about to be slammed with more work than you ever thought possible. "And I think you're ready."

"For what?" I ask. More traumatic trips to wedding boutiques with my mother? I know that Noah sees me as a big-time lawyer who can handle anything, but I am *so not* ready for that.

"To take the lead on this case."

"What an honor," I say. "What a thrill! Who will be working with me on it?" I'm secretly hoping that he'll say that Esther can work on the case with me, but I don't want to sound as if I don't appreciate the opportunity. I will just act thrilled and enthused no matter what associate he tells me he's going to assign to this case. There are five different first years that I'd be happy to work with—Jordan, Ethan, Spencer, Oliver and Ruby are all great, and there are four other second years that wouldn't be bad, either—Stacey, Jon, Jen or Lee have great reputations, too. Maybe I'll even get *two* junior associates to work with! And I won't complain or say a word if one of them's not Esther.

"I don't know if you need any more manpower on the case just yet," he says. "Let's start off by staffing it lean and mean and take it from there, okay?"

Um, that is *so not* okay.

"Okay," I say, trying to hide the look of horror that is no doubt crossing my face at this very instant. At my old law firm, Gilson, Hecht, such a case—a complicated commercial litigation with a fabulously famous client—would have been staffed by at least four attorneys. And Noah wants me to go it alone?

I immediately rush back to my office and start researching the cause of action of dissolution of partnership. Next, I draft a very professional e-mail thanking Monique for her business and asking her to gather the partnership contract and various non-compete agreements that she had with her husband, and then arrange for a messenger service to pick all of it up from her brownstone. After that, I pick up the phone to call Vanessa.

What? After getting all that work done, I think I deserve a little work break, don't I?

"There's no such thing," Vanessa interrupts.

"There is, too," I say in a stage whisper, careful not to let any partners walking through the halls hear me.

"Brooke," Vanessa says, "there is no such thing as 'wedding dress law.'"

"Could you please just research it for me?" I ask, eyes darting furtively to my office door.

"And what client should I bill this to?" she asks. I can't see her since we're on the phone, but I get the distinct sense that she's tapping her foot at me as she says this.

"Healthy Foods," I say, invoking one of Gilson, Hecht's biggest clients, and one that I worked for almost exclusively when I was still at the firm, "I don't care!"

"You want me to bill it to your old client?" Vanessa asks.

"Yes," I say, practically ducking down under my desk as I see Noah walking by my office door with one of the other partners.

"You do realize that your fiancé is now the lead on all Healthy Foods matters, right?" she says.

"Which is exactly why he'll let the billing go though," I explain, "Now type."

"Can you get disbarred for billing personal stuff to a client?" Vanessa asks.

"No!" I say. Yes. In fact, that's the main reason why most attorneys get disbarred. But that shouldn't really stop two women on a mission, should it? And anyway, this research is *important.* "They won't mind at all. And they really do charge way too much for their coffee. I just went to a Healthy Foods the other day and my cappuccino was almost five bucks. The least they can do is help me out with this teensy tiny little issue."

"What am I searching for here?" Vanessa asks. I can hear her beginning to type.

"Try typing in *ethics* and *wedding dress,*" I say. "And put *wedding dress* in quote marks so that you search for the full term, not the two words separately."

"You don't have to tell me how to do a Lexis search, thank you very much," Vanessa says.

"Well," I say, "I *did* have to tell you what to type in."

"That's because what you want me to type in is crazy," she explains. "You want me to find a case where the court holds that it's not a breach of your ethical duties to have a wedding dress designer create your wedding dress for you when you're representing her in a dissolution of partnership action."

"Exactly!"

"Every lawyer knows that you can never find a case that matches *your* exact case perfectly," Vanessa says, speaking to me as if I were a small child. Or a first-year law student.

"When you wanted me to research whether or not 'randomly kissing some sleazy skank' counted as a grounds for divorce," I ask, "did I tell you that was crazy?"

Vanessa doesn't respond, but I do hear the frantic tapping of keyboard keys over the phone.

"I've got something on a lawyer stealing money from a wedding dress designer's escrow funds?" she says, still typing away.

"Nope," I say. "I don't want her money, just her dress."

"How about this one—Southern District of California. Woman sues her wedding dress designer, who promised that she'd design a custom gown, on the grounds that the dress the designer created for her was not actually unique. Seems after this designer created the custom gown for this customer, the designer then began mass-producing the dress. Someone wore the same dress to the wedding that the bride wore herself."

"Oh, my God, I'd be so pissed!" I say. "And who wears white to a wedding? If you see anyone show up to my wedding in white, please kick them out."

"The designer had mass-produced the dress in forest green," Vanessa says. "So, the guest showed up in the same dress as the bride, only hers was green."

"If that happens to me, please still kick them out," I say.

"I'm not really finding any cases that are on point for you, Brooke. Sorry."

"Well, keep looking," I say, as I open a window on my computer to begin a search on Westlaw. I hang up just as Vanessa's saying something about having other work to do and I do, too, to be sure, but clearly my work on "wedding dress law" trumps all of that.

As the partners stop by my office all afternoon to praise me for my good work and dedication to the firm, one by one, like a receiving line to the Queen, all I can think is: *My wedding dress…*

4

Is it inappropriate to start making a mental checklist of who I want to have in my bridal party when I'm sitting in a divorce attorney's office with my best friend? I mean, I can still be supportive of her and her divorce even while I'm thinking about my own wedding, right? No laws against that?

Okay, okay, so maybe it's a tiny bit self-centered of me to be thinking about my wedding party while Vanessa laments the end of her own marriage, but I'm going to ask her to be my matron of honor, and that should probably cheer her up! Although, she'll be divorced by the time I get married, so I guess that would make her the *maid* of honor. Not like she's an old maid or anything!

Perhaps I shouldn't bring this up right now.

"Vanessa, Ms. Cohen is ready for you now," the assistant

says. Vanessa takes a deep breath as she stands up. I stand, too, and give her a big hug.

It's been hard for Vanessa to come to grips with the fact that her marriage is ending—I mean, obviously it would be hard for anyone to go through a divorce, but Vanessa has the added pressure of little to no support from her mother and the rest of her family, in general. They all seem to think that Marcus is the second coming of Christ, despite the fact that he kissed another woman while they were married. Well, he is tall and slim like Jesus, and ridiculously handsome and rather ethereal-looking, so, if it's true that Jesus was actually black, they may have a decent argument.

But then there's that whole kissing-another-woman thing. I'm pretty sure that those people who wear those WWJD bracelets—What Would Jesus Do?—would categorically tell you that the one thing that Jesus would *not* do is kiss another woman while married to Vanessa. It was just that one woman that one night, but still, it broke Vanessa's heart and she still hasn't fully recovered. Not long after she and Marcus separated, I went to dinner with Vanessa and her mother, and her mother repeatedly advised her to "get over yourself and go save your marriage."

My mother couldn't understand why Vanessa was getting a divorce either:

"How could you divorce a doctor?" my mom said to Vanessa on one of our wedding gown shopping expeditions. "Clearly, you are not Jewish. A Jewish woman would never divorce a doctor."

"Being married to a doctor isn't all you'd think it would be, Mrs. Miller," Vanessa said. "Being married to a doctor has its disadvantages."

"Like, for example," I said, "anytime you're in a crowded place and someone screams, 'Is there a doctor in the house?' he has to say 'yes.'"

See how good I am at defusing a difficult topic and changing the subject? I don't want to brag, but in addition to being a big-time lawyer, I also have an undergraduate degree in child psychology.

Oh, please. As if you don't employ the same skills in dealing with your mother as you do in dealing with a small child.

"Well, there's that," Vanessa said, "but I meant more like the fact that he's never home. He's never there."

"Well, yeah," I said, "and the whole doctor-in-the-house thing."

So, Vanessa's really going through with the divorce. And now the only person she can depend on is me.

"You can do this," I say and Vanessa nods unconvincingly back. "Want me to come in with you?"

"No," she says quietly, "I think I have to do this part on my own."

"Well, I'll be sitting right here," I say. "So just let me know if you need me."

"Okay." Vanessa squeezes my hand and I watch her as she walks into her attorney's office.

Should I have insisted that I go in there? Vanessa's been my best friend since our first year of law school and I hate that she's going through something so painful right now. I should have just insisted that I go in with her. I consider for a second whether I should just walk back there and insist on sitting in on Vanessa's meeting. But having your best friend bum-rush your first visit to your divorce attorney probably doesn't set the best tone for an attorney-client relationship, so I opt to stay out in the reception area, like Vanessa's asked me to.

As the door shuts with barely a sound, I sit back down and take out some work that I brought with me to do while I wait for Vanessa. I look at my research on dissolution of partnership. My initial research revealed that this was a fairly straightforward case, and I realized why Noah must have assumed that I could take the matter on by myself. Monique's partnership agreement is well-written and clear—its elegant language should make this matter go smoothly and easily. This research shouldn't really take very long at all.

Which really frees me up to do some more thinking about my bridal party: Vanessa will lead the charge as my matron/maid of honor, with the rest of the party rounded out with Jack's three older sisters. Even though I haven't met Jack's older sisters yet, I just know that when our families meet, they are all going to love each other immediately and Jack's sisters will be my new best friends.

I walk to the other side of the reception area to get myself a cup of coffee—after all, in one short afternoon, I've figured out my entire case *and* planned out my wedding party. Surely I deserve a snack.

"It will be easier to start getting over him once you take

that ring off," a strange voice whispers to me as I'm pouring my coffee. I turn around to see the epitome of tall, dark and handsome leaning over my shoulder. As I melt into his hazel-green eyes, it takes me a second to realize that I'm still pouring the coffee. And that I'm engaged. I look down to see that I've spilled my coffee all over the countertop.

What is it with me and coffee lately? I just got this skirt back from the dry cleaners after my last run-in with an errant cup of joe.

"Me? Oh, no, I'm not getting a divorce," I say, "I haven't even gotten married yet! I'm just here to support my friend who's going through a divorce."

"Oh," he says, already turning to walk away from me, his broad shoulders sinking just the tiniest bit, "sorry about that."

That guy was really hot! I think. *I guess I've still got it! Off the market and still a little heartbreaker….*

I immediately e-mail Jack a message from my BlackBerry to tell him how I get hit on left and right when he's not around. He e-mails back a very detailed message that explains all of the things he plans to do to me later to ensure that I never ever ever stray from him, not even for one minute.

I put my BlackBerry away with a smile and scan the room. (What can I say? Some single girl habits die hard….) The guy who approached me isn't the only hot guy in the room. Everyone in this office is pretty hot, including Vanessa's divorce lawyer herself, Stephanie Cohen. *This would be a great place to meet someone,* I think to myself, looking around the room at all of the good-looking eligible men. Not one is wearing a wedding ring, so they are all clearly single! Or about to be, any minute! What a great place to meet men—I wish I'd known about places like this back when *I* was single. And now that I've discovered this hot spot, I'm already engaged. Life can be so unfair sometimes.

I wonder if Stephanie ever dates her hot clients after their divorces are final and they are free and single again. What? I mean once they aren't her clients anymore, I'm not trying to insinuate she'd do anything unethical. Geez!

As I stir my coffee, I notice the tray of mini cupcakes sitting next to the coffee set-up. Now, I know that I should be on a wedding diet, but now that Monique's not designing my dress, maybe it would be okay to have just one cupcake. It suddenly dawns on me that now that Monique isn't designing my dress anymore, I don't have a dress. I'm back at square one. And I don't even know where to go and look for a dress, since my mother made me have a nervous breakdown at nearly every bridal designer's showroom in town!

Don't panic, you will find another dress. I take the napkin wrapped around my cup of coffee and tear it into halves. *After all, finding a wedding dress is easy! People find wedding dresses every day of the week—how hard could it possibly be? Why, I'll probably find one in the next store that I go to!*

Okay, I didn't even convince myself on that one.

I have no wedding dress! I've got the guy, but no dress. *What am I going to wear down the aisle?* Okay, be cool, be confident. You'll find another dress. Maybe I should just take a tiny peek at a bridal magazine to start getting some ideas. Get those creative juices flowing again.

The *New York Law Journal,* the *National Law Journal,* the *New York Times,* the *Wall Street Journal*.... Nary a *Vogue* or a *Glamour* or a *Marie Claire* to be found. Which is really odd, seeing as Stephanie is so put together and well-dressed. Just because it's a lawyer's office, that doesn't mean that they can't have *any* fun magazines? Don't they know that there are people here who need wedding dresses? Would it kill them to have a *Bride* magazine?

Okay, maybe that's pushing it, since I'm at a divorce attorney's office. Must focus my energy on more important things. Like mini cupcakes.

"Brooke, is that you?" a voice from behind me asks just as I've popped an entire mini-cupcake into my mouth. I turn around to see Monique deVouvray standing right behind me.

"Oh," I say, trying to swallow quickly, "Monique."

"What are you doing here?" she asks in her thick French accent. She's dressed impeccably, just as she was on the other occasions when I'd seen her, but I notice that she's got a large scarf wrapped around her head like she's Bridget Bardot and is wearing enormous Chanel sunglasses that hide half of her face.

"I'm just here with a friend," I say, stirring my coffee. I don't want to tell her that it's Vanessa, since the last thing Vanessa needs right now is for her mother's acquaintances to know about her divorce and how quickly it's moving forward.

"Well, I'm just here to talk to a lawyer so that I know my rights," she says in a hushed voice. "Just talk. I'm not filing for divorce or anything." She looks around the room furtively before looking back to me.

"I won't tell a soul," I say as Monique pours herself a coffee—black. I marvel at the fact that she doesn't even give a second look at the mini cupcakes. Or the hot guy with the hazel-green eyes. French women have so much self-control.

"My prenuptial agreement is very complicated," she says. "As a lawyer, I'm sure you understand that."

"Of course," I say, my voice barely a whisper.

"Robin Kaplan is supposed to be very discreet," she says, evoking the name of the most famous divorce attorney to the stars in New York City. "And I'll count on you to be the same."

"Of course," I say as an assistant comes over to us and tells Monique in a whisper that Robin Kaplan is ready to see her. Monique bows her head as she follows the assistant back to Ms. Kaplan's office.

First the dissolution of partnership and now a divorce. The tabloids will have a field day with this. Monique and her husband are a New York City institution, and have been since they first got together back in the seventies. I consider, for a moment, telling Vanessa about seeing Monique. Maybe it would make her feel better. After all, if a couple like Monique and Jean Luc can't make it, who can? But then I consider that perhaps this conversation would fall under the attorney-client privilege that Monique enjoys with me, since I *am* representing her in her dissolution of partnership from said perfect husband. Who, after all these years, can't seem to make it work. *What if Jack and I can't make it work?*

I begin stuffing mini cupcakes into my mouth.

Vanessa and Stephanie walk out of Stephanie's office just as I'm licking some frosting from my fingers.

"Thank you for everything," Vanessa says, giving Stephanie a hug. I wipe my hands on a napkin just in time for Vanessa to introduce me to Stephanie.

"Did that guy hit on you?" Stephanie whispers as she shakes my hand, nodding her head in the direction of the tall, dark and handsome stranger who spoke to me earlier. "My assistant said that he came over and hit on you."

My goodness, I am *so* on fire that even Vanessa's divorce attorney's assistant noticed! My hotness simply cannot be concealed. Even a trained eye like that of a divorce attorney can tell that I am so fab that I get hit on left and right even *with* my engagement ring on!

"Well, I might be taken," I say as I flip my hair off my shoulders, "but I've still got it."

"That guy hits on everyone," she whispers, "that's why he's getting a divorce."

Or not.

I immediately reach for another mini cupcake.

5

I half expect to hear the theme song to *Dynasty* ring out every time I pull up to Jack's parents' house. Just twenty minutes outside of Philly, it is an enormous home that sits on seven acres of immaculately maintained landscaping, complete with its own double tennis court, Olympic-sized swimming pool and accompanying pool house that is larger than the house I grew up in.

Seeing it tonight, now through my parents' eyes, it's like I'm here for the first time again. I remember when Jack took me home to meet his parents, how that ever-growing feeling of surprise grew like a pit in my tummy as we drove down the tree-lined block, houses getting bigger and grander by the second.

I knew the house would be elegant—after all, Jack's father

is a federal judge for the United States Court of Appeals for the Third Circuit and his mother is a socialite, so, of course their home would look like something out of an Aaron Spelling nighttime soap. It's just that I hadn't expected it to be quite so, well, large. Jack is totally down to earth, and on the few occasions when I'd met his parents, they seemed very unassuming as well. Although maybe I should have known that the house would look something like this from the places we'd have dinner whenever Jack's parents met us in the city. It's a veritable Zagat's Top Ten whenever Jack and I dine with the Solomons: Le Bernadin, Per Se, Danube… the more extensive the wine list, the better. Usually, when my parents come into the city to take Jack and me for dinner they drive us out to Don Peppe's in Queens, an amazing Italian joint just a stone's throw away from JFK airport where the owner's grandmother is the head chef and they only serve homemade red wine.

We stop at the tiny guardhouse at the foot of the driveway to announce ourselves, and as the tremendous wrought-iron gates open for us and we drive up the winding driveway, my father announces, "Your tax dollars at work." I say a little "thank you" to the gods above that Jack decided to head up earlier in the day to spend a little time with his parents before the big meeting-of-the-families dinner and isn't in the car to hear the play by play of the first reactions to the house. On the car ride up, I'd tried to subtly warn my parents about the size of the Solomons' house, since I didn't want their mouths to drop to the floor in front of Jack. But, as it turns out, there's really no easy way to warn your parents about your in-laws-to-be's house without making your parents feel totally and completely inferior. Which is why I ended up not saying anything to them at all.

As we pull up to the front door, I see Jack standing outside, waiting for us. Even though he's over six feet tall, he looks like a little boy against the massive fourteen foot double doors. They're carved out of a rich mahogany that is a striking contrast to the whitewashed brick that covers the rest of the house. My father drives around the courtyard circle to pull right up to the front of the house, but then my mother complains that it is rude to park right in front of someone's house, so we drive around the circle two or three times until my mother is happy with the placement of where my father has parked the car. Jack's sisters and their husbands haven't arrived yet, so there is no way to gauge where we should park. But the grounds are landscaped to the hilt, so I consider all of this driving in circles to be a nice opportunity to take a look around at the beautiful trees and sculptures adorning the property.

Hopping out of the car the moment it stops, I fly up the steps and into Jack's arms.

"Nervous?" he whispers into my ear as we hug. I can smell his aftershave, and it goes down my spine.

"Not at all," I say, running my fingers through his shaggy brown hair, "What do *I* have to be nervous about?"

"We come bearing gifts!" my father bellows, the thick Brooklyn accent of his youth ever-present, as we take off our coats in the foyer. It is a vast entranceway with a beautiful antique table as its focal point, a floral arrangement climbing four feet high in an Hermes vase right in the middle. Servants materialize from out of nowhere to whisk away our coats and then disappear just as quickly as they arrived. My high heels make more noise than I intend as I walk along the cool, ivory marble that covers the entranceway floor, and I begin walking on the balls of my feet in an effort to make less noise.

Jack's mother, Joan, comes floating into the foyer, looking impeccable, as usual. She's dressed in the sort of thing you'd imagine Jackie O, in her Jacqueline Kennedy years, wearing for a simple evening of entertaining at home: black high-waisted palazzo pants and a crisp white shirt with French cuffs. She's even got her thick dark brown hair styled just like Jackie's, shoulder length with just the right blend of subtle movement and helmet head. I can see a smile cross my mother's lips as she winks at my father and I know that at this precise second, she is thinking that she does not have to worry about the mother of the groom upstaging the mother of the bride. You see, she has this thing about high-waisted palazzo pants. She thinks that only women who have something to hide (read: fat thighs) wear them.

She often encourages me to wear high-waisted palazzo pants.

As I kiss Joan hello, the first thing I notice is that she is wearing the pair of Manolo Blahniks that I wanted to buy last month. This realization creeps me out a bit and I wonder if there are any other strange similarities between Joan and me that will mean that Jack is a total mama's-boy freak.

My mother is wearing a form-fitting black shift dress, her best set of pearls, and black pumps with a kitten heel. Am I the only one who didn't get the dress-like-Jackie-O memo today? Are Jack's sisters going to show up dressed for *Camelot,* too?

I, instead, am dressed like Audrey, with a big ballerina skirt and a matching wrap sweater. It makes me giggle when I see that the crimson tie that Jack's wearing with his navy sports jacket and gray trousers matches my ensemble exactly. Not even married yet and already we think exactly alike! The meeting of the parents? For a couple like us, that's no problem! Tonight's going to be a piece of cake.

"You shouldn't have," Jack's mother says, as she reaches out for the package my father is holding. My father and I had a huge fight regarding the package he is holding. When it comes to a hostess gift, my father seems to think that nothing says "Welcome to the family" like a nice cut of beef tenderloin. I tried explaining to him, to no avail, that giving your future in-laws raw meat was inappropriate, even if you are a kosher butcher.

In fact, giving raw meat as a gift is never appropriate in *any* situation, an argument which my father sharply refuted. ("It is never inappropriate to give raw meat as a gift. Never.") I explained that there is nothing that is festive or celebratory about raw foodstuff, even if you did lovingly pick out each cut of meat. It is simply not done in polite society.

Especially when you're going to meet your future in-laws for the first time.

Which is why I have a bouquet of white roses and lilies

in my hand, which I place firmly in Jack's mother's other hand in a vain attempt to distract her from the packet of E. coli that my father has just given her.

We all hug and kiss awkwardly and make the introductions as Jack's father, Edward, walks into the foyer. As my mother curtsies and calls Jack's father "Your Honor," I try to laugh and pretend that she's joking. Since she's not laughing herself, it's a tough sell. Jack sees what I'm doing and begins laughing himself.

See why we're so perfect for each other?

"So," my father says, "open it! I have a feeling you're going to want to open what I brought you right away."

"How sweet," Joan says with a smile.

"I brought flowers!" I call out, in a pathetic effort to distract Jack's mother. But, there's no fighting it. No matter what I do or say, she's about to open the present.

"This is very interesting wrapping," she says, as she puts a perfectly manicured finger underneath the tape that holds the butcher paper together.

"Don't you want to look at the flowers first?" I say in desperation. "They're white lilies! Your favorite!"

She looks up at me for a second, wondering, no doubt, why I'm pushing the flowers on her like one of those urchins who accost you in the streets of Paris, but the fact of the matter is that I just do not want her to open that package. There has got to be some way to distract her. Maybe I should just grab Jack and kiss him passionately and everyone will be so charmed by our young love that they will drop what they are doing (or opening, as the case may be) and forget all about my father's hostess gift. Or maybe I could hit the fire alarm and get everyone out of the house quickly. But then I guess that sprinklers would go off and that would, like, totally mess up my hair and makeup. And, anyway, pretending to set the house on fire the first time your parents come to your future in-laws' house is probably not the best way to make a first impression.

I turn my face away as Joan opens the package and the meat almost falls onto the floor as she looks up in horror.

Why, oh why, couldn't I have just been orphaned at birth like other kids? Life can be so unfair sometimes.

"Oh, my goodness," Jack's mother says, looking somewhat faint, "it's raw meat."

"That's my best cut of beef tenderloin I've got there for you," my father says, beaming.

"How very kind," Joan says, as she passes off the red slab to a servant who appears out of nowhere.

"I'll help you get it on the barbecue," my father suggests. "I've taken the liberty of pre-seasoning it, so we can toss that baby right onto the grill."

"Thank you, Barry," Jack's mother says, "but the chefs have already prepared dinner for us this evening."

"Oh," my father says, looking like a little boy who's been chosen last for teams during gym class.

"Anyhow," Joan stage whispers to my father, "I'm a vegetarian."

"You don't say?" my father says and looks at my mother. My father doesn't trust vegetarians. Especially vegetarians who are wearing six-hundred-dollar leather shoes.

After the dust on Tenderloingate has settled, we sit down at a mammoth table in the Solomon's formal dining room where we learn that the main course is—gasp!—fish. My father is not pleased. ("These fancy chefs of theirs never heard of a surf and turf?")

I'm seated next to Jack somewhere smack dab in the center of the table, with my father on one end, to the right of Jack's mother, and my mother down on the other end, to the right of Jack's father. My mother will later tell me on the car ride home that they were placed in the "seats of honor" at the table. I make a mental note to look that up for truthfulness on the Internet later.

Jack grabs my knee under the table and I giggle in his direction. As I look up, I catch Jack's oldest sister, Patricia, watching us from across the table. I smile at her with a look that says, "Ain't love grand?" but she averts her eyes as soon as hers meet mine.

All three of Jack's older sisters appeared, husbands in tow, soon after my family had arrived and we'd made our way into the salon for pre-dinner drinks.

I know! Who has a salon?

Jack's sisters weren't really what I thought they would be—I envisioned them grabbing me and pulling me aside and showing me the room Jack grew up in. No doubt, in our excitement about the families coming together, we would all jump on his bed and start giggling like schoolgirls as they regaled me with funny stories about Jack's childhood. Tales of braces and first kisses and awkward haircuts and hijinks at various family bar mitzvahs. Isn't that what siblings are for? Being an only child myself, I really had no idea, but I could imagine. Growing up, the closest I'd ever come to a sibling was the life-sized Barbie head that my mother bought me when I was five. But I thought that Jack's sisters and I would be immediately on our way to being best friends forever and sisters for life.

Instead, Jack's sisters came in and greeted me with firm handshakes, clipped smiles and formal introductions to their respective husbands. It was as if I was on a job interview at a law firm, except at most of the firms I'd interviewed at, the partners were much warmer or, at the very least, pretended to be.

Meeting all of Jack's sisters and brothers-in-law was such a blur that I didn't quite catch all of the brothers-in-laws' names, and not just because the names are all nearly identical: Adam, Alan and Aaron. This was because, just as I was being introduced to the various brothers-in-law, Jack's father poured champagne for a toast with my parents, and I was panicked at the mere thought of my mother drinking the happy juice. I didn't want her to embarrass me in any way (more so than usual, I mean), and I *especially* didn't want her to start bragging about my new big case. In addition to the fact that the case was highly super secret, I hadn't even had a chance yet to tell Jack about it or about the fact that because of it, I now needed a new wedding dress. Although maybe my mother wouldn't spill the beans because she was too embarrassed to admit even to her mah-jongg friends that Monique wouldn't be designing my dress anymore. (Me: "Just tell them that we didn't want to spend so much." My mom: "I will do no such thing!" Prompt hang-up of the phone for effect.)

Also, the three brothers-in-law all bear an uncanny resemblance to each other, from their receding hairlines to their pastel Loro Piana cable sweaters to their black Gucci loafers, so I really can't be held responsible for remembering who's who. Now, I know what you're thinking—why didn't I simply study some pictures before I came here? See, that's the thing. I *did* study pictures of all of the siblings, or siblings-in-law, as the case may be, but all Jack really had were the various wedding photos of each couple. The eldest, Patricia, is now forty-five years old and got married seventeen years ago, so you can only imagine how different her husband looks now. The middle sister, Elizabeth (*not* Liz, mind you, it's Elizabeth), is forty-two years old, and got married ten years ago. Lisa, the youngest at thirty-nine, got married three years ago, but by that time, all of the guys were already beginning to morph into each other. Lisa's husband did have more hair on his wedding day, but by now, he just looks like the other two. Apparently, being married to a Solomon sister makes all of your hair…well, you know where I'm going with this one. Don't make me say it.

And don't think that I could identify them by their various married names. As I was informed by Jack's mother one night during dinner at Park Avenue Café, the Solomon sisters do not change their names.

I did manage to work out a positively brilliant system for identifying them, though: I numbered them according to the birth order of the sister they were married to and then memorized what color sweater they were each wearing. So: brother-in-law #1—Adam, in the pale yellow Loro Piana, belongs with Patricia, Jack's eldest sister; brother-in-law #2—Alan, in the light pink Loro Piana, belongs with Elizabeth, the middle sis; and brother-in-law #3—Aaron, in the baby blue Loro Piana, goes with Lisa, the youngest.

"So, have you two given any thought to a wedding date?" brother-in-law #1 asks. He's Adam, and he goes with Patricia. It makes sense that Adam is #1 since Adam and Eve were the first man and woman. See how well my system works? Although, he looks closer to his late thirties than his mid-forties. Was it that #1 goes with the youngest sister and #3 goes with the eldest? Now that I think about it, maybe Aaron was supposed to be #1 since Hank Aaron holds the all-time Major League Baseball record for home runs. (And I know you're thinking that Barry Bonds is now #1 in terms of home runs, but Jack says that for real baseball fans, that doesn't count.)

This would be so much easier with name tags. Or if the proper brother-in-law was seated next to the appropriate sister. The Solomons do this strange table seating thing where you don't actually sit with the person you came with. Jack and I are the only couple seated next to each other, and that's just because this dinner is meant to celebrate our engagement. Everyone else is scattered about, with no regard whatsoever as to who goes with who. Jack's mother said something about us all talking to each other and not to the same person we talk to every day, or some such nonsense like that.

"Mimi and I were just discussing the wedding date before we sat down to dinner," my father says. Yes, my mother's name is Miriam, but my father calls her Mimi. How embarrassing.

"Edward's docket generally is lightest in winter," Jack's mother says.

"Jack and I were thinking spring," I say, looking at Jack and squeezing his leg under the table. "Maybe April?"

"Lots of new appeals in spring," Patricia says, "not the best time of year for a wedding in this family. Adam and I got married in February." I wait for Patricia to look to her husband as she mentions him, thus putting my system back on track, but she doesn't.

"That sounds beautiful," my mother says, ever the people pleaser, "but since so much of my family will be flying in from Miami for the wedding, we really can't take the risk that there'd be snow and they won't be able to get here for the big day."

"That's unfortunate," Jack's mother says. Unfortunate? My mother looks immediately at me and I look at Jack. Jack looks down into his halibut and pretends he didn't just hear his mother say that. Or that it didn't really mean anything.

Before meeting me, Jack had been engaged to a woman for three and a half years without ever having set a wedding date. You'd think his parents would be more appreciative of the fact that I've at least nailed their son down to a season.

"March could work," brother-in-law #3 says, mouth full of salmon, "March is part spring, part winter."

"Sometimes there's still snow in March," brother-in-law #1 says, as he motions to a servant for more wine to be poured.

"No, there's not, Adam," Elizabeth says, looking at light-blue Loro Piana. My system would be back on track, but for the fact that I'm not a hundred percent sure whether she actually just said *Adam,* or if she may have said *Aaron* instead. Or *Alan,* for that matter.

"Sometimes there is, Elizabeth," Lisa says. "April sounds great, Brooke."

"How is he going to have a wedding in April," brother-in-law #2 says, nodding his head in the direction of Jack's father, "when he's working like an animal on his caseload?"

"Maybe he doesn't have to work like an animal," Elizabeth says, looking at her father. Edward clears his throat loudly.

"No, Adam's right," I say, trying to be diplomatic, "we can do March if that would work best."

"I'm Aaron," brother-in-law #1 says.

"Didn't I say that?" I say, taking a huge gulp of wine.

"Yes," Jack says, putting his arm around the back of my chair and brushing his fingers against my shoulder, "that's what she said."

"Anyway," brother-in-law # 3 interjects, "the date is usually influenced by the venue. You have to pick from the dates that your venue has available."

"That's not going to be a problem," my father says.

"It's not?" Joan asks, taking a sip of wine.

"Our rabbi is so happy to see our BB getting married that they'll do anything we ask. They're even going to give us a huge discount on the reception room at the temple," my father proudly tells Jack's dad. Bragging about the discounts he brokers is one of my father's greatest pleasures in life. "And, of course, I'll be supplying all of the meat—my best cuts, of course—so we've got the venue and the catering covered."

"A temple?" Jack's father says. His voice is big and strong and everyone seems to notice at the same time that this is the first word he's uttered during this entire debate. Which only makes his few words that much more powerful and scary. I can tell that this is a strategy he uses with attorneys in his courtroom—lying in wait until you're ready to pounce and make your word gospel. Which, if you're an appellate court judge, is pretty much any time you speak. I look at Jack and he's still got his head down in his plate. Man, he must *really* love his halibut. "Joan and I were thinking about a New York City hotel wedding. Weren't we, dear?"

"We love the Pierre," Joan says softly. I look at my mother and she is trying to maintain a gracious smile with her mouth frozen in place and teeth gritted together.

"Jackie?" I say.

"We like the Pierre, too," Jack says, looking up from his plate, "remember, we went to that charity event there this summer?"

"I forget," I say. Jack regales the table with a story about how we couldn't find a cab after the charity event and ended up taking a horse-drawn carriage at 1:00 a.m. all the way down Fifth Avenue from 59th Street to 23rd. I take the cocktail napkin that has been underneath my wineglass since we came from the salon to the dining room out from under my wineglass. It's an ivory napkin with a large *S* embossed on the front. I tear it into two pieces. And then into four.

"But, Edward," my mother says, smile still firmly in place as she places her hand gently on Jack's father's arm, "two Jewish kids getting married. Wouldn't it be lovely to celebrate such a mitzvah in a temple?"

"Joan and I would be glad to contribute to costs," Edward says quietly to my mother. And then louder, to the whole table: "In fact, it would be an honor, wouldn't it dear?"

"An honor," Joan parrots back. I tear my napkin into eighths.

"Absolutely not," my father bellows, his Brooklyn accent even more prominent than usual. "BB's our only daughter. We've been waiting our whole life for this day. The wedding's on Mimi and me. We'll do whatever our BB wants. Do you want a hotel wedding, BB?"

"Well," I start to say, beginning to take my father's defense, "I did always dream of—"

"Then it's settled," my father says, still a little too loudly, "we'll start looking at hotels next week."

I suppose that in my heart of hearts, I knew that this was

how it would go down. Why on earth would I have thought that our parents would get along? Jack's father is a Circuit Court judge and his mother is active in charity work, while my father is a kosher butcher and my mother is active in her mah-jongg game.

Is it too late to elope?

Just asking…

WHICH fashion designer is about to bid her businessman husband adieu? Her friends, family and investors think things are *très magnifique,* but a hotel bill at the Lowell says otherwise….

6

Back at work. Thank God. I may not have a wedding dress, and the first meeting of the parents may have gotten off to a bit of a rocky start, but at least work is the one thing I understand, the one thing that's under my control. The one area where I know that nothing will go wrong. Especially since today is the initial conference on Monique's case—the first case *ever* where I get the chance to take the lead. Luckily for me, the case is pretty open and shut, so I barely need to prepare for this morning's court date. Granted, I seem to have hit a *tiny* stumbling block on this case—a pesky little countersuit by Monique's husband filed this morning right before I left to go to court—but the case is still pretty straightforward and I should have things squared away with the judge in no time at all. And before the *New York Post* can blow up this morning's "blind item" about Monique into a full-fledged article. Hopefully, while I'm at federal court dealing with the dissolution of partnership case, all of the reporters will be over at family court, poking around for the divorce case that doesn't exist. Yet. I should have this thing settled before they even realize that they're in the wrong courthouse.

It's refreshing to be doing something this morning that I have power over. Especially since last night, after we got back from dinner at his parents's house, I had to calmly explain to Jack—who under normal circumstances is an absolutely perfect fiancé—that he needs to take my side whenever there is a disagreement amongst the families. But it's not like we got into a fight about it or anything. We are not one of those couples who ever fight. Which is surprising since we're both lawyers, but it's true. We never fight. Not at all adversarial. We're just *not* one of those couples you see who compete with one another. In fact, if we were a Hollywood couple, it wouldn't matter *at all* who won an Oscar first or who made more money per picture—we wouldn't get a divorce over it or even have a cross word over it—because we are simply not competitive with each other in the slightest bit and we most certainly never fight.

"How dare you not take my side in front of your parents!" I said last night, the second we walked back in the door to our apartment after dinner at Jack's parents' house. Okay, so I may have been screaming it at the time, but you get where I was going with that one. That was the most calm as I could muster, given the circumstances.

"Sides?" my perfect fiancé said. "It's not about sides, sweetie. It's about our families coming together."

"You're right, honey," I said, "it's not about sides." And Jack was *so* right. It is *so not* about sides at all. It's about our families merging into one. Even if his family does outnumber mine by an alarming ratio of four to one. "Right, Jack. I just meant that you need to agree with everything I say in front of your parents."

My perfect fiancé looked back at me and furrowed his brow.

But, today in court, I will be in control. After all, I am a tough, no-nonsense attorney who does not take "no" for an answer. I am confident, intelligent and self-possessed. I am woman, hear me roar. See, with my can-do attitude, there is no way that I can lose in court today. Especially since it's only an initial conference where we just cover administrative matters, so there's actually no winning or losing to be had. And this isn't the sort of case that *ever* goes to trial for actual winning or losing. It's more of a transactional thing. Also, the judge assigned to my case is an old law school buddy of Jack's dad.

But, I'll still roar if need be.

As I enter the judge's courtroom, I take a peek at the docket and notice something very odd. When I got notice of the countersuit, Monique's husband had checked off the box to indicate that he'd be handling the matter *pro se,* meaning that he'd be his own attorney. It made sense to me at the time since a dissolution of partnership is so routine, but today he has a law firm representing him.

My old law firm.

"This must be a typo," I say to the court deputy sitting at a long table in the front of the courtroom. When I say this to him, a *tiny* voice inside me realizes that it must be true, that my old law firm will, in fact, be opposing me in my first big case that I take the lead on. Which would also be the reason why Monique didn't hire Vanessa. She knew that her husband would be using Gilson, Hecht. Still, I think that it can't hurt to ask the deputy, maybe even flirt a bit, and earn myself a few brownie points with the judge's staff.

"No typo," he says, without even looking up from his coffee, donut and *New York Law Journal.*

"I'm representing Monique deVouvray and her husband is opposing the action *pro se.*"

"Pro se?" he says, looking very annoyed that I've distracted him from his breakfast. This is probably not the way to earn brownie points. I lean over his desk so as to show some cleavage, but it doesn't really work since I'm wearing a turtleneck sweater. Maybe he'll applaud the effort, anyway, though.

"You know what?" I say, not wanting to piss off the man who controls the court's calendar—and my fate on this case for the next couple of months. "Don't even worry about it. I'll just figure it out when you call me."

"You must be Brooke," a thick Southern drawl from behind me says. I turn around to see Miranda Foxley, an associate at Gilson, Hecht. I've never met her before, but her reputation precedes her. Word on the street—or at the Park Avenue law firms, as the case may be—is that she left her last law firm because she slept with a married partner. Happy as I am to see that the case is staffed only with a junior associate, and not a partner, it dawns on me that the whole flirt-with-the-staff-of-chambers strategy isn't really going to work if Miranda Foxley is my opposing counsel.

Standing five foot ten, Miranda looks more like a model than an actual lawyer. Her blazing red hair flows loosely around her shoulders, down her back and it makes my hand instinctively fly up to my own locks since it reminds me that I chopped my own long hair off just a few months ago. Which doesn't really matter today anyway, since I have it back in a bun to look professional for court, but still. And she's unbelievably—annoyingly—thin. I could never understand how Southern women could ever be thin with all of that delicious comfort food they grow up with in the South, but Miranda is. I guess that she is able to ignore a buttered biscuit and fried chicken in a way that I never could.

Today she's got on a fitted salmon-colored Nanette Lepore suit with a little silk camisole underneath that's bordered with lace. I'm in my most conservative charcoal-gray suit with a black turtleneck sweater, black opaque stockings and black pumps. The contrast is striking—she's Susan Dey in *LA Law* and I'm Marcia Clark before the makeover. I bet Miranda's even got garters on under that pastel-colored number.

Thank God I still have an in with the judge by way of my future father-in-law.

"Jack told me all about you," she coos. I hate that she knows my fiancé. Visions of them cavorting naked in conference rooms while working on a "document production" fill my mind.

"He did?" I say, smoothing back my hair with the back of my hand, wishing I'd worn it down today.

"See? No typo," the deputy informs me. "You're appearing against Gilson, Hecht today."

"Yes," I say, "thank you." And then, under my breath, "I can see that."

Our case is called at 11:00 a.m. and Miranda and I make our way into chambers. Judge Martin sits behind a massive mahogany desk with case files piled high on either side. The bank of windows is right behind his shiny bald head and I almost have to squint as I sit down in my chair. He looks much older than Jack's father does and I wonder if that's because he was ahead of Jack's dad in law school or if that's because of his huge pot belly and the two hundred and fifty pounds he's carrying around.

Note to self: Must start wedding diet, stat.

"First," Judge Martin begins, "at the outset, I'd like to tell you, Ms. Foxley, that although I do not personally know Ms. Miller, I do know her future father-in-law and, as such, I will be attending her wedding to his son. I don't think that this should present a problem, but, before we go any further, we should discuss right now whether or not you'll be making a motion for me to recuse myself from this matter."

"I have no objections, Your Honor," Miranda says with her thick Southern accent. I'm certain that she's putting the accent on even thicker for the judge's benefit. "I know that you and Judge Solomon were both Harvard Law, class of 1962." Why didn't *I* think to do a Westlaw background search on Judge Martin?

Or, had she done one on Jack's father?

"Ms. Miller, I assume that you don't have a problem with me being on this case?"

"Of course not," I say, glowing at the mention of my wedding. Surely, by my wedding day, I will have won this case by a landslide and by spring, Judge Martin will be at my rehearsal dinner giving a toast: *Beauty and brains, the total package, that's our Brooke.*

If I were Miranda, I might have considered a motion to recuse Judge Martin from the case. It is *so clear* that I already have an advantage here. It's obvious that the man *already* thinks of me as his surrogate daughter. And, I'm litigating against an associate who is junior to me. This case is going to be so easy that it's almost unfair. But far be it from me to point that out.

Judge Martin glances over the court papers. "So, we seem to have a little bit of a disagreement here."

"Yes, Your Honor," Miranda pipes in, sitting up straighter in her chair. "My client is countersuing. He helped build his wife's business and he is not going to allow her to cut him off from its future profits. It was his personal savings that first—"

"I wasn't aware that we'd be arguing our cases today, Your Honor," I say with an innocent smile, cutting Miranda off. Normally, I wouldn't be so bold as to say something like that, but on a case that I had with Jack three years ago, a similar situation arose where opposing counsel began posturing on his client's behalf before the case even began and that was what Jack said to shut him down immediately. It worked like a charm in that initial conference—simultaneously shutting up opposing counsel and currying favor with the judge—and I was hoping for a similar result.

I wish Jack was here with me right now. If he were here, he'd put the fear of God into this little Southern belle and we could probably force a settlement right now. Since leaving Gilson, Hecht, the one thing I miss most is working on all of my cases with Jack. Not only is he an amazing attorney, but he also used to give me something nice to stare at when I was bored to tears at these things.

"Ms. Miller is correct, Ms. Foxley," Judge Martin says, "this is just to set up our court calendar. I won't have you posturing on your client's behalf. Unless you're ready to talk settlement already?"

"No, sir," Miranda says, looking down at her papers and straightening them out.

"We are ready to talk settlement whenever you are, Your Honor," I say. "In fact, we really were expecting a very basic dissolution of partnership. Totally by the books. We weren't at all expecting a contentious litigation."

Wow, didn't that sound, like, totally dramatic? I'll have to remember to tell Jack about that little zinger later.

"Counselor?" Judge Martin says, looking at Miranda for a response.

"Sorry, Your Honor. My client is firm. He wants to proceed with litigation."

"So, then let's set up a calendar for the discovery process," Judge Martin says, taking out his calendar, a huge red leather book that he places on his desk with a big slam.

"Would it be all right to take a very brief recess?" Miranda asks. This is highly unusual. An initial court conference is generally so brief that there's no time to take a break.

I give a disapproving glance in Judge Martin's direction, indicating that I do not want to take a break and that I'm ready to continue with the conference. He already took my side when Miranda started posturing and I just know that he won't allow a recess if I indicate to him that I don't want one. The control I'm *already* exerting over this case is embarrassing. I've got this guy eating out of the palm of my hand. But, it's okay, since I'll only be using my superpowers of litigation for good.

"I'll allow it," Judge Martin says. "Let's take five minutes." He must have misconstrued my disapproving glance as saying: I really need to go to the ladies' room.

Anyway, a five-minute recess will give me enough time to call Jack and get some tips on how to deal with Miranda. You're not allowed to bring cell phones into a federal courthouse, but Jack showed me a tiny trick that's hardly even *that* illegal to sneak your phone in to court—you just turn your phone off as you go through security and hide it in an inside pocket.

Granted, I'm still not allowed to tell him that Monique is my client, but I can ask him about litigation strategy without revealing anything about the case. After all, asking him for tips on how to deal with an annoying adversary (with a totally put-on Southern accent) is not a breach of my ethical duties to my client.

I dial the number and hear the familiar ring tone for Jack's cell phone. It's the song "Hello, I Love You" by the Doors. I have the same one on mine. As I hear it ringing, I can hear the actual phone coming down the hallway.

"What are you doing here?" I say, as Jack rounds the corner, practically walking into me in his effort to covertly answer his phone while avoiding the glare of any federal marshals lurking in the hallway who might confiscate it.

"What are *you* doing here?" he asks right back, talking into the phone. "You didn't tell me you were coming to court today."

"You're supposed to turn the phone off when you pass through security," I remind him, taking my own phone away from my ear.

"I taught *you* that trick, sweetie," he says, shutting his phone and grabbing me for a little kiss. "Are you here on a case?"

"Super-secret client," I stage whisper. "I'd tell you, but then I'd have to kill you." I try to say this last bit all flirty and sweet, just like Calista Flockhart on *Ally McBeal*. I love that I'm still flirting with Jack even though we're already engaged. I hope that I still feel that way when we're old and gray. Well, okay, I'll probably never be old and gray. I'll be old with a totally kick-ass natural-looking dye job, but you know what I mean.

"Super-secret client?" he laughs, running a hand through his shaggy brown hair. "Me, too. What judge are you assigned to?"

But I don't need to tell him what judge I'm assigned to because we both figure it out at the exact same time.

Miranda rounds the corner and calls out to Jack: "Oh, *there* you are! We've been waiting for you! I've been stalling all morning, just like you taught me to! Brooke, I don't know what I would've done in that conference if your fella hadn't coached me on it last night." She walks over to us and stands between Jack and me. Then, as if it was the most natural thing in the world, she rests her hand on his shoulder and sighs audibly, sort of the way Scarlett O'Hara did to Rhett when he came to rescue her from a besieged Atlanta.

Jack looks at me and I look at him. Neither of us say a word. We don't need to. Turns out that there *is* a Gilson, Hecht partner on the case, after all.

My fiancé.

7

"Your Honor, you can't *possibly* let him litigate this case against me. I mean, how can he be objective for his client? It's so obvious that he is completely, madly, desperately in love with me!"

What I fail to mention to the judge here—and the real reason why I'm so adamant to get Jack thrown off this case—is that Jack's also a much more experienced lawyer than me, and during our five years together at Gilson, Hecht, he really did teach me everything I know. How on earth am I going to use all of the litigation tricks I know on the person who taught them to me in the first place?

"I can be objective for my client, Judge Martin," Jack says. "I may be completely, madly—"

"And desperately," I add.

"Yes, and desperately," Jack says with a laugh, "in love with counsel, but we're all professionals here, and I'm quite certain that we'd be able to keep work separate from our private life. In fact, we worked together for five years at Gilson, Hecht before Brooke left for SGR."

"Ha!" I say, "but when I was at Gilson, Hecht, you were totally in love with me."

"I seem to recall that *you* were totally in love with *me,*" Jack says, turning to face me.

"Oh, please!" I say, "Your Honor, look at the man! He can't even keep his eyes off of me! Jackie, you're going to have to find another partner to litigate this case."

"Are you afraid of a little competition?" Jack whispers, eyes still glued to me.

"Your Honor, look!" I say, pointing at Jack, "He's *flirting* with me right here in your chambers!"

"This is a unique situation we are in here," Judge Martin says, rubbing his hand on his bald head.

Unique, indeed. Most couples, when they argue, don't actually have a United States District Court judge refereeing it for them.

"Judge Martin, I'm ready to go forward with this case," Jack says. "If Ms. Miller has a problem with it—"

"It's my case, Jackie," I say through gritted teeth, "back *off.*"

"Ms. Miller," Judge Martin says, "if you'd like to make a motion, I'd be happy to entertain it right now."

The judge wants me to make a motion? Right now? When I'm not even prepared for the conference, much less an oral argument? No way. No way in hell. And he wants me to argue it against Jack? Now that Jack's here, Judge Martin's totally going to favor him, and not me! I can just see Judge Martin at our rehearsal dinner: *Brooke certainly gave it the old college try, but she was just no match for our Jack. Beauty and brains, that's our Jack.*

I don't think so.

"No, Your Honor," I say. "I'm ready to go forward."

"Fine, then," the judge says. "Are you familiar with the term *Chinese Wall?*"

Miranda sits in her chair, furiously taking notes while Jack and I manage a little giggle. You see, when I was at Gilson, Hecht, Jack and I had a case where we had to construct a *Chinese Wall.* Now, a Chinese Wall is not a real wall—it's a term of art used in law to describe a situation within a law firm where there may be a conflict between certain clients. It means that the attorneys working on conflicted cases must keep all privileged information private and cannot discuss the information amongst themselves.

Four years ago, Jack and I represented Healthy Foods, one of the firm's biggest clients, while our corporate department represented Organic Life, their competition, in a totally unrelated transaction. The two clients weren't against each other in their respective matters, but since they were competitors in the market, the judge ordered the firm to construct a Chinese Wall within Gilson, Hecht so that we didn't share privileged information.

"Now, the judge has ordered us to construct a Chinese

Wall within the firm so that we do not inadvertently share information about our clients," the partner on the Healthy Foods case announced in a large associate meeting just after the firm was retained by Organic Life. "Remember, even the most seemingly innocuous information could turn out to be privileged. Does everyone understand? However, for our purposes here, since the term *Chinese Wall* is so un-politically correct, we're going to call it an Asian wall."

"Was that a joke?" Jack whispered to Vanessa and me.

"I can't believe we had to give up billable time for this meeting," Vanessa said. I, myself, was always glad to have any excuse not to work.

"Actually," a fifth-year associate piped up, "only people are Asian. Objects are Oriental. Like an Oriental rug."

"Okay," the partner said, "then I suppose we can call it an Oriental wall." Danielle Lewis, the head of the corporate department furrowed her brow and whispered something to the head of litigation.

"That's way more offensive than Chinese Wall," someone in the crowd called out.

Vanessa raised her hand. "Maybe we should just call it a Swiss wall, since they're neutral."

"Let's just call it the Great Wall," the partner offered and the other partners all shook their heads in agreement. "We will construct the Great Wall within Gilson, Hecht and I trust that all of the associates assigned to these matters will keep the details of their respective cases confidential."

Jack, Vanessa and I refused to use the term *Great Wall*

and instead referred to it as "the wall formerly known as Chinese" for the duration of the litigation. For some reason, the entire time we were on the case, I always had a massive craving for eggrolls.

"Yes, Judge, we are familiar with the concept," Jack says to Judge Martin.

"Ms. Miller?" the judge asks me.

"Yes, Your Honor," I say, but to be honest, I'm already beginning to think of the wok that I registered for at Crate and Barrel, hoping that someone buys it for me for my bridal shower.

"Great. So, then, I'll expect," he says, jotting down notes as he speaks to us, "that you two will construct a Chinese Wall at home and have no discussions whatsoever about the case."

"Yes," Jack and I say in unison. I'd never actually heard of a judge directing two lawyers to construct a Chinese Wall in their home, but it was giving me some great decorating ideas for our apartment. A silk screen in the living room would look totally fab.

What? It's not like I wasn't taking the case seriously. It's just that when you're a big-time lawyer like me, you have to multitask and think about apartment design while you're working! Geez.

"I'm sure that the two of you have much more interesting things to discuss at home anyway," the judge says. "I'd also like to fast-track this case. I understand from Ms. Miller's papers that both parties are very well-known celebrities and they'd like to try to avoid unwanted media attention, so that's why I've sealed all court records on the matter. I think it's best to get this matter resolved as quickly as we possibly can. Am I correct?"

"Yes, Your Honor," Miranda and I say in unison, while, at the same time, Jack says, "Yes, Judge Martin." Sort of like on *Cheers* when Norm comes in and everyone in the bar would say: "Norm!" but Diane would say: "Nor-man." Although, "Your Honor" is actually more formal than calling a judge "Judge," but you get the general point I'm trying to make.

"So, then in that case, the discovery process will begin this week and I'll see all of you in three months for our next status conference."

"Thank you, Your Honor," we all say as we record the next status conference in our BlackBerries. I try to keep my cool even though the judge has set an incredibly tight discovery calendar. In my old firm, it would have been no problem, what with Gilson, Hecht's enormous staff, but in my new firm, where I'm handling the case on my own, this has the potential to become a real nightmare. Although I must admit, I probably won't have any trouble getting extensions on my deadlines since I'm sleeping with opposing counsel.

What? The judge merely said we had to construct a Chinese Wall—he didn't say that we had to stop sleeping with each other!

I pull my hair out of its bun as soon as the door to chambers shuts and I walk down the hallway toward the elevators with Jack and Miranda.

"This is no fair," I say, as soon as we are halfway down the hall, safely out of earshot of Judge Martin and his chambers staff. "You never even ever wanted to be a lawyer!" My argument, though childish and whiny, is true. It's a known fact that Jack only became a lawyer after his dream of becoming an actor fizzled. Thus, his predilection for courtroom theatrics.

"My word," Miranda says, "this is going to be some case, isn't it?"

I resist the urge to tell her to shut up and leave Jack and me alone. Jack asks Miranda to excuse us and this inexplicably causes her to put her hand on his forearm. There's that hand again. I resist the urge to scream, "Get your man stealing hand off of my fiancé!"

Not like I'm jealous or anything. This must be a litigation technique she's trying to employ to throw me off. Trying to make me so jealous that I don't concentrate on my case at all and focus all my energy into the wrong things. Oh, please. Amateur hour. As if I'd fall for that for one second! She's going to have to try a lot harder to faze a tough no-nonsense adversary like me.

And why would I ever get jealous? Jack and I have a strong relationship, and just because my last serious boyfriend cheated on me and left me for another woman, that doesn't mean that Jack will do the same thing. Because Jack's not him. And Jack is more than just another serious boyfriend. He's my fiancé. Things are different with him. Better. More secure.

Right?

"Y'all have a lot to discuss," Miranda says as the elevator

doors open, "Jack, I'll see you back at the office." I can swear I see her press her documents tightly to her chest, which has the effect of pushing her breasts up to expose massive cleavage in her lace-trimmed camisole. My eyes dart to Jack's to see if he's noticed.

"Thanks, Miranda," Jack says, his eyes still on me, "why don't you get started on discovery and we can talk it over this afternoon?" I can't help but wonder whether or not she takes off her fitted jacket when she's back at the office and attends meetings in only her lace-trimmed camisole.

What a hussy.

The elevator doors close and Jack and I stand face to face.

"No fair?" Jack says, "Is that the sort of tough argument you'll be presenting me with in court? Honestly, Brooke, I thought I taught you better than that."

"This isn't funny," I say (okay, I'm actually whining it, but give me a break, I'm under a lot of stress here!). "This is the first case I've ever taken the lead on and I want to do well."

"Well," Jack says, leading me down the hallway to the other end, where no one is standing. "This is a high-profile client for the firm and I want to prove that I have what it takes to be a rainmaker. To pull in the big clients and keep them happy."

"Okay, my argument was, like, totally more compelling," I say as we stop at the end of the hall.

"Whatever happened to: 'You're going to get the case and be amazing. And I'll be the loving, doting fiancée who is here to help you every step of the way.' Remember saying that to me?"

"Well, yes," I say, "but that was before the biggest case of *your* career coincided with the biggest case of *my* career, silly."

"But I'm a partner," Jack pleads, "so I need the big case more than you do at this stage."

"Totally flawed argument," I say, "clearly *I* need the big cases more so that I can *become* a partner."

Jack runs his hand through his hair.

"Since when do you care about taking the lead on a case? When we were at Gilson, Hecht together, you never cared about being on the big cases. In fact, you always tried to get on the smaller cases and the cases most likely to settle quickly," Jack says, putting his case files down on the windowsill. "Let's face it, Brooke, you don't even like working that much. Why on earth would you want to take the lead on a case?"

"Who likes working?" I say. I think, but don't say: *Duh!* "But these Manolos don't exactly buy themselves."

"I'll let you buy all the Manolos you want," Jack says, putting his arms around me, "you can even buy baby Manolos when we have a daughter."

"They don't *make* baby Manolos," I tell Jack with a pout, as he puts his finger under my chin and tilts my head up to face him.

"If you wanted baby Manolos," Jack says, leaning into me so that our faces are only mere inches away from each other, "I'd get you baby Manolos. I'd get you anything you ever wanted, you know that, don't you?"

"Yes," I say. "Can you tell what I want right now?"

Jack smiles, his baby blues sparkling, and leans down to kiss me. Every time I kiss Jack, it feels like the first time. His soft lips touch mine and I just melt. I really do. It could be any time, any place, but when Jack kisses me, the rest of the world just floats away. I close my eyes and with Jack's arms around me, I could be on some island in the Caribbean for all I know.

Or a federal courthouse in Manhattan, as the case may be. "Ahem," I hear a voice say from behind me. I turn and see Judge Martin standing in the hallway, right behind us. Jack doesn't release me from his grip, but my arms fall down as if to say: *Didn't I tell you that this man is completely, desperately, madly in love with me?* Case closed. I think I've proven my point. "Counselors, are we going to have a problem here?"

And it was just as good a question as any to ask. Would it be a problem litigating my first major case against my fiancé while we're planning our wedding together? Won't thoughts of taffeta and floral arrangements distract me from being the tough, no-nonsense attorney who does not take "no" for an answer that I am?

But, I am woman, hear me roar! I can do anything I set my mind to. I've faced much tougher obstacles in my day. After all, I am a woman who has endured going to three of my ex-boyfriend's weddings and I managed to totally humiliate myself at only *one* of them! And, I've only been sanctioned by the court on *one* of my major litigations. All in all, a pretty darn good track record. All I have to do now is plan the wedding of my dreams (well, the wedding of my mother's dreams, anyway) and win the big case!

What could possibly go wrong?

8

In my next life, I've decided that I'd like to come back as Monique deVouvray. Not only is she beautiful and glamorous, but she is also the epitome of grace under fire. In the face of intense media scrutiny, she doesn't cower. She's not bothered at the line-up of paparazzi outside her home, nor is she concerned with gossip columnist after gossip columnist calling her to find out why her husband Jean Luc is registered as a long-term guest at the Lowell Hotel. She doesn't care that her publicist gets called three to four times an hour to give a statement about the fact that her husband's stay at the Lowell has become public and she doesn't even appear fazed that this little tidbit of information seems to be the top story on *Entertainment Tonight* for four nights running. (Which I find especially impressive, considering she designed

Mary Hart's wedding dress for her back in 1989.) Monique didn't even bat an eyelash at the fact that gossip blogger extraordinaire Perez Hilton himself flew into town from L.A. just to be blogging from a coffee shop that's closer to the action.

No, in the face of her world seemingly falling apart, Monique deVouvray is throwing a party. And I feel like I've walked into the pages of *Mrs. Dalloway* as I come to her townhouse to meet with her after my initial conference in court. People are scurrying about—florists, chefs, photographers and musicians—and there is a party planner standing in the eye of the storm, barking out order after order to prepare for what will be, no doubt, the party of the season: the renewal of the vows of Monique deVouvray and Jean Luc Renault. I walk through the entranceway of their Upper East Side townhouse, wide-eyed, just gazing at the spectacle before me.

"Brooke," Monique calls to me from the stairway across the main foyer, "come with me upstairs. I am ready for you." I rush through the crowd to Monique and we walk up the stairs, arm in arm like little French schoolgirls. We go up to her studio, not her office, since she doesn't want the press—or any of her party planners, for that matter—to find out that I'm actually her lawyer. Instead, today I am playing the part of Monique's 3:00 p.m. bridal appointment.

To make this ruse work, she's insisted that I come to her townhouse carrying only my pocketbook, not a briefcase, and that I bring only a tote bag with high-heeled shoes and a strapless bra, no legal files. The plan seemed to work perfectly as I slipped by the paparazzi undetected, but let's face it, it's only a matter of time before I appear in court and pull a strapless bra out of my work bag. Monique still has no idea how her husband's stay at the Lowell got leaked to the press, but she seems certain that it wasn't anyone at the Lowell. I get the distinct feeling when she tells me this that she is sure of this hunch based on past experience with Jean Luc staying at the Lowell (but I dare not ask her if I'm right). Instead, Monique guesses that it was one of her staff at the townhouse. Since she employs a staff of over twenty people at her townhouse, she can't be too sure of where the leak came from, and to this end, she has insisted that we pretend that I am one of her brides and that she fit me for a gown each time I come to her to discuss the case.

"We may have hit a tiny stumbling block on this case, but it's nothing I want you to worry about," I say, as Monique brings out the muslin I'll be trying on for fit today. I can't help but wonder if she'll be pretending to fit me with one of her real brides' muslins, or if she's actually creating a new dress for me to make this ploy seem real.

"So, then, why are you telling me?" Monique asks me, as we are interrupted by a florist coming in with a sample floral arrangement: white and baby-pink hydrangeas, white roses and fuchsia orchids. Absolutely breathtaking. And appropriate for the occasion—the white and pastel colors give that bridal feel you'd want for a ceremony celebrating a marriage, but then the fuchsia mixes things up enough to make you remember that this is a vow renewal, and not a first wedding.

Monique looks at the flowers critically before nodding her head in approval, signaling the florist to scurry off.

"Well," I slowly say as Monique helps me slip into a decoy muslin, "it seems that your husband has hired my old law firm." Monique slides the muslin onto my body and then helps me up onto a small round stand that's set up right in front of the three-way mirror. It's like a tiny stage for me and my wedding dress and I love it—the dress drapes over the stand, and the six inches that the stand lifts me off the ground makes me look tall and thin, as if I were wearing nine-inch heels. It is the perfect vantage point for me to stare at myself in my wedding dress.

Um, I mean fake wedding dress.

"That is not a problem," Monique says, smoothing the muslin out, "I am unconcerned."

"Well," I say, this time even more slowly, "the lead attorney on the case seems to be Jack Solomon." I give a nervous laugh which Monique does not even seem to notice. She's busy studying the muslin she's just put me into before grabbing some pins. I'm tempted to remind her that this is just a fake dress that we're working on here, but then I decide that I should at least get to enjoy the experience of Monique making a wedding dress for me, faux or not. "My fiancé, Jack Solomon."

Monique laughs, careful not to disturb the pins she's put in her mouth as she begins to work on my faux dress. She's about to say something as we are interrupted again, this time by a chef, coming into the studio with a small tasting.

I love that he is decked out in full chef regalia—the white jacket, the white hat and black and white checkered pants—thus giving the occasion all of the pageantry it deserves. I try to place the chef's face, since I'm sure that I've seen him before on the Food Network. His jacket is embroidered with simply his first name: Daniel.

"Madame and mademoiselle," he says dramatically in a French accent that's even thicker than Monique's, "may I interrupt?"

"You may," Monique says, now looking at my dress through the mirror.

"The Dover sole," he announces, placing the tray on a nearby table with a dramatic flair, as if he were presenting us to the royal family. Or presenting us to the royal family's dinner, as the case may be. "I would be honored if you would take a taste."

Monique walks over to the table and I'm unsure of what to do. I'm pinned into this muslin and the bottom part of the dress is a straight line from my hips to my ankles. I can barely breathe in it, much less walk. With the line she's given the skirt, I'm not really sure if my legs have enough room to actually get off of this elevated stand to get myself over to the Dover sole. But the smell—the smell is simply delicious. It's lemon and butter and basil and all of a sudden, I absolutely, positively *must* have a taste. I turn to the chef, ever so slightly, so as not to fall, and try to take a step in my muslin.

As I move my right leg to walk, the dress catches on my left and I stumble a bit in my effort to move. I straighten myself up a bit—good, no one seems to have noticed my little near slip—and I try to regain my composure. I smile and gather a bit of the fabric in my hands so that I'll be able to walk. There, now that's it. I'll just take teensy tiny little baby steps and make my way off of the stand slowly. When I get to the end of the stand, I'll just gracefully ask Monique for a bit of help and then they'll ask me if I'd like a taste of the Dover sole. You know, just to be polite. In all of my time around Monique, one thing I've learned is that French people are exceedingly polite, contrary to the stereotype. I begin shuffling my feet, centimeter by centimeter, inch by inch, and as I get closer and closer to the edge, I can practically taste the Dover sole on my tongue. Just as I near the edge of the stand, Monique turns to Daniel and says, "Daniel, I'd like to introduce you to Brooke Miller. She is one of my brides."

And then I fall face-first off the stand, smack in the middle of Monique and Daniel.

How do you say "Timber!" in French? Well, that's okay if you don't know. It really was more of a SPLAT! than anything else and I'm pretty sure that SPLAT! is universal.

"Ah, Brooke!" Monique says, as she and Daniel both lean down to me to help me up, "are you all right? My goodness, Brooke, did the pins get you?"

"No, they didn't." Yes, they did. All twenty-two of them, in fact. But when you're at your client's office pretending to be a bride and you fall off a stand because you're salivating over a piece of fish, you tend to lie to save face. Better late than never, I always say. "I'm okay. Absolutely fine."

Monique and Daniel have to team up to lift me together. They grab me under my armpits and raise me upright like a stiff board since I still can't really move my legs in the dress.

"Let me just get this one for you," Monique says, gently taking out a few of the pins that have lodged themselves into my thighs.

"It is a pleasure to meet you," I say to Daniel once I'm upright, putting my hand out for him to shake.

"You are a very lucky girl to be having your wedding dress designed by Monique," he says, kissing the top of my hand.

"Yes, I'm very lucky," I say, and feel an expected gush of sadness as I say it.

"Now, please," he says, "try the Dover sole."

With all of the tiny pin pricks still stinging on my legs, I don't even want to try the fish anymore. I should just let Monique do her tasting quickly so that we can get back to business and start discussing our case.

Okay, I didn't even convince myself on that one. It literally takes all of my self control not to dive right onto the plate. Daniel takes a fork and puts a bite onto it.

I take a bite and it melts in my mouth. Everything about it—the taste, the consistency—is absolutely perfect. There are so many different flavors exploding on my palate, one by one, that can only be described as deliciously complex. Now I finally know what they're talking about on *Top Chef!*

"It's perfect," Monique says to Daniel and I nod my head in agreement. All I can think is, *would it be rude to take another bite?* Thankfully, Monique takes another forkful and motions for me to do the same. The second bite is just as close to pure heaven as the first one and we both let out an "Mmm!" at the same time. Daniel beams back at us.

Would it be a breach of ethics to try to get myself invited to the party tonight? After all, if I don't get to have the gorgeous wedding dress of my dreams, I should at least get to attend the most fabulous party of the season, right? Okay, the truth is that I just can't wait to taste all of the other courses this chef has got up his sleeve. And the hors d'oeuvres. I can only imagine what he would come up with. But that's as good a reason as any to want to attend a party, right?

I'll definitely start my wedding diet…tomorrow. This weekend at the latest.

"Now, we must get back to work," Monique says as Daniel walks out of the studio. She helps me back onto the stand and then continues pinning the dress again, which I take as a cue to start discussing the case.

"Did you know about this?" I ask. "That Jean Luc would hire my old firm? You don't seem surprised at all."

"No, I did not know," she says, "but that was the reason I didn't want to use Gilson, Hecht—Jean Luc does use them on quite a few corporate matters of his own. Will it be a problem?"

"It won't be a problem for me," I say, "but you need to think about whether or not it will be a problem for you. If you are at all uncomfortable with this, we can discuss it more."

"I have faith in you, Brooke," Monique says, now examining the bodice of the dress, "I just want *you* to think about if you really want to do this."

"I do," I say, as Monique pins the bodice, lowering the neckline. It highlights that part of my body that I hate most—where my arms meet my torso—and makes me look like I have chicken fat protruding from my armpits. Not my best look. Not *any* woman's best look, is it?

Okay. So I understand that this isn't really my wedding dress that she's working on. Really I do. But would it kill her to put me in a style that's more flattering to my figure?

"Monique, I just want you to know how much I appreciate this opportunity. I'm going to work so hard for you on this case."

"I know you will," she says, smiling at me gently. "But, I suppose I don't have to tell you my own personal opinion on what it's like to work with the man you love."

"Well," I say, the lawyer in me coming up with a rationalization before I even have a chance to fully think my response through, "we won't actually be working together. We'll be adversaries."

"But, isn't that worse?" Monique says, tilting her head to the side.

"Jack and I have worked together before," I explain, "and the truth is, it's never been a problem for us before. So, it won't be a problem now."

"Good," Monique says, "Now let me help you out of this muslin."

"Let's talk spin," I say, as Monique helps me get out of the dress. It's like an obstacle course with the millions of pins that she's put all over the fabric, but she holds the dress at just the right angles for me to take it off unscathed. Well, more unscathed than I already am. "That blind item in the *Post*. Do you want to sue?"

"I think that would make it more conspicuous," Monique says, putting the muslin back in the closet and then sitting down on the couch as I put my clothes back on. "This party tonight should put everyone's suspicions to rest, once and for all. After tonight, there will be no doubt in anyone's mind how committed Jean Luc and I are to each other. The funny thing is that Jean Luc and I thought of the idea together. I guess there are still some decisions we can make as a team."

I see Monique's eyes begin to tear up at the edges, and I look away to pretend not to see.

"I agree," I say, walking to the window where I look down at the swarm of reporters waiting by the door, "I think you're making the right decision."

"Then, it's time for me to get ready for my party," Monique says, and stands up from the couch where she'd been sitting.

"Well, have a wonderful time tonight," I say. "Do you need me to be here for anything? You know, in case any legal issues pop up."

"You are so funny, Brooke," Monique says with a laugh. "How would it look to the reporters if one of my brides were to be here? The one who is a lawyer?"

"You can also invite a bride who is an accountant," I offer. "Or a banker. Do you have any brides who work in investment banking?"

Monique laughs loudly and I laugh along, too, trying to pretend that I'm not desperate for a piece of free fish.

"Well, have fun," I say, conceding defeat. "I just know it will be a huge success."

"And so will your case," Monique says as she walks me to the stairs. "Speaking of which, what comes next?"

"Discovery," I explain. "It's the part of the case where each side gets to ask the other side for information—questions, documents, depositions—they're all part of the pretrial process that the federal court calls discovery."

"What a funny name for it," Monique says as we stop at the top of the stairway.

"I never really thought about it before," I say, "but, I suppose it is."

"I guess it's because I'll be *discovering* a lot of things about my husband?" she asks with a laugh. "Things that the court assumes that I don't already know? Well, Brooke, I can assure you—after over thirty years together—I already know all there is to know about him."

"There's always more to find out about someone," I say, thinking of a particular case I had when I was still practicing at Gilson, Hecht. In a routine discovery process, some e-mails sent by the CEO of a company were revealed that his shareholders probably didn't know about and that his wife most definitely did not know about. Apparently, he'd purchased a mail order bride over the Internet and was keeping her and their two love children in a home in Minnesota. Even though this bit of information showcased his ability to multi-task, one of the most important qualities you'd look for in a CEO, he was still fired and served with divorce papers from wife number one the very next day. "You'd be surprised about how much you can learn about a person you really thought you knew."

Column Five

You didn't hear it from us...

OVERHEARD over a glass of wine at the reception following Monique deVouvray and Jean Luc Renault's renewal of the vows ceremony: "Why is it that every time a couple renews their vows, the relationship crashes and burns six months later?"

Sour grapes? Or *in vino veritas?*

9

"And she says to me: 'yes, that would be fine,'" I tell Jack as our taxicab lurches up Park Avenue. We're fifteen minutes late already and I don't want to keep my parents waiting at the florist. God forbid they give my mother a glass of champagne to celebrate. Then the next thing you know, she'll be passed out in a patch of begonias and my father will have negotiated a real "steal" on the floral arrangements by using flowers that were previously used the weekend before at a funeral.

"Fine?" he asks, tilting his head down to look at me. I love it how, when we sit together in a taxicab, he always puts his arm around the back of the seat so that I can get close to him.

"Yes," I explain. "I ask Elizabeth to be a bridesmaid and she says—and I quote—'yes, that would be *fine.*'"

"I thought you said it was Patricia?" he says, turning to face me.

"Which one's the oldest?" I ask. "It was the oldest."

"Patricia, then Elizabeth, then Lisa," he says, counting them off one by one on his fingers for me.

"Right," I say, "then it was Patricia."

"That is so like her," he says, baby blues narrowing.

"Really?" I ask, excited to get some Solomon family gossip. Jack never speaks badly about any of his family members. Ever. Come to think of it, he never really talks about his family at all, so I was excited to get the inside scoop. As an only child, there's really not much to talk about with each other (Dad: Did you hear that your mother is making meat loaf for dinner again? Again? Me: Why don't you just ask her about it? She's standing right there.) I mean, what's the point of being part of a big family if you don't get to gossip about each other?

"No," he says, "not really. I just thought I was still doing that whole 'you have to agree with me all the time thing.' "

"Yeah," I say, giving him a peck on the lips. "That's pretty much always in effect."

"Maybe you called her the wrong name and that's why she wasn't that excited about it," he says, looking down at me with a smile.

"Um, still in effect!" I say and Jack smiles even wider.

We sit in silence, looking out our respective windows, me leaning on Jack, as the cab drives through the Helmsley building over Grand Central Station and into midtown Manhattan. The florist is on 61st Street, between Park and Madison, so we're almost there. But that's not the reason why we stop talking. We stop talking because there's nothing to actually talk about. We can't talk about work—the Monique case is the biggest case that either of us is working on, and we can't talk about the wedding. Jack knows I'm still ever-so-slightly on edge about the fact that my parents have been bullied into having a wedding at the Pierre when what they really wanted for me was a traditional Jewish ceremony at a conservative temple on the South Shore of Long Island.

Our taxi stops right in front of Maximo Floral Concepts and I hop out as Jack pays the fare. The entranceway to the floral shop is done up to the hilt, with massive vines of ivy intertwined with crimson-red roses completely covering the stone-wall entranceway. As you walk through the cherry-wood doors, the delicious aroma of lilacs and lavender hits you and you can't help but stop and take a deep breath. The second we get inside, Jack squeezes my hand and leans over to give me a kiss.

"The newlyweds!" my mother cries out as we walk inside.

"We're not newlyweds, we're recently engaged, Mom," I say as I look around for the bottle of champagne.

"Ah, the couple of the hour!" the florist says, walking over to us with two glasses of champagne.

So, *he's* the culprit. I grab my celebratory glass of champagne and shoot my mother a stern look. She walks to the other side of my father with her glass, well out of my reach.

"I am Maximo," the florist says in grand style, throwing

his arms out wide as if he were a magician, with an accent that is definitely either Spanish or Italian. He bows slightly before extending his hand for us to shake. He shakes Jack's hand first and then takes mine delicately and gives it a little peck as only a Spaniard would. Or an Italian.

"Oh, Maximo," my mother titters. I give Maximo a tight-lipped smile and then shoot another glare in my mother's direction. I'm not sure why she's flirting with him since it's well known that Maximo owns this shop with his life partner, Federico.

"So, I was thinking white roses," my mother says, taking my hand and leading me through the showroom. "Maximo has a gorgeous display back here that's even in our price range!" She throws her head back and says the "price range" part loudly for Maximo to hear. He politely laughs at her lame joke.

"My guy on the island can do it for cheaper," my father says, leaning against a very expensive-looking trellis.

"We can't have Long Island flowers for a New York City hotel wedding," my mother says, dropping my arm from hers and walking over to my father. Since deciding to have the wedding at the Pierre, she has very much embraced the idea of a New York City hotel wedding. I'm just happy that she has something to brag about to her mah-jongg game now that Monique's not designing my dress anymore.

"What?" my father asks, "now *you* hate Long Island, too?"

"No one hates Long Island," I say with a smile as I walk over to Jack and pull his arm close to me.

"Oh," my father says, "then it's just the Long Island *temples* that everyone hates."

"No one hates anything, Mr. Miller," Jack says, breaking from my grip and walking over to my father. "It's just that, well, it's silly. You see, my parents always dreamed that I'd be getting married at the Pierre. When they got married, they had just graduated from college and they didn't have a dime. Their parents could barely afford to throw them a proper wedding and they weren't even allowed to invite all of their friends. Now that they've worked so hard to achieve so much, they just want me to have the wedding that they never had. I hope you can understand."

"Our Jackie is such a mensch," my mother says and throws her arms around Jack. My father looks over to me and we just look at each other. I know that he's thinking: *But didn't they plan three other weddings already?* but won't say it.

Truth be told, I'm sort of thinking the same thing, too.

"Let us give the lovebirds some time to walk around and see our selection," Maximo says, coming between all of us and taking Jack's and my hands. "Now, go, lovebirds. Go and get inspired." But, since he's Spanish (or Italian), he says the "inspired" part as if in slow motion: een-spy-yeyrd. Which sort of does have the effect of inspiring me.

Jack takes my hand and we begin to walk through the showroom. From the outside, it was hard to tell how large Maximo's showroom would be, it looked like it would be the size of any regular Manhattan store, but as we walk through it, it keeps getting larger and larger, like one of those dreams where you discover that your very own house has extra hidden rooms that you never even knew about.

"Why couldn't you have been this diplomatic the other night when we were at your parents' house?" I ask Jack, as we walk through a gazebo lined with pink hydrangeas.

"You're right," Jack says, as he guides me toward a tiny bridge with a stream of running water flowing under it. "I agree with everything you just said and you are always 100 percent right. About everything. Always. Ever."

"I'm serious, Jack," I say, looking down at the water. The waves are so delicate, so beautiful and the sound of the trickling water makes me wish that I could see the bottom of the pond.

"You know how hard it is for me to have a relationship with my father," Jack says, tugging at my arm so that I'm forced to turn and face him. "You know how hard it is to stand up to him. My family isn't like yours."

Jack looks at me, baby blues deep and dark as night, and runs his fingers through his hair.

"I know, Jackie," I say. "I know."

"They are nothing like your family. And I'm just doing the best that I can with him," Jack says. "Can't you try to understand that for me?"

"I know," I say. "I just wish that you knew what was important."

"I know what's important," he says, mouth fighting back

a smile, "Didn't I tell you that you can buy as many Manolos as you want?"

"And baby Manolos," I say. "Which don't even exist. You promised me those, too."

"Even baby Manolos. So, does this mean that you're dropping the case?" he asks, eyes wide with anticipation.

"God, no, Jackie," I say, "this is the first client I've ever brought in and my first shot at being the lead attorney. Why should *I* be the one to drop the case? *You* should drop the case. There are a million different cases you could lead at Gilson, Hecht right at this very moment!"

"But, this is a high-profile client," Jack says, "and I need to show the big boys at the firm that I can handle the big clients. Especially Mel. How can I tell him now that I don't want the case he brought in especially for me?"

"Mel loves me," I say, "just explain the situation to him."

"Mel would not understand. And anyway, word on the street is that Old Man Trattner is going to be coming in to visit the firm at the end of the month, and I want to make sure that I've got this high-profile case on my desk."

"I always forget that he's still alive," I say, remembering the days when I was an associate at Gilson, Hecht. When associates first get to Gilson, Hecht, they always think that the fact that the last named partner is still alive is like a law firm urban legend—that he doesn't really exist, that he's just a ghost used by partners to put the fear of God into associates ("You think working until midnight is bad? Back when Old Man Trattner was still here, he would have made us work straight through the night and checked up on us at 3:00 a.m. to make sure we hadn't dozed off!"). But the truth is, Milt Trattner just moved out to California and is teaching anti-trust law at U.C.L.A. "Isn't he, like over one hundred years old? Is it even safe for him to fly?"

"He's one hundred and three. But that's not the point. I'm a partner now in a firm that has four hundred attorneys, and I have to start making a name for myself."

"Well, I'm almost a senior associate now," I say, "and I need to start taking the lead on cases and bringing in clients if *I* want to make partner."

"If that's the way you want it," Jack says, "then that's fine. You keep your case and I'll keep mine. But just one warning—I am going to cut you into twelve little pieces and feed you to the jury. So get prepared for it!"

"Don't be silly, Jackie," I say, "dissolution of partnership cases don't go to trial."

"It's a movie quote," he says, smiling down at me.

"Since when do you quote movies?" I ask.

"I quote movies," Jack says.

Since when does Jack quote movies?

"Lovebirds!" Maximo calls out, "are you een-spy-yeyrd?"

"Very," Jack says.

"Well, good," Maximo says, "I am glad. And I am glad that you found our little pond. You throw a penny in and make a wish now, no?"

Jack and I look at each other and Maximo announces that he has a penny for each of us to toss.

"I give you a moment to come up with a wish."

"I don't need a moment," Jack says, "I know what I wish for."

"Me, too," I say, looking at Jack.

"Then, let's do it," Jack says as Maximo smiles and hands us each a penny.

We both close our eyes and throw our respective pennies into the pond.

10

"You do not look like James Bond," I say.

"Of course I do," Jack says, not even looking at me, waving the zappy gun menacingly at the row of crystal bowls we're browsing. We're at Tiffany and Co. today to register since my parents' friends apparently went to Tiffany to buy us an engagement gift and we were—gasp!—not registered there yet. ("The Goldmans said that you are still not registered at Tiffany's. I could *not* believe my ears. Still not registered at Tiffany's? *Still?* Well, when they told me I was horrified. Horrified!")

"You don't," I say, grabbing the gun from him to zap the Harmony bowl onto our registry. I've bought that bowl for so many engaged couples that I've lost count. I know that I should be thrilled that *I* am now the one registering for it, but all I can do is be annoyed at Jack for acting so juvenile. Who is this man-child and what has he done with my fiancé?

Why does Tiffany's even give out these stupid zappy guns to couples who are registering, anyway? You would think that a classy joint like Tiffany and Co. wouldn't want to give couples a scanner to scan merchandise directly onto their registry. You'd think that they'd ask you to write them a formal note on perfumed stationery detailing just exactly which items you would like on your registry instead of letting all of their couples make a scene in the store by having them walk around debating the merits of the basketweave pattern versus the plaid. More importantly, don't they know that the men who hold the scanners will instantly revert to children and start using the scanning guns as toys?

I had this image of us walking into Tiffany's—a modern-day Audrey Hepburn and George Peppard—behaving elegantly as we registered for all of the things that we would need for our glamorous new life together. I even wore a black shift dress and beige raincoat. Instead, my fiancé began playing with the gun like a six-year-old, thus testing our relationship to its very brink.

"Gimme that," he says, grabbing the gun from my hands, "those Russians are on our tails." And with that, he begins to skulk behind the glassware.

"What in God's name are you doing?" I whisper loudly as I follow him behind the rock-cut beer mugs.

"Shhh!" he says, pointing at another couple around the same age as us who are also registering, "the Russian couple!"

"First of all," I say, "they're not Russian, Jackie."

"Yes, they are," he whispers. "And use my code name, Hannibal."

"Excuse me?"

"Hannibal," he says, crawling past the wineglasses straight toward the bowls. "You said that I had to be George Peppard today."

"Get up!" I say, pulling Jack up off the ground from his shirt collar, "His character's name was *not* Hannibal."

"Well, I'm George Peppard from the *A-Team,*" he says, "George Peppard from *Breakfast at Tiffany's* was a huge wimp."

"You can't just pick whatever George Peppard you want to be," I say.

"The Russians!" he says, pulling me behind the wall that separates the personal shoppers from the rest of the floor.

"Stop this," I say, "You're George Peppard from *Breakfast at Tiffany's.* Start behaving accordingly."

"A-Team!"

"Who are you and what have you done with my fiancé?"

"Please, Brooke," he whispers, "we don't want the Russians to attack. We're vulnerable by the glassware. Let's move to the sterling silver."

"You do realize that you're supposed to be the normal one in this relationship," I say as he drags me across the floor to the sterling silver. And he's right, there's much more cover in the sterling silver section. It's just that my father will kill me if I register for any sterling silver that could be gotten for cheaper out on Long Island at Morell's.

"Do you see the Russians?" Jack asks, his back to the display case.

"Okay, they are not Russian!" I say. "They are just another couple registering for their wedding, just like us."

"Well, actually, Brooke," Jack says, "both of my grandmothers were born in Russia, as was my grandfather on my mother's side."

"Could you focus on the task at hand, please," I say, taking the gun away from him.

"Shouldn't you just be happy that I came?" Jack asks. "Most men make their fiancées do all the work by themselves. But, I'm here. So, can't you just appreciate that and let me have a little fun instead of being bored to death?"

"Oh, my God, Jackie, you're bored to death?"

"Kind of," he says, "but I know it's important to you, so I'm here."

"Jackie," I sing, grabbing him for a kiss. "That is so sweet of you."

"Of course, sweetie," he says as he glances back to the table filled with crystal bowls. "But you can do Bloomie's with your mother, right?"

"Right," I say with a smile.

"Hey, are these the Georgetown bowls?" Jack says, picking up a crystal bowl and turning it over. It's a large crystal bowl, but rather plain. It lacks the elegant lines of the Harmony bowl, and has big sides that look cumbersome—like they'd always get in the way. I never would have chosen it myself, but if Jack wants it, I suppose I don't mind.

"Miranda says that we should register for the Georgetown bowl," Jack says, getting the scanner ready to zap.

Miranda? Why is *Miranda* telling him what to register for?

"Why is Miranda telling us what to register for?" I ask, taking the bowl from his grasp under the pretense of taking a closer look at it.

"She says it makes a great salad bowl," he says, baby blues shining. He seems so excited about having suggested something for our registry that I barely have the heart to tell him that I really don't care what Miranda thinks we should register for, since she's not our friend. She's just someone who works for Jack.

Not like I'm jealous of her or anything. But, really. How dare he invoke her name while we are in the temple of Tiffany and Co. (And if you don't think that shopping at Tiffany's is a religious experience, clearly you've never been there.)

"It's at a good price point," Jack says, smiling. "Didn't your mother tell us that we should register for things in a wide variety of price points?"

"Zap it in," I say, forcing a smile. I think to myself that I can always delete it off of our registry later online.

"Will do," Jack says, and turns around to zap the totally boring Georgetown bowl into our registry.

"Gotcha!" the faux Russian guy says, coming from out of nowhere, pointing his zappy thingy at Jack. Jack clutches his chest and pretends to fall to the floor. I do what any woman in my position would do—stand there with my mouth wide open, waiting for faux Russian guy's fiancée to arrive so that we can roll our eyes at our respective men-children.

"Brooke," he chokes out, "just remember how much I love you. (Cough.) I want you to go on without me and live a happy life. (Cough, cough.) Don't mourn me for the rest of your life. And—whatever you do—don't register for that Metropolitan vase. I really hate it." He coughs a bit more, just for good measure, and then collapses completely onto the floor, moaning all the way.

I am not amused. Again, and I really can't stress this enough, *he's* supposed to be the normal one in this relationship.

"Who *are* you?" I say, and take his gun and start zapping silver serving spoons indiscriminately.

"Boys and their toys," a woman, whom I can only assume is the faux Russian fiancée says to me, rolling her eyes. "Just give them a phallus and they can play all day." Um, okay, can't we just call them little boys? Was that phallus remark really necessary? That comment totally ruined Tiffany and Co. for me for the day. Perhaps forever.

But, maybe they really *are* Russian. That post-perestroika tough-talking sort of Russian woman who simply tells it like it is. After all, she does have pitch-black straight hair, pale skin and bloodred lipstick. I ask you, what says Russian woman more than black hair, pale skin and red lipstick? And her fiancé has pale blond hair, even paler skin and a tall, skinny frame that totally screams Baryshnikov in *White Nights.*

Or, she could just be totally correct. There was something

disturbingly phallic about the zappy guns at Tiffany's, with their long noses and thick bases.

Eeew. Now I've grossed myself out.

"Let me give you a hand there," faux Russian says to Jack, as he helps pull Jack up off of the floor.

"Thanks," Jack says, brushing off his pants and running his hand through his hair.

"No problem," faux Russian says. "I'm Yuri. And this is my fiancée, Natasha."

"Nice to meet you," I say, shaking their hands as Jack introduces us. Out of the corner of my eye, I can see the edges of Jack's mouth creep into a sly smile.

"So," Jack says, putting his arm around my waist and giving me a squeeze, "you guys are Russian, huh?"

Jack smiles, and I must admit, I smile a bit, too, at the ridiculousness of the situation, but really, all I can think is: *Who is this man and what has he done with my perfect fiancé?*

11

"So, how's the Monique case going?" Noah asks me, peeking his head into my office.

"Great," I say, smiling at him, "just great!"

And why shouldn't I feel great? After all, I've got the litigation totally under control. I've researched the law on dissolution of partnership, studied Monique's partnership agreement, analyzed her non-compete clause, and even had the case fast-tracked in an effort to avoid unwanted media exposure. So, I've got it all in the bag.

"Litigating against your fiancé is going all right?" Noah asks, furrowing his brow. When he found out that Jack was the Gilson, Hecht partner on the matter, he wanted me to pass the case off to another associate, but I stood firm. I'm really going to prove myself on this matter and nothing's going to stand in my way.

"Of course!" I say, "In fact, it's even better than I could have imagined. With Monique's husband, it would have been a bit of a challenge to negotiate a settlement. But, with Jack against me, it'll be a piece of cake! The man is putty in my hands. I almost feel sort of sorry for him, you know?" Now, I know I was laying it on a bit thick, but Noah Goldberg is one of the founding partners of the firm and I just want to assure him that my case is going well.

And, okay, Jack may not be actual *putty* in my hands—he didn't drop the case when I asked (read: begged) him to—but, I know that he'll treat me with kid gloves in this litigation and I plan to exploit that to the fullest extent allowed by law. You see, in a normal litigation I know exactly what Jack would do. Seeing that his opposition is a firm that's much smaller than Gilson, Hecht, with much fewer resources, he'd begin the discovery process by burying the other side in a massive document production that would take them weeks to produce. He'd request thousands of pages of documents from the other side that they, in turn, would have to get from their client, review for relevancy and attorney-client privilege, and then number, stamp and photocopy. Given that our case is fast-tracked, the deadline would be even sooner than a regular document production, and in requesting as many documents as he could think of, he'd force the other side to concentrate all of their energy into putting together the requested documents instead of working on case strategy, which would then allow him to use all of that time to work on his own case strategy and easily win the case while the other side is inundated with minutiae.

But, my Jackie would never do that to me. Thank God, really, because I have a million wedding dress appointments to go to in the next two weeks.

"Putty?" Noah says to me, "Really?"

"Yes," I say in a stage whisper, "it's almost embarrassing."

"That *would* be embarrassing," he says, "if you hadn't just been served with a discovery request." He walks over to my desk and throws a legal document on top of the case law that I was reviewing. "So much for putty."

Served?

How can that be? Jack and I had a very romantic dinner last night and he didn't mention a *thing* to me about serving me with discovery requests. How could he do this to me when I was such a fabulous fiancée last night? I even cooked for him! Well, not so much cooked as ordered a Heat-and-Eat meal from Fresh Direct, but I *did* totally unpack the box and then heat it up for him! *And* picked up a bottle of wine and a cheesecake on the way home, to boot! He is really taking this Chinese Wall thing seriously.

I don't even need to look at the document Noah's just dumped on my desk. I already know what it is—it's fastened with two staples across the top, like all discovery requests, with a "blue back" attached, which, as the name implies, is a blue piece of paper secured to the back of a document that folds over the top of the first page by one inch. The fancier law firms use that one inch where blue back folds over the top to announce, in bold-faced type, the name of their law firm. I don't even have to look to see what this familiar blue back says:

Gilson, Hecht and Trattner
425 Park Avenue
New York, New York 10022

Jack has served me with a discovery request. A document request, to be specific.

I immediately pick up the telephone. "I've just been served," I say to Vanessa.

Oh, please. As if your first order of business after being served *wouldn't* be to call your best friend?

"Served? Like in that movie?" Vanessa asks. "Has someone challenged you to a dance off?"

"This is not funny!" I say. "Jack has just served me with a document request! And he's requesting a lot of documents here!"

"Just get the junior associate to do it," Vanessa says. "Why are you panicking? It's not like *you're* going to be the one reviewing all of those documents. You're just going to supervise the darn thing, so don't be so dramatic."

"I'm the only person on the case," I say, twirling the phone cord around my index finger.

"Oh, that is not funny," Vanessa says.

"I know," I say, now twirling the cord around my whole hand. My engagement ring peeks out from in between the cord, all sparkles and fire, and I unwind my hand from the cord.

"What types of documents is he requesting?" Vanessa asks, and for a moment I consider faxing the document request to her to get her opinion on the case. But then I remember that she, too, works at Gilson, Hecht and could turn to the dark side just as quickly as Jack had.

"Tons and tons of things," I say, flipping through the request. "And it's due in two weeks."

"No," Vanessa says, "in the Southern District of New York all discovery requests get thirty days for response."

"We're fast-tracked," I say. "I agreed to turn around discovery requests in two weeks."

"Well, that was stupid," she says, matter-of-factly. "Unless you did it so that he can't spend as much time with Miranda Foxley, man stealer to the stars."

"Man stealer to the stars? She's slept with *celebrities?*" I ask, my ears perking up at the thought of such delicious gossip. Even in the face of hours and hours of work, a girl's still got time for some juicy celebrity gossip. "Who has she slept with that I would know?"

"Oh, no," Vanessa says, "she hasn't slept with any actual celebrities."

"Why'd you call her man stealer to the stars then?" I say.

"Everything just sounds better when you say 'to the stars,' doncha think?" she says.

"Let's see, *tailor* to the stars, *chef* to the stars, *yoga instructor* to the stars.... Yes, actually it does," I say. "But it's making Miranda sound more fabulous than she is. Let's just call her 'man stealer extraordinaire.'"

"Done," Vanessa says. "But my point is the same. Is that why you got the case fast tracked?"

"I didn't think he was actually going to serve me with discovery," I say. "This is a dissolution of partnership, for God's sake! We shouldn't even be litigating!"

"Just request an extension," Vanessa says. "Judges love it when parties play nice. You can ask Jack for an extension of a week or two. That way you won't have to miss all of your wedding dress appointments and you'll also get in good with the judge when he sees that you and Jack are being professional."

My wedding dress appointments. I still don't have a wedding dress. I still don't have a wedding dress!

"That would mean that Jack wins," I say, twirling the cord once again.

"Now you're being ridiculous. It's not about winning or losing," she says as I hear her slam the door to her office shut. "It's about the wedding dress! Get your priorities straight, for God's sake, woman."

"Anyway, you can't ask for extensions on a fast-tracked case, especially when it was your own motion that requested the fast-track," I say, leaning back in my chair. "The judge will realize that you don't actually need the case to go fast and think that you're just trying to manipulate his court calendar."

"I wish your judge was a woman," Vanessa says. "A woman

would totally understand that you need an extension to go wedding dress shopping."

"So true," I say as Vanessa begins to tell me the horror of her latest first date. We'd been so excited about this one, since he had tickets to see *The Drowsy Chaperone* on Broadway, which Vanessa and I were both dying to see. We got even more excited when he asked her to go to dinner beforehand. The only thing, he said, was that he got the tickets with another couple, and would she mind it much if they went on a double date as their first date? Well, the theater is the theater, so Vanessa told him that she wouldn't mind one bit and then put on her cutest skirt and cropped jacket to go on the date.

Imagine her surprise when she gets to the restaurant to meet her date and finds out that their dinner companions are her date's parents. Who would also be accompanying them to the show.

"Ironic," I say, "considering you were going to see *The Drowsy Chaperone.*"

"Are you mocking me?" Vanessa says, and I can't help but giggle. And I do feel badly that I'm laughing at Vanessa, but come on! A double date with the guy's parents?

And then I take a peek at document request number thirteen and immediately stop laughing. Document request thirteen is a request for all e-mails sent by Monique that relate to the partnership she had with her husband. Requests that ask for e-mails are always a nightmare—it means that the lawyer reviewing them will have to go through each and every one of their client's e-mails one by one to analyze them for relevancy, just like you would a normal document. But they usually take three times longer to review than regular documents, since e-mails are generally single-spaced. And God forbid there be an attachment.

I could object to the request on the grounds that it is overly broad—it could take me months to go through all of Monique's e-mails—but chances are that the judge will tell me that it's relevant to Monique's husband's countersuit. Which is true. There's only one thing I can do here. Besides throwing myself on the floor and crying like a baby, that is. Or calling my fiancé to yell at him. Or my mother. Or my therapist.

No, there is one thing that I *really* must do here: I need to get myself to Monique's computer as soon as humanly possible.

"Van," I say, "I'm sorry, but I've got to go."

Just asking...

WHAT prominent French businessman, married to a former model turned fashion designer, took a quiet jaunt to the Cayman Islands for the weekend?

His friends say he was just in desperate need of a tan, but sources tell us he's hiding his funds in anticipation of his impending megadivorce. Sources say when this one hits, it'll be bigger than the Loni/Burt, Alec/Kim and Charles/Denise splits...combined.

12

"Where were you?" my mother says, bursting through the door to my office. I'm shocked to see her there for two reasons: the first is that my mother never visited me at work. The second is it's 8:00 p.m. that night.

"What are you doing here, Mom?" I say, getting up from my desk to give her a kiss hello.

"We had a 7:00 p.m. appointment at Amsale," she says.

"I totally forgot," I say, trying to figure out what day it is. "I'm so sorry."

"You forgot?" she says, "about shopping for your own wedding dress?" And with that, she puts the back of her hand to my forehead. And then her other hand to her own forehead.

"What are you doing?" I say, swatting her hand away.

"You must be ill," she says, "I'm testing to see if you have a temperature."

"I feel fine," I say, walking back behind my desk and sitting down, "Why would you think that I'm sick?"

"Well, you would have to be deathly ill," my mother explains, as she sits down on one of the visitor's chairs in my office, "to forget about shopping. Wedding dress shopping, no less."

"I'm not ill," I say, "I'm just insanely busy at work is all."

"I have never known you, in your thirty years on planet Earth, to choose work over shopping," she says, reaching over my desk to feel my forehead again. "Surely, you must be delirious."

"I'm not delirious," I say leaning back in my chair out of reach of her arm, "I'm just very busy at work. And I didn't *choose* work over shopping. I really had no choice in the matter." I toss the document requests over to her to prove my point.

"What is this?" she asks, picking up the document request with two fingers as if it was a dirty turtle I'd found in our backyard. "Is this piece of paper supposed to validate the fact that you missed our appointment at Amsale?"

"I'm just showing you how busy I am," I say, taking the document request back.

"Yes, I know all about it," she says, "it's what you told me last night when you missed our appointment at Vera Wang."

"There's nothing I can do about it," I say, looking back

down at the documents I was reviewing when my mother first walked in.

"That was your excuse on Monday, when you missed our appointment at Reem Acra," she says, grabbing the documents I'm reviewing and throwing them down on the floor behind her.

"What are you doing?" I say, getting up from my chair to retrieve the documents.

"What are *you* doing is the better question here, BB," she says, grabbing my arm as I pass her. She stands up from her chair and we are face to face. "What are you thinking? Don't you want to get a wedding dress?"

"Of course I want to get a wedding dress, Mom," I say, "it's just that I have all of this work to do."

"When you were at Gilson, Hecht you were never this diligent about work," she says. "I remember meeting you on many an occasion at Saks when you'd snuck out of work for the afternoon. And now, when you *really* have something that you need to shop for, you don't have time?"

"I need to prove myself here, Mom," I say, "you just don't understand."

And of course my mother wouldn't understand. The longest job she ever held was working at the Five and Dime when she was sixteen years old. And that was just an after school job. She had the luxury of meeting my father in college and being married by the time she was nineteen. Pregnant with me at twenty-two.

"What I do understand is that I'm trying to get my only daughter—my only child—married here," she says. "What's important is life, not work. You've finally found Mr. Right. Don't you want to celebrate that?"

"While I was waiting around for 30 years for Mr. Right to come around, Mom, I got a career and a life. I still have to honor my commitments. You're the one who taught me that."

"But, BB, now you've found Mr. Right, so you can relax a little. I'm not telling you to quit your job. I'm not telling you to drop your big case. I'm just saying to give yourself a little time off so that you can look gorgeous when you walk down the aisle to go join Mr. Right in holy matrimony."

"This is the last night I work this late, Mom, I promise," I say, as she releases me from her grip and I bend down to retrieve the documents she's thrown on the floor. "Once I get done with this document production, it's back to wedding dress shopping full force."

"And all things wedding?" she asks, her right eyebrow arching upwards.

"All things wedding," I say, "I promise." My mother smiles and I know that it is because she thinks that she has won. But the truth is, the documents are due at 9:00 a.m. tomorrow morning. I couldn't work on them any longer if I wanted to. So, after I have these documents sent over to Jack's office, I can finally rest and get back to planning my wedding.

My mother hugs and kisses me before she walks out the door and I immediately get back to work. The documents themselves are out being photocopied and numbered, so all that's left to do now is draft a privilege log and reread the request to make sure that I've given Jack all of the documents he's requested.

I open a Word document to begin drafting the privilege log, but first indulge in a little activity I always find myself doing to procrastinate when I'm at work. I click open an Internet browser and then type in the familiar Web site of my old law firm: www.gilsonhecht.com. First I type in my own name, and wait for the search screen to come up, telling me that no result was found. Then, I type in Vanessa's name and look at her profile:

Vanessa Taylor, Esq.

– Howard University

– New York University Law

• Member of the NYU Law Review

– Admitted to practice in the State of New York, Southern District of New York, and Eastern District of New York

vtaylor@gilsonhecht.com

She looks absolutely adorable in a fitted black Theory suit which she's paired with a pale pink cowl-neck top. Since she wears her hair so short, she's always wearing beautiful earrings to complement her look. In the picture, she's got on long gold drop earrings that have tiny pink stones dangling from them.

Next, I go to the *S* section of the "Our Attorneys" page where I pull up Jack's profile:

Jack M. Solomon, Esq.

– University of Michigan, *magna cum laude*

• President, Drama Society

– Harvard Law School, *summa cum laude*

• Articles Editor of the *Harvard Law Review*

• Moot Court

• President, Student Bar Association

– Admitted to practice in the State of New York, State of Pennsylvania, Southern District of New York, Eastern District of New York, Eastern District of Pennsylvania, Second Circuit, Third Circuit.

jsolomon@gilsonhecht.com

Just seeing his firm photo smiling back at me is always enough to make me smile myself. And I figure that it's okay to procrastinate by doing this, since when I worked at Gilson, Hecht, I'd go and visit Vanessa and Jack in their offices to procrastinate. Since I'm at a new firm, it's only fair that I still get to procrastinate with them.

Before turning back to my work, curiosity gets the best of me and I pull up Miranda Foxley's profile:

Miranda Foxley, Esq.

– University of Texas

– Emory Law School

– Admitted to practice in the State of New York, Southern District of New York, and Eastern District of New York

mfoxley@gilsonhecht.com

I absolutely cannot get over how slutty she manages to look in her attorney portrait. Even in a suit, with a background of a bookshelf filled with legal treatises behind her, she still manages to look like she's in the mood to have sex. Red hair blazing, completely unkempt and out of control, there's a seductive look on her heavily made-up face and a camisole under her suit jacket that is a little too lacey and way too low-cut for a traditional office photo; there should be one of those cartoon captions over her head that says, "Hey baby, wanna wrestle?"

"Are you still here?" a voice says to me, and I instinctively sit up a bit straighter in my chair and then click off of Miranda's firm photo as quickly as a thirteen-year-old boy caught with a dirty magazine. I look up from my computer screen to find Rosalyn Ford leaning in the door frame of my office with a smile.

"Rosalyn," I say, almost out of breath. "Hi."

"Burning the midnight oil," she says, "I'm impressed."

"It's not like I really have a choice," I say, lifting up the discovery request to demonstrate my point, and attempting a lame smile. "These privilege logs don't exactly write themselves."

"Well," she says, "you always have a choice. You know that. But, you look busy. So, I'll just leave you to your work."

"I'm sorry," I say, "I don't mean to be so cranky. It's just that I'm a bit stressed out right now."

"Don't worry about it," she says. "We've all been there. You'll figure it out. How about I take you to lunch tomorrow?"

I want to tell Rosalyn no, that I have too much work to take a lunch break tomorrow, but it's never a good idea to say no to a partner. Especially one like Rosalyn, who's consistently been supportive of my work and my career here at SGR.

"Great," I say. "Thanks." I try to keep smiling, but I can't help but think about what my mother would say about taking a lunch, but making no time for dress shopping.

"Have a good night," Rosalyn says as she walks out. I draft a quick e-mail to my assistant to tell her that if my mother calls tomorrow between the hours of twelve noon and 2:00 o'clock, she should be told that I am in a meeting. Then I get back to my work.

Four hours later, I've got my documents back in my office and boxed up, my privilege log drafted and everything proofread. With my head so heavy, it's about to hit the keyboard, I quickly draft a cover letter, print it and sign it. As I place the letter in the box of documents, I feel like something is missing. I pick the letter back up and walk with it over to my desk.

My mother is right. What's important is life, not work.

So, I should be focusing on my life. But I am such a woman of the millennium that I can inject a little bit of life *into* my work. I open my desk drawer and rifle around a bit. Finding the loudest, most obnoxious shade of red lipstick that I've got, I quickly put it on my lips. I pull the letter out of the box and put it onto my desk. Once I've smacked my lips together a few times to make sure that I'm even, I then lean down to the letter and plant a big kiss right on the letter, next to my signature line.

With a smile, I put the cover letter back in the box, tape it up and then call Federal Express to pick it up.

13

As I cab across town to meet Jack at a loft on 37th Street to hear a wedding band play, all I can think about is Jack's reaction to the big lipstick kiss I planted on my cover letter.

When the cab stops at the building, so far west that it's almost on the West Side Highway, at first, I think that the cab driver's made a mistake. There is just no way possible that there is a big fancy black-tie wedding going on inside this building. The entranceway is bordering on industrial—classic nondescript 1970s-style construction with just a single door entrance. As I walk in, I announce myself to the security guard, who really looks as if he couldn't care less who is coming or going. I get into the elevator and try to figure out which button is for the penthouse. Most of the buttons have their numbers worn away from use, so I just hit the one for the last floor in the lineup and hope that it takes me to my destination.

I look down at the silk organza gown and open-toe satin shoes I'm wearing and feel a bit overdressed as I look around at my surroundings. But as the elevator lets me off on the seventeenth floor, I realize that I'm in the right place.

The elevator doors open into a beautiful entranceway, elegantly decorated with an antique armoire and rug. I walk through to the area where the reception is being held and it is a vast space—fourteen-foot ceilings if they're an inch—with white-lace-tableclothed tables set up around the perimeter and a medium-sized dance floor in the middle. Enormous crystal chandeliers hang from up above, and the floor-to-ceiling windows are dressed with delicate white fabric which pools at the bottom, flowing onto the floor.

Why didn't Jack and I think about having a wedding like this? A hidden Manhattan space, big enough to fit both of our families (and just our families and closest friends, mind you) that's nestled in a tiny corner of the city. It occurs to me that we never once tried to figure out what we wanted as a couple. Instead, we just deferred to what our parents wanted—Jack's parents, a big New York City hotel wedding, and mine, a traditional Long Island temple wedding—to disastrous results. I wonder what we would have chosen, if we had made the decision all on our own.

"Come here often?" a low voice behind me asks.

"Well, no," I say, spinning around. "But maybe I should."

"Can I kiss you hello or are you still wearing that awful flashy lipstick?" Jack says, with a sly smile.

"Oh," I say, giving him a kiss on the lips, "just admit that you loved it."

"I loved it," he says, taking my hand and leading me into the room where the reception's being held. I take a glance over at the band, Moore Music. They're playing an old big band number that is exactly the type of thing that I want for our wedding. The band is absolutely perfect.

"Did you really love it?" I ask. "Or are you just saying that because that's what I want to hear?"

"I thought it was adorable," he says, "I love it when my woman stakes her claim on me."

"What?" I say, putting my hand on my chest for dramatic effect. "I have no idea what you're talking about."

"Let's see," he says, "you were the junior associate on all of my matters five years running, so I'm pretty sure you knew that Miranda would be opening the documents for me and would be the first to see your grand declaration of love."

"Oh, that's right," I say, "I must have forgotten. Now that I'm at a law firm where I have tons of responsibility, I must have forgotten about big firm bureaucracy entirely. I hope that Miranda didn't mind."

"To the contrary," Jack says. "She told me to ask you what shade of lipstick that was. She's thinking of buying herself the same one."

"Cute," I say. It takes all of my energy not to say something catty about Miranda and how she probably has her own stash of loud, flashy lipsticks to choose from. But saying something like that would make me seem jealous. Or threatened. Which I most certainly am not. Because Jack's not like my last serious boyfriend who left me for a loud, flashy man stealer. So what's there to be jealous of?

"Well, I try," Jack says, pulling on the lapels of his tuxedo. We'd decided that, since we were coming to see the wedding band at a black-tie affair, we should dress up so as to blend in with all of the other wedding guests. "How did I do?"

"Very well," I say, putting my hand on his chest and leaning in for a kiss. I smell his aftershave and it goes down my spine. I keep my eyes closed for a moment longer than I should.

"What do you think of the band?" Jack asks, with his arms still around me.

"I love them," I say, "you?"

"Same," he says, "That was easy enough. See, I told you planning our wedding would be a breeze."

I hold my tongue.

The band announces the happy couple, for the first time as husband and wife, and the groom grabs his bride's hand to begin their first dance.

"So, how was your day?" Jack says as we watch the bride and groom dance in the middle of the dance floor. Her white tulle gown becomes a huge blur to my tired eyes as she spins around and around.

"Great!" I answer a bit too quickly. One thing that Jack always taught me—never let your adversary know where your head is at in a litigation. I certainly don't want him to know that I was in any way fazed by his incredibly rude litigation tactic. Yes, rude! It's one thing to use that tactic on *other* lawyers, but it is quite another to do such a thing to your fiancée who really has better things to do with her time than review ninety thousand pages of discovery documents and get tons of paper cuts. Doesn't he know that when you're engaged, people ask to see your hands all the time? Note to self: must seriously talk to the judge about the paper cut/hand issue.

But, I won't let Jack see me sweat. I will just act like the tough no-nonsense attorney that I am. I am woman, hear me roar!

Although he probably figured out how hard he made me work on that document production since I came home three hours after he went to bed last night.

But, come on, I ask you, who was the one who was *really* punished in that scenario?

"You look a little tired, Miller," he says, grabbing my hand and leading me out onto the dance floor, as the first dance ends and the dance floor begins to fill with wedding guests.

"Tired?" I say, "why, no. I slept like a baby. Didn't you?"

"Well, I would have slept better if my fiancée had been there to keep me warm," Jack says, drawing his arms around me even tighter.

See? I told you so. Loss of consortium is always harder on the man than it is the woman. Although, I must admit, Jack *is* very good at keeping me warm. In fact, I'm getting a bit warm right now, the closer and closer he holds his body to mine.

"Well, I would have been home sooner," I say, "but I've got this big case that I'm working on. The guy that I'm litigating against is a real animal."

"Growl," he whispers into my ear and then takes a little nibble. Animal, indeed! "Well, if you can't handle such a large-scale litigation, maybe you should just concentrate on keeping your fiancée warm and drop the case."

"Am I hearing that you're ready to talk settlement already, counselor?" I whisper back into his ear.

"No way in hell, Miller," he says, and spins me. I almost lose my footing as I come back to face him.

"Why not?" I ask with a smile, now on steady ground, "Isn't it in both of our clients' interests?"

"My client isn't settling," he says, drawing me in close.

"You have an ethical obligation," I lecture Jack, "to go to your client with any settlement offer that I make to you."

"That rule only stands if there is an actual offer," Jack lectures me right back. "You haven't made me any sort of firm offer."

"Oh," I say, sidling up to him, "I'll give you a firm offer."

"That's my line," Jack says, looking down at me, baby blues shining.

"Right," I say, feeling my face heat up, "I confess, maybe I am just a *touch* tired."

"I knew it," he says, "I knew that the document request would work. I must admit, I figured you'd just come home to me and convince me to drop the suit in a very, very unethical way, but—"

"What way did you have in mind, counselor?" I ask, as he spins me and then pulls me in to him. Our faces are so close that his features all begin to blur into each other right in front of my eyes.

"Something," he says, voice lower, "that I can assure you the Bar Association would frown upon."

"Do tell," I say, putting my cheek next to his.

"Surrender," he whispers back.

"Never, Jackie," I say and pull back. We stare each other down, each one waiting for the other to back down, but we both stand firm.

"Never say never, sweetie," Jack says, "Now, I *know* I taught you that."

I try to formulate a response, but just then, Savannah Moore, the bandleader of the band, comes over to introduce herself.

"Everyone's about to sit down for the first course," she says, "let's sneak into the caterer's office for a few minutes to talk about your wedding."

We follow Savannah out of the reception room and down a long hallway. She's a tiny little thing, dressed in a black bias-cut cocktail dress, just like the other two female singers in her band. I like that they are all dressed the same, even though Savannah is clearly the star. Doing it this way makes the band look like a cohesive unit and she obviously understands that. All of the singers dance to the music in unison, and they are all clearly having a blast up on stage, which is another thing I like. If the band is having fun, I can't help but think that our guests will be having a great time, too.

Savannah turns around, her bouncy red hair flipping over her shoulder, as she gets to the caterer's office door. She looks just like Ann-Margaret with her lithe frame and thick red hair. I can practically see her singing along with Elvis to "Viva Las Vegas." Actually, that might be a really cute dance number for the wedding. I wonder if Jack's dad would think that an Elvis impersonator at our wedding would be considered tacky.

Savannah knocks gently on the caterer's office door, and then, not hearing a response, motions for us to come in. I detect a slight Southern accent that she's trying to overcome as Savannah begins to tell us about how many pieces come standard in her band (eleven—four singers, four strings, drums, piano and a flute player), the price (so expensive that I'm embarrassed even to say it here, God knows how I'll stir up the courage to tell my dad), and how many hours they play (four, with an additional hour for the ceremony for a nominal fee). Even as she explains the most mundane of details, Savannah is high-energy and sweet.

"You know who you remind me of?" Jack asks her, after she's completed her spiel on the basics.

"Yes," Savannah says with a smile, "I get that a lot."

"You do?" Jack says, "Well, I was actually thinking of this associate I work with."

He'd better not be talking about who I think he's talking about.

"Right, sweetie?" Jack says, looking at me. "She's just like Miranda!"

"She is most certainly *not* like Miranda," I say a little too quickly, smiling widely as if the comparison doesn't bother me one bit. Which it doesn't, of course.

Only, Jack's been raving all week about how fabulous she is. Savannah, not Miranda, I mean, but it's almost the same.

All I can think is, *Why couldn't he have just said Ann-Margret like a normal person?*

"Well, you remind me of Ann-Margret," I say, hoping to change the subject.

"Why, thank you, Brooke," Savannah says, smiling, "I'm very flattered. I get that a lot, and I consider it to be such a huge compliment. She was really largely talented, and—"

"Ann-Margret was from Sweden, Brooke," Jack says, cutting Savannah off without even realizing it, "I detect a slight Southern accent from Savannah. Am I right?"

When did Jack become such an expert on Southern accents? Is this what Miranda's been helping him with under the guise of working on the Monique case together?

"Guilty!" Savannah says. "I'm from a tiny little town outside of Savannah. But my father always wanted bigger things for me, so he named me for the biggest city he could think of."

Clearly, Savannah isn't sure whose family is paying for the wedding yet, so she's trying to be equally nice to both of us.

Big mistake.

"Well, it's time for me to get back up there and do my thing," Savannah says, "you two can take as long as you'd like in here to talk things over, and then you can feel free to come back out and listen to a few more numbers. Sound good?"

"Sounds great," Jack says, rushing up to his feet to shake Savannah's hand.

"Thanks so much," I say, "thank you for everything."

"My pleasure," Savannah says, as she walks out the door and shuts it quietly behind herself to go back to the party.

"Maybe we should see what else is out there," I say, once the door has closed. "Just to make sure that there aren't any other bands that we missed. We wouldn't want to sign with someone so quickly that we regret it later."

"She's the only female bandleader in the entire Tri-State area," Jack says. "For some reason, I like that. It's so cool that she's a woman doing it in a man's industry. And doing it so well. She brings a certain grace to the whole thing. And, of course, there's her stellar reputation."

"I still think we should see other bands," I say, picking at a stray cuticle.

"But I thought you were sold? Didn't you just say a half hour ago that they play the exact type of music that you want for our wedding?" he says.

I shrug in response.

"*And,* her band looks great. Don't you want a good-looking band that's fronted by a gorgeous woman like Savannah?" Jack asks.

"We're finding another band."

"You know what I think? I think your judgment is clouded because of this litigation," Jack says, pulling his chair closer to mine. "Why don't we talk settlement on our case and then that will clear your head for more important things—like our wedding?"

"Well, I didn't want to do this, but—" I say as I lean back in my chair from Jack and put my hand inside my dress.

"No, please do," Jack says, his eyes following my hand intently as I fish around the inside of my dress. "I insist. Do you need some help with that?"

"No, I think I've got it," I say, as my fingers wrap around the thing I'd been groping for. Jack stands in front of me, eyes wide and glued to my chest like a sixth-grader as I pull out the papers. Now, I don't know exactly what Jack expected me to pull out from the inside of my dress. How exciting could a thing that would fit inside of the folds of my dress be? I guess it was just the excitement of seeing my hands so close to my breasts.

But, unfortunately for Jack, the thing that I was looking for wasn't anything sexy or spicy—it was a set of discovery requests of my own.

"Counselor," I say, pausing for effect and giving the statement the requisite pageantry that such a statement deserved, "consider yourself served."

14

"I hate that one," Vanessa tells me, "it makes your finger look fat."

"Have you been hanging out with my mother?" I say, looking up at her.

"I called it fat," she says, "not fleshy. There's a difference."

"Which is worse?" I ask as she takes the ring I've just tried on and puts it onto her own slender finger.

"See? Fat," she reports. "And I have very thin fingers."

I knew I shouldn't have brought someone who's skinnier than me shopping. Even if it *is* only ring shopping, who ever wants to look fat? I should have just brought Rosalyn. The other day at lunch, she volunteered to come with me, but it was hard to get a word in edgewise throughout the whole lunch as she regaled me with tale after tale of how she works a full caseload, but still manages to carve time out from her work for each and every one of her son's Little League games.

Anyway, I thought it was more appropriate to bring Vanessa, my maid/matron of honor. Even if I haven't asked her yet to be in my wedding party, she's still my best friend.

We're on 47th Street, the Diamond District, at a friend of my father's who is supposed to be giving us an amazing deal on wedding bands. ("If he doesn't discount it by at least half," my father cautioned, "you are to call me immediately.")

It's been difficult to find something that will match Jack's grandmother's engagement ring. An Asscher cut diamond with regal trillions flanking it on either side and channel-set diamonds around the rest of the platinum band, I'm finding it difficult to match its old-fashioned traditional style with the more modern wedding bands that I like. Moishe (his real name) told me that it will be impossible to find a ring that's in my personal style to match the engagement ring, but I just know that if we try hard enough, we'll be able to make the two styles come together beautifully.

"That one's no good," Moishe says, taking the ring from Vanessa and putting it back in the showcase. "Let me run downstairs and take a look at the other stuff we've got. You two look at earrings while I'm gone."

I should mention here that I find it very disconcerting that an Orthodox Jewish man with a painful comb-over who weighs more than Vanessa and me combined has better taste in diamonds and assorted other baubles than Vanessa and me combined.

"So, my divorce is moving along quickly," Vanessa says as we walk over to the earring display case.

"Oh, my God, Van," I say, "is this too hard for you? Maybe we shouldn't be doing this today."

"Of course not!" she says, pointing to a pair of delicate ruby studs. "I can be happy for you even though my world is falling apart."

"Your world is not falling apart," I say, motioning for Moishe's son to come open the display case for us.

"Yes, it is," Vanessa says, looking at me, "but I'm okay with it."

"No, it's not," I say, as Moishe's son rubs the ruby earrings with alcohol so that Vanessa can try them on, "you have your friends, your family, your apartment."

"Friends?" she says as Moishe's son hands her the earrings to try on, "I don't have any friends. My so-called *best* friend hasn't even asked me to be in her wedding party."

"I wanted to!" I say, "but it never seemed like the right time. Of course I want you to be in my wedding party! You *are* my wedding party! Vanessa, will you be my matron of honor?"

"No," she says, looking at her reflection in the mirror with the earrings on.

"Was I supposed to get down on one knee for that or something?" I ask. "Maybe that's why I got such a chilly reception when I asked Jack's sisters. Is there some bridesmaid protocol that I'm not aware of?"

"You asked them before me?" Vanessa says, eyes widening in disbelief.

"Is that why you said no?" I ask.

"No," she says, looking at me, "it's because by your wedding I'll be a maid. Not a matron anymore."

I grab Vanessa and give her a hug. Vanessa's not really a hugger, but as I hold her to me, I feel her hug me back.

"Let's just leave," I whisper into Vanessa's ear, "I'll come back later."

"No way," Vanessa says, pulling back. "This is your day to look at wedding bands. It's all about you."

"No, it's not," I say, "it's all about the lunch after the wedding ring shopping. I think we've done enough for one day and there's a Burger Heaven right around the corner. Let's go get burgers and fries and talk all afternoon. We can always come back later if we want."

"Okay," Vanessa says and we make a beeline to the door.

"Ladies!" Moishe says as he huffs and puffs on his way back up from the basement.

"Don't worry, Moishe," I say, walking back to his counter, "I'll come back this week and we can finish up then."

"No—" he says, but I cut him off. These guys on 47th Street can be so pushy! I guess he doesn't realize that after the deal he made with my father, it's a foregone conclusion that I'll be getting Jack's and my wedding bands from him.

"Moishe," I say, putting my hand on top of his, "you don't have to worry. We're not going to go to someone else. It's just that we've had enough jewelry shopping for one day."

"Brooke—" he says.

"I promise you! We're not going to anyone else!" I say

with a laugh, looking back at Vanessa, who is nodding as if to say, "After all of the time and expertise you've expended with us, would we go to someone else?" Moishe is finally able to get a word in edgewise.

"The earrings," he says, as his son puts his hand out.

Vanessa's hand flies to her ears upon realizing that she is, in fact, still wearing the ruby studs, and she begins to quickly take them out of her ears.

"I knew that," she says.

I ask you, is there any greater pleasure in life than a burger and fries with a Vanilla Coke? There's nothing that such a combo cannot fix. It's comfort food at its best—the perfect mix of salty and sweet. For God's sake, it is the American Way. Vanessa and I sit at a booth at Burger Heaven where I've thankfully got her mind off her divorce. Instead, we're discussing the fact that her mother has been setting her up on a multitude of dates—almost five a week for the past four weeks. This before her divorce is even final. We can't decide if it's because Millie thinks that dating other men will send Vanessa flying back to her own estranged husband, or if she's just trying to get her daughter married off again as quickly as humanly possible. The smart money's on the former.

"And so he says, 'I really feel like I should see you home in a taxi.' Even though we were only two blocks from his apartment and mine was twenty blocks uptown."

"That's so sweet!" I say, sipping my Vanilla Coke. Dating in Manhattan can be funny like that—most people don't have cars, so the most chivalry a girl can hope for is for her date to hail her a taxi at the end of the evening. Taking you home in a taxi makes a man total marriage material, as far as I'm concerned.

"No, it's not," she says, dipping a French fry in ketchup, "he picked a place that was two blocks away from his apartment. That's totally rude."

You see, Vanessa has never dated in the city before, so she has no idea how hard it is and how often you have to drop your standards and expectations. She met her husband on her first day at Howard University and by senior year, they were engaged. She's never had to be an adult in the world without her husband standing beside her. She's never had to go through endless amounts of bad first dates, hopeless blind dates and awkward bar hook-ups. She never wondered, night after night, if she'd ever find the right person. If she was destined to end up alone.

Until now.

So now, at age thirty, she's doing—for the very first time—what the rest of us did in our twenties. And it makes me wonder: is it better to have struggled for all those years only to finally find love now, like me, or to have found love all those years ago, and then lose it and have to start all over again, like Vanessa? It's sort of like when you play that morbid game with yourself, wondering whether you'd rather die quickly in an accident without even knowing it was coming, or if you'd rather be ill for a long time first, and get to say goodbye to your loved ones and make peace with your universe.

Is it bad that I'm getting married and I just equated relationships with death?

Anyway, the point is that Vanessa is entering the New York City dating scene for the first time and it's been a bit of culture shock for her. You see, she was with Marcus, a handsome, charming surgeon, who was always the perfect gentleman. Except, of course, for that one tiny incident where he kissed another woman while married to Vanessa, thus precipitating their divorce, but you know the general point I was trying to make.

"I still think it's very gentlemanly for him to see you home in a taxi," I say, taking a bite of my pickle. "And rather out of the ordinary. Usually a guy gets brownie points just for hailing you a cab. Actually getting *into* one with you and taking the trip to your apartment with you? Call *The New York Times* because it's front-page news. Oh, wait, were you annoyed because you thought it meant that he assumed he was coming upstairs?"

"No, you're missing the point. He didn't see me home at all," she says, dipping another fry into the ketchup.

"You just said that he said that he felt like he should see you home."

"That's right," she says, "that is exactly what I said."

"What am I missing here?"

"He said that he *felt* like he should see me home," she says, taking a bite of her burger and then a sip of her Vanilla Coke. "So I said, 'Oh, that's so sweet!'"

"It *was* sweet," I say, swiping a fry off of her plate.

"And then he said, 'Oh, but I'm not going to.'"

"Excuse me?"

"Yes," she says, "You heard that correctly. Then he said, 'Oh, but I'm not going to.'"

"He did not," I say, swiping another fry off of her plate and sticking it into my mouth. In my shock over what she was telling me, I even forget to even dip it into the ketchup first.

"Yes," she says, "he said, 'I *feel* like I should see you home.... But I'm not going to.'"

"Charming," I say, "was he trying to get brownie points under the guise of it being the *thought* that counted?"

"At least it's not as bad as the guy who wrote me an e-mail the day after our blind date and said: 'I know you've been out of the dating world for a while, so here are a few pointers....'"

"I thought we agreed never to speak of that again," I say, taking a sip of my Vanilla Coke, "Anyway, I still think you made that e-mail up."

"The one thing I learned from all of your years of dating and countless bad date stories," she said, "is that you just can't make this stuff up."

"No," I say, "you cannot. So what did you do?"

"I said goodnight and hopped into the nearest taxi," she says. "Isn't that what you would have done?"

"Yes," I say, "but then I would have also called my mom to yell at her for setting me up with such a jerk, cried about how depressing my life is, and then had a pint of Häagen Dazs while sitting on the couch watching *Blind Date*."

"Oh," Vanessa says, "I did all of that, too."

This is why I'm so glad to have Jack, I think, but don't say out loud.

Or rather, don't mean to say out loud, but say out loud since I'm on a sugar high from the two Vanilla Cokes I've had. When I was single, I used to hate women who said stuff like that out loud to me. How could I have just said that to Vanessa! "Not like he's that great or anything."

"You don't have to say that to make me feel better," she says, "didn't we cover this? I can still be happy for you even while going through my divorce."

"Well, he served me with massive discovery," I say.

"That makes sense," she says, "since you're litigating against him. You totally should have blown it off, though, for wedding dress shopping. I've been stuck with your mother alone for three nights in a row."

"Sorry about that," I say.

"Strangely," she says, "I've been having a lot of fun with Mimi. She's had some really great advice."

"Well, I'm glad you're having fun with my mom," I say. "I guess."

"It would have been more fun with you," Vanessa says. "Stop working so hard, would you?"

"I will," I say, "and, anyway, you'll be pleased to know that I got him back."

"Are you going to tell me some sort of kinky sex story now?" she asks, slurping the remains of her Vanilla Coke. Our waiter swoops in and grabs her glass for a refill. "Because I may be happy enough for you to hear about wedding stuff, but for a kinky sex story, I just do not have the strength."

"Here's your Vanilla Coke," the waiter says, setting down Vanessa's Vanilla Coke with a strange look. He lingers for a brief instant, waiting to hear, no doubt, my kinky sex story.

"No," I say, "I served *him* with discovery requests."

"Why the hell did you do that?" Vanessa asks, "are you trying to create work for yourself?"

"No," I say, "I'm just doing what I would do against any adversary."

Vanessa puts down her burger in righteous indignation and glares at me. Okay, okay, so I *wouldn't* normally do that. I would normally just be trying to settle and make as few billable hours for the client as humanly possible. And when I say "as few billable hours for the client," I really mean: as little work for myself as humanly possible.

Oh, please. As if you wouldn't do the exact same thing.

"You do realize," Vanessa says, "that now Jack will have to work more hours with Miranda Foxley, man stealer extraordinaire. You do realize that, don't you?"

Clearly, I had *not* thought about that. But now that Vanessa's brought it up, it's the only thing that I can think about. I stir my Vanilla Coke slowly as I formulate a plan.

"There's only one thing I can do now," I say, looking Vanessa straight in the eye.

"Why do I have a feeling that I'm going to be involved in this in some way?" she says, stirring her own Vanilla Coke. "Please don't make me do anything that would get me disbarred."

"You need to start spying on Jack and Miranda," I say, "just to make sure that there isn't any hanky-panky going on."

"Hanky-panky?"

"You know what I mean," I say. "Just make sure that everything's on the up and up. But don't let them know you're spying."

Why is it that we nice girls must constantly be on the lookout for man stealers? That's what destroyed my last serious relationship, and you can be sure that I'm not going to let that happen again. Maybe if Jennifer Aniston had asked Courtney Cox to spy on Brad, they'd still be happily married right now.

"That doesn't sound very ethical," she says, narrowing her eyes as she takes a sip of her Vanilla Coke.

"Do you want to maintain your post as matron of honor or not?" I ask.

"Maid," she says, as the waiter dumps our bill on our table.

"Whatever," I say. "Do you?"

"I've been in a lot of weddings before, Brooke," she says, "and no bridesmaid detail ever included spying on the groom."

"Thank you so much for agreeing to do this for me," I say.

"But, I haven't agreed to anything yet," she says.

"Close enough," I say, as I pick up the check.

Sightings...

CONFIRMED. Halle Berry will be the next celebrity bride to walk down the aisle in one of Monique deVouvray's creations. Insiders spotted Berry shopping for wedding bands with an unidentified brunette on 47th Street, talking about wedding plans, kinky sex and, of course, Monique's dress.

Berry's publicists deny the couple's even engaged, but insiders say that she shopped at Moishe's Jewelry Emporium before ducking into Burger Heaven for a late lunch.

15

"That sort of thing really wouldn't come under the umbrella of what a wedding photographer does," Melissa says to me, putting her hand to her forehead as she sits back in her chair.

Melissa Kraut is the wedding photographer Vanessa recommended to me and we're in her fabulous studio in Chelsea. Vanessa met Melissa when she represented her, pro bono, through Volunteer Lawyers for the Arts, back when Melissa was just starting out with a camera her parents gave her and Central Park as her backyard studio. Back then, she was a starving artist who needed Vanessa's help in protecting the intellectual property rights in her work. Now that she's doing wedding photography, she's hardly starving any more and she's got her own studio and her own legal team at her beck and call. Even though Vanessa no longer represents her, they've stayed friends. In fact, Melissa even set Vanessa up on a date the other night. It didn't really work out, since to hear Vanessa tell it, "he was so short he only came up to my boobs," but I thought it was nice of Melissa to think of Vanessa nonetheless.

I have this vision of Melissa covering my wedding for me, and then being so inspired by the photos of me that I become her muse and she takes even more and more photos of me, and then eventually exhibits them in Vanessa's mom's art gallery and I become a big international supermodel. The first supermodel *ever* to be only five foot four and a half.

What? It could happen. They have short models on all the time on *America's Next Top Model.*

"Think of them as action photos," I explain, "action photos of the groom."

"Still, it's a little out of the bounds from what a wedding photographer would normally do. Surely you understand that." I'm suddenly very aware that I'm leaning forward, practically hanging over Melissa's desk, and she's leaning so far back on her chair that she's in considerable danger of actually falling out of the window.

"Getting acquainted with your subject?" I ask, leaning back in my chair with my hand demurely on my chest so as to feign innocence. "Is getting acquainted with your subject what you consider out of bounds?"

"You want me to spy on the groom for you."

"Spy sounds so harsh," I whisper, sotto voce, "don't you think?"

"I think I'd like for you to leave."

★ ★ ★

"That sort of thing really wouldn't come under the umbrella of what a wedding videographer really does," Jay says to me.

Jay is a friend of a friend of a friend of a friend of my father who's based out of Queens, and he's promised to give me a "real deal" on my wedding video. We're meeting at a pastry shop on Lefferts Boulevard and instead of the non-fat decaf cappuccino I promised myself on the way over, I'm halfway into a regular cappuccino with a chocolate chip cannoli on the side. To be fair, though, it's not really my fault. This meeting with Jay has been the *tiniest* bit stressful. And not just because the wedding photographer I met with kicked me out of her office. My father told me that there was a very slight chance that Jay has connections to the Mafia, so I should be careful not to say anything negative about the Mafia when I'm with him.

Now if that isn't an elephant in the room.... *Don't say Mafia. Don't say Mafia.*

And, at any rate, my father told me, I shouldn't really be concerned, because Jay wasn't high-ranking in the mob—at the very most, my father surmised, he was a soldier.

Note to self: must rent first season of *The Sopranos* to find out what a "soldier" is.

"Think of it as background footage for the wedding video," I say, making an effort not to sound desperate, "it would be great fun!"

Oh, God. I just said "great fun" to a man who may or may not be connected.

"Great fun?" he says, taking a swig of his espresso. Busted.

"Well," I quickly say, "you know. Fun. Sort of fun. We can all get to know each other before the wedding!"

"I've never really taken footage before of a groom at his office," Jay says, "but I've done some surveillance in my day, so if that's what you're looking for—"

"Surveillance?" I say, almost choking on my cannoli, "I don't need surveillance! Who said anything about surveillance? No, it's just that my fiancé, Jack, just loves to work and so you'll just be getting background footage of him in his natural habitat!"

"Whatever you want to call it," Jay says, looking at the door as someone walks in. "Where does he work?"

"He's a lawyer," I say, "He's a partner at Gilson, Hecht and Trattner."

"Fancy," he says, taking one more swig of his espresso and finishing it. "Isn't that the firm that represents Jean Luc Renault?" I'm momentarily taken off guard by this question, since Jay doesn't really look like the type to cover couture fashion.

"I believe so," I say, "Why? Do you follow fashion?"

"Are they going to be covering Monique and Jean Luc's big divorce? I'm not a pap, don't think I'm one of those scum-suckers, but when that whole thing goes down, details about the divorce are going to be selling for a fortune."

"No, they're not getting divorced," I say, ever the protector of attorney-client privilege.

"Well, smart money's on the rumors that say that they are," he says.

"Well, they're not," I say, grabbing my Sweet-n-Low packet and tearing it in half. And then into fours.

"How do you know?" he asks.

"I just know," I say, looking back up at him. "So, do you think you'll want to do my wedding video?"

Jay looks at the door again as another person walks in. Even though he's had nothing to eat, he takes out a toothpick and puts it into his mouth. He flips the toothpick to the side of his mouth with his tongue and says: "You're on."

"Great!" I say.

"Let's go to your fiancé's office first."

"Great!" I say, taking another bite of cannoli. "Now?"

"No time like the present," he says and I stuff the rest of the cannoli into my mouth, followed by a big swig of my cappuccino. "I've got my camera in the car. I'll drive you into the city."

Now, my mother always taught me that I shouldn't get into a car with a stranger. But, surely a friend of a friend of a friend of a friend of my father would not be considered a stranger, now, would he? Even if he may or may not have the capacity, connections and mental wherewithal to fit me for concrete shoes and then drop me into the Hudson.

Forty-five minutes later, we've listened to the entire side A of Frank Sinatra's *Ring a Ding Ding* album, on tape cassette, natch, and we're pulling into a parking garage a block away from the Gilson, Hecht offices. Normally, parking in midtown costs more than most people in America would pay for a down payment on a house, but Jay seems to know the manager of the garage.

"This is a surprise," Jack says, as he looks up from his desk to find Jay and me at his office door.

I walk into Jack's office first, with Jay following me with his camera on his shoulder, as if I'm Ed McMahon coming with an oversized check.

"We just thought we'd get some footage of you at work," I say, giving him a peck on the lips. "You know, for the wedding video."

"Great," he says, getting up from his desk. "Have you eaten yet? I can take a break right now and we can run down to the cafeteria for something to eat."

"Keep filming," I say to Jay. And then, to Jack: "No, honey, I just had a quick bite. And, anyway, I want Jay to get some footage of you working for the wedding video."

"You want footage of my office for the wedding video?" Jack asks, brushing his hand through his shaggy brown hair.

"Why, of course!" I say, as if to say: "Doesn't *everybody* have footage of their fiancés working at their offices on their wedding videos?"

"Okay," Jack says, reluctantly going back behind his desk.

"Just look natural," I tell him.

"Right," Jack says, looking around his office, no doubt, for Alan Funt to jump out from behind his potted plant. Or at the very least Ashton Kutcher.

"Anyway, I have way too much work to do today to stay here," I tell Jack, already kissing him lightly on the lips and heading out to leave. "That you assigned to me."

Jack laughs and tells me that he loves me as I walk out. I

grab Jay and whisper to him that if he *just so happens* to see a red-headed Southern belle who looks as though she has a penchant for married men, he should feel free to tail her for a little bit. I leave out saying the more dramatic: "If you do, I'll make it worth your while," since that part's really implied and I'm not *actually* an extra in an episode of *The Sopranos.* I'll just be referring to the show later purely for research purposes.

As I hit the button for the elevator, I wonder if I have time to make a quick visit to Vanessa's office. I turn around, about to make my way down the hallway, and see an old junior partner I used to work for.

"Hi there, Larry," I say with a forced smile. I never liked him much when I was an associate at Gilson, Hecht, and my absence from the firm most certainly has not made my heart grow any fonder.

"Miller," he says, "Just who I wanted to see. Are you available for a meeting right this minute? Go grab a legal pad, I need you."

"What?" I say. What on earth is he talking about? Did this guy actually miss the fact that I left the firm almost a year ago? Did he really *not* notice? And if so, why did Jack force me to spend *days* working on a carefully worded politically correct Exit E-mail Memo that ensured that I didn't anger anyone/piss anyone off/get me disbarred?

Make no mistake: the Exit E-mail Memo is a true art. When associates at large Manhattan law firms leave, what they *really* want to say is:

From: "Brooke Miller" <bmiller@gilsonhecht.com>
To: "NYC office" <allusers@gilsonhecht.com>
Subject: I am so out of here, SUCKERS!!!

I hate you. All of you. You have truly made my life a living hell from the minute I walked in the door here, and, while I learned a lot, I would much rather have been working as a gas station attendant at some gas station in God's Country, USA. Which, come to think of it, is really how most of you made me feel most of the time, so I guess I broke even.

I really only ever worked here because you paid me so darn much as a first year and I had massive student loans to pay. Now that I've dug myself out of debt, if I have to look at any of your ugly faces for another second, I might actually have to stab myself in the eye.

Signing off,
Faceless associate #536

Brooke Miller
Gilson, Hecht and Trattner
425 Park Avenue
11th Floor
New York, New York 10022

*****CONFIDENTIALITY NOTICE*****
The information contained in this e-mail message is confidential and is intended only for the use of the individual or entity named above. If you are not the intended recipient, we would request you delete this communication without reading it or any attachment, not forward or otherwise distribute it, and kindly advise Gilson, Hecht and Trattner by return e-mail to the sender or a telephone call to 1 (800) GILSON. Thank you in advance.

What I actually said was:

From: "Brooke Miller" <bmiller@gilsonhecht.com>
To: "NYC office" <allusers@gilsonhecht.com>
Subject: a fond farewell to everyone at Gilson, Hecht and Trattner

---

As many of you know, today is my last day at Gilson, Hecht and Trattner. It has been an amazing five years here, and in the time that I've been at the Firm, I have had the honor to work with some of the most outstanding attorneys practicing law in New York City today. I've made some of my best friends in the world here and I truly treasured my time spent here at the Firm.

It may be time for me to move on to a new adventure, but I will always look back on my time at Gilson, Hecht fondly.

Best regards,
Brooke

Brooke Miller
Gilson, Hecht and Trattner
425 Park Avenue
11th Floor
New York, New York 10022

*****CONFIDENTIALITY NOTICE*****
The information contained in this e-mail message is confidential and is intended only for the use of the individual or entity named above. If you are not the intended recipient, we would request you delete this communication without reading it or any attachment, not forward or otherwise distribute it, and kindly advise Gilson, Hecht and Trattner by return e-mail to the sender or a telephone call to 1 (800) GILSON. Thank you in advance.

The "Thank God I at least met my fiancé here so it wasn't a complete, total, utter waste of time" part was implied. As was the "I hate you. All of you." part.

"I've got a meeting with Janobuilder Corp. Didn't you

use to work on their matters when you were a first year?" Larry says to me, seemingly out of breath. Or at the very least out of patience.

"Yes," I say, "but I don't work here anymore."

Clearly, Larry did not get my carefully worded politically correct Exit E-mail Memo. An argument for sending the "I hate you" e-mail?

Larry doesn't respond. He merely turns on his heel and begins muttering angrily.

I turn around and begin pushing the button for the elevator furiously. My pulse begins to climb as I realize that I must get out of this building immediately before someone else tries to assign me more work. Vanessa will just have to understand. I'm sure that this sort of situation is covered by her maid of honor duties.

Anyway, it's time to get back to my own law firm. Where I can be accosted with work by partners in my *own* hallways.

16

Do not cry. Do. Not. Cry. You are not going to cry. You are a tough, no-nonsense attorney who can handle anything. Even the twenty boxes of documents that Jack just sent you to review. Piece of cake, right? After all, each box should take approximately four to five hours to review, so it's not that big a deal. That's only, well, let's see, eighty to one hundred hours of work ahead of you.

Eighty to one hundred hours of work. That is, like, so *not* a piece of cake.

And I'm due at the Pierre in forty-five minutes.

There's only one thing that I can do now—only one thing that anyone in my position would do, really—feign illness to get out of this afternoon's festivities. Which is absolutely fine by me. After all, I don't even *want* to get married at the Pierre. The wedding's only there since Jack's parents bullied my parents into it. And, I don't really care what they serve for dinner. My father's going to dominate the day anyway with his talk of his beloved meats and I'm sure they'll serve the glass of obligatory champagne to celebrate, so my mother should be prancing around with a lampshade on her head in no time flat. And I'm sure my father's already worked out some sort of side deal with the chef, so, why should they need little old me to help with menu selection? They probably won't even notice if I don't show up!

I practice my cough and slouch down in my chair—method acting at its best to sound fatigued—as I dial the number for my mother's cell phone. As it rings, I practice a lame, "Hello?" into the air and it's perfect. Which makes sense, since when the twenty boxes of discovery documents were delivered to my office just a moment ago, it actually made me feel physically ill.

"Knock, knock," a voice announces at the door. I hang up the phone quickly and sit up in my chair. "It looks like someone has got quite a bit of work cut out for her."

"Jack," I say as I get up from my chair to greet him. "What are you doing here?"

"I thought I'd pick you up to take you to the Pierre," he says, baby blues gleaming. I smile and forget about my work for a moment. Work that he assigned to me. But that's not what's important. What's important is my relationship with Jack. This is the man that I fell in love with. This is the man that I want to spend the rest of my life with. I knew it all along. Turns out I *can* do it all—I can have the perfect fiancé, work hard and win my case. All in three-and-a-half-inch heels. "And, of course," Jack continues, gazing over at the stack of boxes he's messengered to me, "I wanted to see the look on your face when you got our documents."

This is the man who is making my life a living hell. This is the man I am going to decimate in court.

"Is this your idea of a joke?" I ask, holding up a handful of documents.

"These are the documents *you* requested," he says.

"I just took a quick look at the first box, and already there are tons of duplicates," I say. "That's going to make it take me twice as long to go through this as it should."

"The Federal Rules of Civil Procedure don't say anything about having to mine the documents for duplicates. And there was a tight turnaround time on these, so it's not like we had time to have a paralegal check for dupes, anyway." Jack is smiling as he says it.

I am not smiling. "And there are tons of documents in here that aren't even responsive to my requests."

"Well," Jack says, his smile sort of turning into a smirk, "I just wanted to make sure that we didn't leave anything out. The judge would be furious if he thought that we weren't giving you exactly what you deserve, sweetie."

As we walk out of my office and down the hall, Jack starts telling me about our wedding videographer, Jay.

"So, is he supposed to be taking video of my filing

cabinets?" Jack asks as we walk toward the elevator banks. "Is there going to be attorney-client privileged information on our wedding video?"

"Well, Jackie," I say, "we just want to get footage of you in your natural habitat."

"But, my natural habitat isn't at the office," he says.

"It isn't?" I ask, with an innocent look on my face, as the elevator doors open up for us.

"No," he says, walking into the elevator with me and then kissing me as the doors close. "My natural habitat is anywhere that you are."

Swoon.

Jack and I kiss the rest of the way down the elevator, and then hop into the first taxicab we see. Fifteen minutes later, we are rounding the corner to the Pierre Hotel on Fifth Avenue, just across the street from Central Park. A uniformed doorman opens our taxi door and I walk out slowly.

The lobby is grand and lush and looks every bit the "testament to understated elegance" that their Web site promises, with its original 1930s detailing still on glorious display.

As soon as I walk in, I feel instantly reminded of something. From the black-and-white marble entranceway to the exquisite crown moldings on the wall to the lush royal-blue carpeting, I get the distinct feeling of déjà vu. And it's not because I've been here before for events. There is something about the Pierre that reminds me of somewhere else.

Jack's parents' house.

And Jack's parents look right at home, seated in chairs on

the landing in the near right corner, talking quietly as they wait for us. My parents, on the other hand, stand out like a stripper in church (or pair of strippers, as the case may be), milling about toward the far left corner of the lobby, looking around curiously and waiting for us. The lobby is so large that they haven't even seen each other yet.

Ladies and gentlemen, on one side of the lobby, we bring you Barry "the Butcher" Miller, who hails from the South Shore of Long Island, measuring five foot nine inches and weighing in at 250 pounds, 360 if you also count his wife, Mimi. On the other side of the lobby, we've got Edward "the Judge" Solomon, who comes to us from the mean streets of Philadelphia, measuring six foot two inches and weighing in at 225, and a hell of a lot more if you count his wife, too, since she's wearing palazzo pants today.

It's the clash of the parents: Round Two. Ding!

Now, I know what you're thinking—the first meeting of the parents didn't exactly go as planned. So, why on earth would I be bringing them all back together again? Well, I seemed to have this crazy notion that inviting everyone would be a good way to get the families to start getting along better.

And why should that be so difficult? After all, we're here to celebrate a joyous occasion—the marriage of the Solomons' youngest and my parents' only—so of course everyone will soon come around and iron out their differences. Just being here all together today at the Pierre is the first step in becoming a big happy family. The type of big happy family an only child like myself has always dreamed of.

As I stand between the two sets of parents, in the middle of the lobby of the Pierre, a thought crosses my mind for the very first time—this might not work out the way I had originally planned.

Thank God I didn't invite the siblings.

Both sets of parents meet Jack and I in the center of the lobby and we all awkwardly greet each other. The wedding coordinator spots us and waves. When I found out we'd be working with one of the Pierre's wedding coordinators, I had this vision of our wedding coordinator being some hilarious European gay man, straight out of *Father of the Bride* (Steve Martin incarnation, of course). Or even J. Lo in *The Wedding Planner* with her totally fabulous hair and makeup (but without the whole stealing the fiancé thing). What the families really need now is an outrageous personality who can take our minds off our differences and get us to focus on what's important. We need someone who can take the emphasis off the families and put it where it belongs: onto the bride and groom. Well, really just the bride, because, let's face it, weddings are really all about the bride.

Oh, please! As if you wouldn't want the world to revolve around you when you're planning your very own wedding?

So, what we need is someone to defuse this time bomb of a situation we've got going here. We need a referee, a distraction, or, at the very least, someone to gang up on. In a word, we need Martin Short speaking with an unintelligible faux Euro accent. What we've got instead is Catherine Glass. Shiny blond hair swept up into a French twist, pearl earrings and a navy-blue suit, she looks entirely nondescript, nonoffensive, and just plain old non. Isn't the wedding coordinator supposed to be some crazy colorful character? Or at the very least as fabulous as J. Lo? What a disappointment.

Catherine shows us to her office, where she has a conference room table set up with nine different types of table linens, four different menus, dozens of photo albums of past events at the Pierre piled up high, and seven chairs going around it. She sits at the head of the table, where her oversized leather notebook is placed, and my family files onto one side of the table with Jack's family across from us. I consider, for a moment, asking everyone to get up and all sit randomly, the way we all sat at the Solomons' house for that fateful dinner, but then I think better of it, hoping instead that no one will notice that we are lined up as if we were contestants on *The People's Court*.

"So," Catherine begins, barely looking up from her notebook as she takes notes, "how many guests were we thinking of inviting to this affair?"

"We'd like to keep it small and intimate," my mother says, folding her hands in front of her on the table. I do the same and smile back at my mom.

"Yes, we totally agree," Jack's mother says and I allow myself to take a deep breath. Maybe this afternoon won't be as difficult as I thought it would be. See, we're all in agreement already! "I'm not sure how many people you'll have from your side, but we were thinking that six hundred might be a good number to shoot for."

"Six hundred what?" my father says.

Jack's mother laughs. "Barry, you're so funny."

"Six hundred guests?" I say, looking at Jack. He and I had always talked about having a small wedding. Jack picks up an album and begins leafing through the pages.

"Yes," Jack says, barely looking up from the album, "only six hundred. We should definitely cap it at six."

"I know that your family is bigger than ours," my mother says with a smile, "but how could you possibly have six hundred guests?"

"Well, Edward has many business contacts that he's got to include," Jack's mother says.

"Are you inviting the entire United States judiciary?" my father asks, looking at Catherine. I know that he's hoping for a laugh from her, but she keeps a clipped smile on her poker face. I wonder if she'd play the role of dispassionate observer if she knew that my father was paying for the whole thing and tends to be a fairly huge tipper, even when it's inappropriate and/or discouraged to give a tip.

"Perhaps we should talk menu first," the wedding coordinator asks, pen poised and ready to write. "What were we thinking for an entrée?"

I see my father's expression brighten, ready, no doubt, to start talking sirloin.

"We were thinking lobster," Jack's mother says first and I see my father's face fall. My mother, all of the sudden, seems very interested in her fingernails.

"Lobster?" my father says, attempting a smile, "but, Joan, this is a Jewish wedding."

Everyone just sort of stares at everyone else for a moment and I just silently pray that I don't have to explain to the Solomons that lobster is *so not* kosher, which is why my father objects to serving it at a Jewish wedding.

"We were thinking filet," my mother says, taking a deep breath as she looks up from her hands with a broad smile on her face. "Filet mignon." The "'which my husband will lovingly pick out and supply himself" part is implied.

"Excellent choice," the wedding coordinator says, barely lifting her head up as she jots down notes.

"Maybe we should do a duet—the lobster and your meat," Jack's mother says. I'm sure I'm just imagining it, but it seems like she says the words *your meat* as if she's talking about my father serving meat from mad cows. I know she's a vegetarian, but surely she knows how high quality kosher meat is?

"*Now* you want a surf and turf?" my father says. No one seems to have any idea what my father is talking about, but I do. If only Jack's mother had served the beef tenderloin my father brought her that first night they all met, maybe some of this hostility could be avoided.

"Joan and I really had our hearts set on lobster," Jack's father says. "Don't you like lobster, Brooke? Whenever we go to the Palm, you always order lobster instead of the steak."

"Well, I…." I manage to eke out. I always make fun of Jack for his inability to stand up to his father, but now, sitting here in the hot seat, with Jack's father's eyes on me, accusing me of loving the non-kosher creatures of the sea, I can almost understand where Jack is coming from. I really can't imagine having a man like Edward as my own father. I can't even imagine having him as the judge in one of my cases. (Judge Solomon: "Isn't that right, Brooke?" Me: "Yes, Your Honor! I'm guilty!" My client: "You're fired.")

"Brooke and I love lobster," Jack says, running his fingers through his hair. Et tu, Brute?

My father turns and looks at me as if he's King Lear. But he needn't worry about me.

Now, I know I eat lobster all the time in my regular day-to-day life. And Jack's right, I would probably eat lobster every day if I could, but the point is, you simply cannot serve lobster at a Jewish wedding. Well, actually, you can (which has now been made exceedingly clear to me today by the Solomons), but the point is, when your father is a kosher butcher and he is paying for the whole thing, you simply cannot serve lobster at a Jewish wedding.

Don't panic, I think. Be calm. Be cool. Use your super litigator skills to make this man and his father realize that they do not, in fact, want to serve lobster at a Jewish wedding. They want to serve the meat that my father will pick out lovingly cut by cut. But, be so smart as to make them think that they came to this conclusion themselves. The sort of Jedi mind trick young engaged women everywhere are forced to use on their fiancés and future in-laws every day.

"You can't serve lobster at a Jewish wedding!" I cry out very, very fast. I catch my breath and realize that I've jumped a bit out of my chair in my zest. So much for The Force.

"Anyway," my father says, "some of our family members

keep kosher and they would not appreciate being served lobster at this Jewish wedding."

"Do you keep kosher?" Jack's mother asks, furrowing her brow, with the same tone I'd imagine her using if she'd asked my father, "Do you practice cannibalism?"

"That's not really the point—" my mother begins, before being cut off by my father.

"My Aunt Devorah does, for one," my father says, "if you've got lobster on the plate, she won't be able to eat the meat that's next to it. She can't eat something that's touched lobster. So, what's my Aunt Devorah going to eat?"

"No one really ever eats the entrées anyway, Barry," Jack's mother says to my father, reaching across the conference room table and putting her hand over his. "She'll probably just fill up at the cocktail hour and skip the main course altogether!"

"Probably not," my father says, "since at the rate we're going, we'll probably be serving *cheeseburgers* at the cocktail hour!"

"Well, we *are* from Philly," Jack's mother says.

All I can think is, *Please don't say Philly cheese steak. Please don't say Philly cheese steak.*

"You are not serving Philly cheese steak at my only daughter's Jewish wedding," my mother says, now leaning onto the table.

See why we're related?

"Well, of *course* we wouldn't serve cheese steak at the wedding!" Jack's mother says, laughing, and I breathe a sigh of relief. Those crazy Solomons! They almost had us going there for a minute. But, she was just kidding! And thank

God, since there is no one thing in the world that is quite as offensive to a kosher butcher from Long Island than a cheese steak from Philly. Eating meat and cheese at the same time is enough of an offense to a kosher butcher as is, but the thought of using Steak-Umms in a sandwich is really just too much for my father to handle.

But, she was kidding! Which means that this thing can turn around in an instant. We can still salvage this day. In fact, we'll probably all end up going out to dinner after this appointment. We'll have lots of laughs and drink too much and after a while, we won't even be able to *remember* a time where we didn't all get along famously.

"But," Joan says calmly, "we may do a little Philadelphia *homage* at the rehearsal dinner we're planning for the night before the wedding for our out-of-towners."

Almost under his breath, my father says: "You are going to serve meat and cheese at my daughter's rehearsal dinner?" My mother and I lock eyes, both afraid to look at my father, whose face is probably bright red by now, fists clenched into tiny little balls under the table.

"Let's move on to the cake," the wedding coordinator asks, changing the subject. "What price range are we thinking about for the cake?"

Yes, cake. That's it—let's talk cake. That Catherine is good. Nothing can divert one's interest quite like baked goods. Maybe she even has samples for us to taste and we can all have some and get on a huge sugar high and become the big happy family that I just know in my heart that we are destined to be.

Hell, at this point I'd even let my mother chug a glass of champagne if it would defuse some of the tension.

"We don't want anything too outrageous," my father says, "right, BB?"

"Yes," I say, happy that my father and I have regained our composure, "something understated and moderately priced."

"We don't have to go moderate," Jack's mother whispers to me from across the table, "why don't you just let us take care of the price of the cake?"

"It's not just the price of the cake," my father says, even though Joan's remark clearly wasn't meant for him, "I just don't want it to look overdone and tacky."

"Will we be giving out lamb chop party favors?" Jack's dad asks. "That's not tacky at all."

"People love lamb chops," my mother says. "Especially my husband's. There are people who drive all the way from Westchester just to get a taste of Barry's chops."

"Jack," I say, staring at my fiancé, still concentrating very hard on the albums Catherine has laid out for us, "do you have anything to contribute to this conversation?"

"Whatever you guys decide on," he says, "is fine by me."

"Just put us down for the most outrageous one you've got," Joan says. And then, in a whisper, "on us!"

"I think we've made it clear," my father says, taking a deep breath as he does, "that there is no greater pleasure in our life than to pay for BB's wedding entirely. So Mimi and I would really appreciate it if you would let us do that."

My mother smiles a Stepford wife smile and says: "Really. It's *our* dream to throw BB the wedding *she's* always dreamed of."

"Thanks Mom and Dad," I say, "you know, Catherine, there are so many wonderful choices you've got here for us. But, unfortunately, I've got a ton of work to do at the office, so I'm finding it hard to focus right now. I'd very much like to think about it and then come back with my parents and make my final decision."

Wow. Don't I sound, like, totally lawyerly?

"That sounds like a great idea, Brooke," Catherine says, closing her notebook and giving me a warm smile. "Call me to set up the next appointment."

"I think I'll go powder my nose," my mother says, pushing her chair back and getting up from the table.

"I think I'd like to come with you," I say, as I stand, too, and round the corner to the other side of the conference room table. I give fake air kisses to Jack's parents and ignore the fact that they try to draw me in closer for a hug. My mother does the same. When I come to Jack, I give him the same air kiss I gave his parents and I can see in his eyes that he knows why I don't kiss him. My father reluctantly stands and says a proper good-bye to the Solomons.

"See you at home," Jack says to my back as I'm already half-way out the door.

"See you at home," I say without turning around. It's the first time since Jack and I got together that I don't kiss or hug him good-bye.

Once my mother and I determine that the coast is clear (read: Solomon-free—*thank God* I didn't invite the siblings!), we go back to the conference room to pick up my father. The plan is for me to walk them to the parking garage and catch a ride back to my office on their way back to Long Island.

My father stands up as my mother and I walk into the room—he always stands when a lady enters or leaves a room—and I throw my arms around him for a big hug. As he hugs me back, I realize that I'm crying.

"I hope those are tears of happiness, BB," my father says, "because I'm going to throw you the most beautiful wedding in the world."

"I'm sorry," I say, running my fingers along my eyelashes to catch the tears.

"You have nothing to be sorry for," my mother says, patting my head and then kissing it. "This will all work out. Jack will come through, just like he always does, and everything will be smooth sailing."

"I know," I say, but for some reason, the tears keep coming. My father takes his handkerchief out from his inside pocket.

"We're just around the corner from Barneys," my mother says. "Why don't we duck in there and see what wedding dresses they've got?"

"I don't think I really feel like it, Mom," I say, as we begin walking downstairs toward the lobby.

"Call Ripley's Believe it or Not," my father says, "Our BB actually doesn't want to shop. I thought that shopping was the cure to everything for my little Miller girls?"

"I just have too much work to do," I say, carefully wiping my eyes and handing my father's handkerchief back to him. My mascara covers the ornate monogram that my mother has put onto all of my dad's hankies.

"Hey," my father says, "I have an idea. Let's all go to Don Peppe's for dinner. There is nothing in this world that a little homemade red wine can't fix. After a tiny glass of red and a huge plate of pasta, you'll feel a world better. And after a cappuccino and cannoli, I promise to drive you back to your office. Whaddya say, BB?"

It would take a forty-five-minute car ride to get to Queens from midtown and even if we were seated right away, it would still take at least an hour and a half to order and eat. And you never get seated right away at Don Peppe's. Then it would be another forty-five minutes to get back into the city, assuming we don't hit any traffic, so that means I couldn't possibly be back at my desk any sooner than three hours. And then eighty to one hundred hours of work awaits me.

But, then again, I'm not exactly rushing to go home to see Jack tonight, so what's the hurry to get back to work?

"Sounds perfect," I say as we reach the parking garage. We all pile into my father's car and head toward the Midtown Tunnel.

17

Back when we were a loving, newly engaged couple who were merely living in sin and not fighting in both the courtroom and the bedroom, Jack and I had our morning routine down pat. I'd wake up first at 7:15 a.m., and hop in the shower while Jack snoozed the alarm until I was done in the bathroom. When I got out of the shower, I'd throw my hair into a towel, and get the coffee ready (that brewed every morning at 7:20 a.m., thanks to the kick-ass coffeemaker with timer settings that Jack's cousins Judy and David bought for us for an engagement gift) while Jack showered. Then, we'd read the paper and eat breakfast together while my hair dried and I stared at Jack lovingly.

Since the Monique litigation began, things have not exactly been the same. Especially since the incident at the

Pierre. Now, I sleep until 7:30 a.m. (those fifteen minutes make all the difference when you've worked past midnight...) and Jack takes the *New York Post* with him to work since I've usually grabbed *The New York Times* on my way out while he's still in the shower.

Today, as I'm about to run out of the apartment with the *Times* firmly tucked under my arm, the phone rings. I briefly get that panicked feeling you get when someone calls you and wakes you up in the middle of the night. Why is someone calling here at eight-thirty in the morning? I look at the caller ID and see that it's Vanessa.

"Whatever you do, do not look at the paper," Vanessa says.

"Is something wrong?" I ask, sitting back down at our breakfast bar. I look at the clock and see that it's 8:31 a.m. Jack will be out of the shower any minute.

"No, nothing's wrong," Vanessa says, trying to sound nonchalant, "just don't look at the *New York Post*."

If I have any chance of making it out of the apartment before Jack gets out of the shower so that I can avoid him like the coward that I am, I've really got to leave now.

"What's in the *Post*?" I ask, eyeing the paper that's on my kitchen counter. It's still wrapped in a roll, secured by a rubber band, and I wonder if I take the rubber band off, if I'll be able to get it back on so as to make it look like I haven't touched it.

"You are definitely *not* on the cover of the *Post*," Vanessa says, "so do not look at it."

Is this how she's trying to get me to not check out the *Post?* Telling me *not* to look at it? Does she know *nothing* about reverse psychology? This woman is clearly not ready for children.

As I eye the newspaper, all I can think is: this is about Monique. This is all about Monique and Jean Luc. No doubt, my videographer has been tailing Jack and me, going through our garbage nightly, and by now knows all the sordid details of the dissolution of partnership. Hell, he probably already knows that Monique went to see Robin Kaplan, divorce attorney to the stars.

This is bad. This is very bad. The second Monique finds out about this, she is going to fire me. And then Noah will fire me! And then I'll be jobless! On a lighter note, I won't have to do the document production that Jack served me with the other day, but what kind of self-respecting bride walks down the aisle in five-hundred-dollar shoes while collecting unemployment?

Actually, unemployment might not be so bad. My skin will be clear from the lack of stress from work, and I'll finally be able to find the time to go shopping for a wedding dress. Hell, I'll have time to take a class to learn how to *make myself* a wedding dress! I mean, how hard could couture *really* be?

I'll also have time to work out and finally start that wedding diet everyone tells me I should be on. Maybe I can even start taking tennis lessons like my mom! Then, by the time Jack and I get to Hawaii for our honeymoon, I'll already have a killer backhand! (And much tighter glutes....)

While contemplating how much one can reasonably expect

to make on unemployment and how many hours of tennis practice I'd need before I would look totally cute in a tennis skirt, I grab the paper from the kitchen counter and rip off the rubber band. I'm immediately relieved that the article is not about Monique and Jean Luc at all, so I can rest easy. I will not be getting fired today. Unemployment would have been nice, but it's not happening for me.

Not today, at least.

Instead, right there, on the front page, for all the world to see, is the headline: Move over Hepburn and Tracy: It's a Real Life Battle of the Sexes!

"Oh, my God," I say into the phone and almost drop the receiver.

"I told you not to look!" Vanessa says, her voice an octave higher than usual.

"Then you shouldn't have told me *not* to look!" I say, "don't you know anything about rearing children?"

"I'm your maid of honor," she says, "not your babysitter!"

"Same thing!" I yell into the phone.

"What are you looking at?" Jack says, coming out of the shower. He's draped in just a towel, and using another to dry off his shaggy brown hair, and I momentarily forget that I'm still angry at him because of what happened at the Pierre.

"Nothing," I say, trying hard to keep my eyes fixated on his baby blues, but instead just staring at his hairy chest and freckly arms.

"So, you saw it?" he asks, coming over to the kitchen counter. He drops the towel he was using to dry off his hair onto a kitchen stool and uses his other hand to pull up the towel that's around his waist. My eyes are firmly glued to that other hand. "Brooke?"

You are still angry with your fiancé, I remind myself. *Stop staring at his towel. Stop staring at his towel.*

"Oh, yes," I say, eyes flying back up to his face with a "Who, me?" expression on my own, "Vanessa just called me about it."

"Don't blame me!" I can vaguely hear Vanessa screaming into the phone. "Tell him that I told you *not* to look at it!"

"Van," I say into the phone, "I'll call you back."

"So, I guess that you already saw it?" I ask Jack.

"I did," he says, "but I thought you'd get upset, so I was hoping that you wouldn't see it. And you've been running off with the *Times* lately, anyway, so I thought that maybe you'd miss it."

Um, hello? As if I *don't* go to www.nypost.com every day to read Column Five?

"Sorry," I say, "did you want the *Times?*" I take the paper out from under my arm and hand it to Jack.

"I don't want the *Times,*" he says, pulling me toward him, "I want to start having breakfast with you every day while we're reading the *Times.* Like we used to. I don't want you to run out of the apartment every day while I'm in the shower."

"I'm sorry," I say, as Jack sits down at one of the kitchen stools, his arms still holding mine. Then he drops his arms so that his hands are holding mine. "I'm just under a lot of stress here. I have a ton of work. Which you should know, since you assigned it to me."

"I don't think it counts as me assigning it to you since we don't work at the same law firm anymore," Jack says, baby blues smiling.

"And I've got wedding plans to think about," I say, looking down at the kitchen counter.

"I'm sorry about the Pierre," Jack says, putting one finger under my chin and lifting it up so that our eyes meet. "I'm sorry."

"I don't want us to fight," I say.

"Me, neither," he says, pulling me in for a hug. "I'll talk to my parents."

"Thank you," I say, feeling my eyes begin to tear up for a minute, but then smiling through it. I can smell his after-shave and it gives me a tiny shiver. "Thank you."

"Can I get you a cup of coffee?" Jack asks.

"I'd love one," I say, and Jack jumps up from his seat and tends to the coffee. I look down again at the front page of the *Post*. I hate the picture that they've got printed. Is there any chance that they've used a different picture of us for the online version of the paper? Maybe I should e-mail them a copy of one of our engagement pictures to use online. In the print edition, they've got a shot of the two of us leaving the federal courthouse on the day of our initial court conference. For a second, I wish that I had worn a sexy Nanette Lepore suit just like Miranda had that day, with a camisole that was too low-cut for a court appearance, instead of the conservative dark suit and turtleneck that I actually chose. Then I begin to wish that I even *owned* a sexy Nanette Lepore suit with matching camisole.

Note to self: must pick up sexier suits next time I'm at Saks if I'm going to make a habit out of being photographed while leaving court.

Jack and I aren't the main headline of the paper today, but we're the big inset on the lower right-hand corner of the front page. Either way, you can't miss us. The teaser tells me to flip to page nine, so I do. The same headline leads the full page article:

Move Over Hepburn and Tracy:
It's a Real Live Battle of the Sexes!

By Shawn Morgan (AP Press)

Forget the movies: it's a real life case of *Adam's Rib* in the Southern District of New York as Manhattan lawyers Brooke Miller and Jack Solomon, who are engaged to be married next spring, showed up in federal court yesterday to fight on opposite sides of a tightly sealed federal litigation. Why are the papers so tightly sealed? What's at stake? And more importantly, who will win—the women or the men?—when this litigation finally becomes public and the trial date is set?

I allow myself to exhale as I realize that the court records were sealed before the press could get wind of the fact that the case is about Monique and Jean Luc dissolving their business partnership. I glance down at the photo that accompanies the story: Jack and I kissing in front of the federal courthouse, standing smack dab in the middle of Foley Square without any regard whatsoever to the people walking by. My ego loves it, but the rest of me can't help but wonder: how on earth is this news?

I'm momentarily distracted by the photo credit—Jay Conte, aka our wedding videographer—as my BlackBerry begins to vibrate. I pick it up and see an e-mail from Judge Martin's courtroom deputy.

From: "Judge Martin's Chambers 2"
<deputy_martin@sdny.uscourts.gov>
To: "Brooke Miller" <brooke.miller@sgr.com>;
"Jack Solomon" <jsolomon@gilsonhecht.com>
Cc: "Judge Martin" <martin_b@sdny.uscourts.gov>,
"Judge Martin's Chambers 1"
<assistant_martin@sdny.uscourts.gov>;
"Miranda Foxley" <mfoxley@gilsonhecht.com>
Subject: Today's NYPost

Counselors:
In light of the media frenzy you were trying to avoid in your matter appearing before Judge Martin, when reporters came to the courthouse to try to find out the identity of the parties litigating in our sealed litigation, we thought it prudent to pretend to "leak" information about the case

so that they would stop digging for information. As such, we had Judge Martin's assistant "accidentally" tell the press that the reason this case was sealed was because the lead lawyers on either side were actually an engaged couple.

If you look at today's *New York Post*, you will see that this story has appeared on page nine.

Best,
Brandon William
Courtroom Deputy to Judge Martin

*****CONFIDENTIALITY NOTICE*****
The information contained in this e-mail message is the property of the United States Federal Government. If you are not the intended recipient, we would request you delete this communication without reading it or any attachment, not forward or otherwise distribute it, and kindly advise the Southern District of New York by return e-mail to webmaster@sdny.uscourts.gov. Thank you in advance.

Jack's BlackBerry begins to buzz next, so I read him the e-mail.

"See," he says, returning to the kitchen counter with our coffees. "All's well that ends well. And our case is still firmly under lock and key."

"But, what if they keep digging for dirt?" I ask.

"Don't worry," Jack says, taking a sip of coffee. "It will be some other story tomorrow. I'm sure some reality show reject will be involved in some scandal and we'll be yesterday's news. Maybe even before today's over."

I can't help but smile. I can never stay mad at Jack for too long.

"Well, for today, I hate the way I look in this photo," I say to Jack as I sip my coffee. "So conservative and stodgy."

"Conservative and stodgy?" Jack says, "Nah, you look just like Jackie O in the White House."

My fiancé is well trained to know that anytime I'm feeling insecure, a reference to a fabulous celebrity is just what I need to get my confidence back. And, for me, it's got to be a classic, old-time star—no Julia Roberts or Reese Witherspoon comparisons for me. He has his pick of the sixties icons: Jackie O (too conservative), Audrey Hepburn (too plain) or Marilyn Monroe (too fat). Even a fleeting Lauren Bacall comment (too sharp) is enough to turn my day back around.

Is it any wonder that we end up back in bed?

18

"Nothing?" I say to Vanessa as soon as we're alone in the bathroom at Mega, a monstrosity of a restaurant in midtown. "You've got nothing?"

"Not a thing," Vanessa says as she applies lipgloss while looking in the mirror. "Mainly, he just assigns her work and then they go work in their respective offices."

Even though Jack spent the last two weeks making up the Pierre debacle to me ("What do you not understand about agreeing with everything I say in front of your parents?" [rest of scene deleted, as unsuitable for children under the age of seventeen]), I still have Vanessa, my darling matron/maid of honor checking up on him. I even made Vanessa take Miranda out for frozen yogurt in an effort to keep your friends close, but your enemies closer. All Vanessa really learned from that scouting expedition was that Miranda prefers chocolate to vanilla, but even that seemingly innocuous information could turn out to be very valuable some day.

Oh, please. As if you wouldn't defend your man, too.

"How can that be? She's the man stealer extraordinaire! No late-night rendezvousing in the tenth-floor library?" I ask, looking at Vanessa out of the corner of my eye.

"Wait, did *you* ever have a late-night rendezvous with Jack in the tenth-floor library?"

"No!" I say, laughing.

"You did, too!" Vanessa says, "I can tell!" She begins laughing while simultaneously staring me down.

"Let's just say, don't go near the treatises on real property law," I say, eyebrow raised for effect, "if you know what I mean."

"I know what you mean," Vanessa says, putting her lipgloss back into her gold Chanel clutch. "And, ew."

"Don't hate," I say, touching up my own pout in the mirror. "Appreciate."

"You're not allowed to use that expression if you're over the age of twenty-two," Vanessa says.

"Don't try to change the subject," I say, turning to face Vanessa, "you're supposed to be getting me dirt on Jack and Miranda. Now, spill."

"There's nothing to spill, Brooke," Vanessa says. I pause for a second, waiting for the inevitable *yet*.

"So, you mean to tell me that you've got nothing," I say, smoothing out my skirt and adjusting the sling-back of my left shoe.

"That would be correct," Vanessa says.

"Then what am I paying you for?" I ask, as we start walking to the door.

"You're not paying me," Vanessa reminds me.

"It's just an expression," I say. "I just can't believe you don't have any dirt at all."

"*What am I paying you for* is not an expression," Vanessa says to me as she holds the door open for me to leave the ladies' room. "It's a nasty way of saying—"

"Well, hiya, ladies!" Miranda says, her Southern accent milked for full effect, strolling into the ladies' room. "How are y'all doing? This is quite a bridal shower, Brooke. Where I come from we don't have bridal showers like this."

"Me, neither," I mumble under my breath. I wanted my bridal shower to be small, but Jack's family insisted on inviting nearly every woman that's invited to the wedding to the shower. We either had to hold it here at Mega, or at Madison Square Garden.

"Jack's sisters must really love Brooke if they threw a shower like this for her," Vanessa says with a smile. "We really should be getting out of here, though. We'll see you out there!" Vanessa grabs me by the elbow and leads me out to the party room.

"Here she is," Jack's sister, Lisa, announces as soon as Vanessa and I enter the room, "the woman of the hour, Brooke!"

Everyone turns around and oohs and aahs at me, and all I can think is, *who* are *half of these people?* My idea of the perfect bridal shower is a couple of friends and tons of family gathered together in someone's home. Vanessa had wanted to throw a small tasteful shower in her apartment, but that idea was quickly vetoed by the sisters Solomon. Instead, in grand Solomon tradition, they have made for me the mother of all bridal showers, the bridal shower that ate Cleveland. Actually, the party room here at Mega is so incredibly large that most of Cleveland could probably fit inside. When I first walked into the party room, I noticed a sign announcing that the room's capacity is 325. I'm quite certain that we are pushing that limit today.

So, I didn't exactly get the shower I wanted, and I most certainly didn't get the guest list that I wanted. When Jack realized what a large-scale affair the shower was becoming, he quickly decided that he had to make sure that his female work colleagues were invited so that no one would take offense. Which really makes no sense to me since Jack's already a partner and once you're a partner in a law firm, can't you just do as you please?

Well, Jack doesn't seem to think so. Which is why Miranda Foxley, the man stealer, was invited (and had the nerve to show up and no, I do not think that she came just to try to be my friend, I think that she came because she is undoubtedly trying to steal my man and lull me into a false sense of security just before she pounces on said man). Along with a bunch of other female partners and associates who I really wish weren't here, either.

I survey the twenty-something tables that have been set up, each with an ornate floral arrangement floating on top.

It is a total and complete sensory overload. The smell of the peonies overpowers me and makes me sneeze. Vanessa doesn't seem to notice as she meets and greets various Gilson, Hecht associates and partners, along with some of our girlfriends from law school. But for me, the room is a swirly mess, from the forty-foot-high ceilings, to the bright orange linens dressing the tables, to the massive table of multicolored presents. I can barely get my eyes to focus.

Mega's party room has a Cirque de Soleil theme, so the chairs are dressed in a deep magenta and the carpet is purple and yellow. At the end of the bar, there is a giant martini glass (with the requisite giant olive placed inside) and the wait staff are all dressed as court jesters in hot pink and teal.

"Let's leave our bags on our chairs," Vanessa says, "okay, Brooke?"

As Vanessa leads me toward our table, my eyelids begin to droop. It dawns on me that for the last two weeks, the most sleep I've gotten on any one given night was about three to four hours. Now, this *should* have been because Jack and I were making up the whole time after the debacle at the Pierre, and to be sure, that's partly it, but what's really drawing my eyes downward is the fact that I've been working nonstop. I've been working on the Monique case for fourteen hours a day, weekends included. I'm exhausted all day long, just praying, waiting for the moment when I can get into bed, but then when I finally get under the covers, I'm too exhausted to actually go to sleep.

Even Vanessa noticed it this morning, when she picked

me up for our hair appointments, not-so-subtly suggesting that I get my makeup done to hide the circles under my eyes. ("You can't show up at your own bridal shower looking like the Bride of Frankenstein.")

We get to our table and Vanessa puts her place card on top of her plate and her gold Chanel clutch on her chair. I pull my chair out and plop down in it.

"Are you okay?" Vanessa asks, leaning down to whisper into my ear.

"I'm just so tired," I say, putting my hands over my eyes. "And this Technicolor Dreamcoat mess is not helping me to relax."

"It's fun," Vanessa says, trying to sound optimistic. "The decor is fun."

With my eyes still closed, hands over my eyes, I hear Vanessa call over a waiter and order an iced coffee for me. So, basically now, in addition to her maid of honor duties of spying on the groom, Vanessa also has to rally the bride at her own shower. I'm sure at Vanessa's own shower she was a happy, well-rested bride who did not look like she was about to pass out. I'm sure she was a gracious bride who knew all of her guests.

"Rocket fuel is on its way," Vanessa whispers and I hear her pull out her chair and sit down next to me. She takes my place card out of my limp hand and puts it onto the table.

"So, you must be Vanessa," Jack's middle sister, Elizabeth, says. I manage to pull my head off my hands and open my eyes.

"I am," Vanessa says, with a smile, standing to shake Elizabeth's hand.

"I'm Elizabeth," she says, "Jack's sister."

"Yes," Vanessa says, "Middle sister, married to Alan. Did I get that right?"

As I look over at Vanessa in her bright orange Milly dress chatting effortlessly with Jack's sister, actually remembering who she is and which brother-in-law she corresponds to, I realize that I hate Vanessa. I hate my best friend. Jack's been briefing me on who's who for months now, and I still can't get it straight. Jack told Vanessa who everyone was last night at dinner and she's already a pro.

But then the waiter brings me my iced coffee (my fourth of the day so far), with two Sweet-n-Lows and skim milk, just the way I like it, and I love her again. I love my best friend. I drink the iced coffee in two big slurps, careful not to spill any onto my white shift dress, and then move in on the ice water at my table setting. Picking it up (I was instructed by Vanessa that I cannot walk around with anything but clear-colored beverages while wearing a white dress), I walk over to Vanessa and Elizabeth, ready to start acting like the charming bride-to-be that I know I can be. If only I weren't quite so tired.

I notice that Vanessa is smiling at Elizabeth with her lawyerly I'm-so-excited-to-work-on-this-lame-ass-case-with-you face and I realize that she's just making nice with Jack's family for me. I guess she really does deserve to be my maid of honor. Or matron. Whatever.

"We worked really hard on those," Elizabeth is saying to Vanessa, just as Lisa, the youngest sister walks over to join us.

"Yes," Lisa says, "we wanted them to be evocative of the flowers we'll be having at the wedding, but not the same exact ones, so that the real flowers will be a big surprise!"

Vanessa already knows, in painstaking detail, what flowers I've picked out for my wedding. She's segued into the classic you-are-so-funny-and-clever-in-the-way-that-you-handled-that-judge/witness/child-under-the-age-of-five! face and I do the same. *Yes, you were so clever with the flowers, sisters Solomon!*

"Are you Lisa?" Vanessa says, eyes squinting as she waits to hear if she's guessed right.

"Yes!" Lisa says, "you must be Vanessa." Vanessa will later tell me that everyone guessed she was Vanessa since she was one of the only black people there. I will take this not as an indictment on me and the types of friends that I have, but as an indictment of Gilson, Hecht, and law firms in general, and how they really need to make more affirmative action initiatives in terms of hiring.

"*There* you are!" my mother says, rushing over to Vanessa and me. "I've been looking *all over* for you!"

I suppose that I don't have to mention here that my mother is wearing a crisp white linen suit.

"Love your suit," I say to my mother, in much the same tone that Hannibal Lecter uses when he says that very line to the Senator.

"Why, thank you, BB!" my mother cries, oblivious to my tone, "I saw it at Saks and I just couldn't resist! How often do you get to be the mother of the bride at your own daughter's bridal shower?"

Jack's two sisters shrug and smile. My mother either doesn't realize or doesn't care that Jack's mother actually got to do that very thing on three separate occasions.

"Well, you look fabulous, Mimi," Vanessa says, giving my mom a hug.

"If you wear white to my wedding," I say, drawing my mother in for a hug and then whispering directly into her ear, "you are dead to me."

"You preapproved this outfit, BB," my mother says, trying to release herself from my grasp.

"You tried it on for me in Saks in blue," I say, "this is not blue."

"Oh, BB, you're so funny," my mother says, laughing like a crazy person, "that's my BB. What a nervous little bride-to-be! Oh, Joan, I didn't even see you walking over here! Hell-o!"

"So lovely to see you," Jack's mother says to us, giving us both a hug and a peck on the cheek. "What a wonderful day, isn't it?"

My mother and I both smile and try not to laugh. I know exactly what my mother is thinking right now because Joan is wearing, yet again, palazzo pants.

Did they have a fire sale on these things at Armani or something? This pair is navy, and she's wearing them with navy sling-backs and a light-blue cropped jacket with three-quarter sleeves.

"My cousin made these delightful cards for us to put on the table," my mother tells Joan, taking pale-pink index cards out of her pocketbook. "You put them on the table and everyone writes down marital advice for BB. Then, BB reads them aloud when she's opening her gifts."

"Oh, Mimi," Joan says, feigning disappointment. "We won't be playing any games at the shower. The girls and I figured there were simply too many guests for such things."

"Oh," my mother says, keeping her smile glued to her lips, "of course. But…"

Joan walks away, Jack's sisters in tow, toward the front of the room before my mother can finish her thought. Or maybe it was the back of the room. It's hard to tell which end is which with all of the brightly colored ribbons floating down from the forty-foot ceiling.

"That's an adorable idea," Vanessa says in a hushed voice. "Why don't we do these at our tables and at your family's tables?"

Vanessa is referring to the fact that even though, I, myself, am an only child like my mother, my father's family is actually quite large. So large that he has seven aunts. His father's family was a traditional eastern European family with the eight children to back it up. I've spent a lifetime trying to remember who is who and which cousins correspond to which aunt. I definitely have Aunt Devorah and Aunt Jean's families figured out, but as for the other five that don't live in New York, I'm completely hopeless. Every once in a while, I'll have dinner with one of Aunt Devorah's brood and we'll outline an ornate plan to create a massive Miller family tree, but that plan usually falls by the wayside by the following Tuesday.

If Vanessa knows the names of all seven of my great-aunts, I will have to strangle her on the spot.

"All of the tables are mixed up," my mother says, with a frozen smile. "Each table is half Jack's family, half ours. Half Jack's friends, half yours and BB's."

"Right," Vanessa says, "well, it was a cute idea anyway."

My mother smiles at Vanessa, trying to keep her composure, and I reach over and hug my mother. This time it's a real hug, not one where I grab her and then whisper threats in her ear.

"And you look beautiful today," I say to her.

"May I have everyone's attention?" Joan says at the front of the room. Or what must be the front of the room, since that's where she's now standing, trying to quiet the massive crowd. Somehow, out of nowhere, a podium with a microphone has materialized. "Is this thing on?" she asks, tapping the mike.

Jack's sister Patricia nods her head at her mother and adjusts the mic upward for Joan.

"I just want to welcome all of you here and thank you for coming. I know that I speak for my family and Brooke's family, too, when I tell you that we are all so happy to be sharing this very happy occasion with all of you. Now, I invite all of you to take your seats and enjoy your lunch!"

Inexplicably, everyone begins to applaud before scurrying about to find their seats. My mother walks with Vanessa and me back to our table—Table One, of course. Since Vanessa and I already set down our place cards, I'm anxious to rush back to our table so that we're able to put my mother next to either Vanessa or me. The rest of the table is made up of Jack's mother and his three sisters, and I just know that Jack's mother and sisters will feel the need to mix the families up. I wonder if they've already moved Vanessa's and my place cards around so that we don't sit with the person we speak to every day.

Vanessa and I had hoped that we'd be at a table with some of our friends. Since I've been working so hard, I've barely seen any of my old friends from Gilson, Hecht and I definitely haven't seen any old friends from law school. Hell, I've barely even seen my friend Esther, who works at my very own law firm. And she's been getting really serious with her blind date guy and I'm ashamed to say that I've been so busy that I haven't had time for her to tell me all of the juicy details.

But, instead, we're sitting at Table One. My only saving grace is that Vanessa told me that it's good form for the bride to visit all of the various tables at her shower, so once I've had a bite to eat, I'll be free to get up from the table.

My mother links her right arm into my left and Vanessa's right arm into her left and we begin to walk back to our table. As I walk arm in arm with my mother and Vanessa, I realize that maybe it isn't such a bad thing for the three of us to be sitting at the same table. There's strength in numbers, right? Sure, Jack's mother and three sisters still outnumber us, but on our side, we've got two attorneys and a pushy matron from Long Island, so we're nothing to sneeze at.

"Vanessa," my mother asks, "do you know what we're having for lunch today?"

"I had my hands full with the table seatings," Vanessa says, "I wasn't really involved with the menu. But, I've taken summer associates here for lunch before and they have great salads. It's like something out of *Architectural Digest* the way they pile them so high. You'll love them."

"Well," my mother says, "I hope I can get mine with the dressing on the side."

"Oh, me too," Vanessa says.

Salad? I can't have a salad for lunch! I'm so tired that I feel like I'm hungover and everyone knows that the one thing you need most when you're hung over is grease. A nice, big plate of delicious grease. What are the chances that they'll be serving a side plate of French fries with those salads? I consider asking Vanessa that very question when I see the waiters set down a few plates of the salads that they'll be serving today. In an instant, I forget all about the fries. In fact, I can't think at all. I stop dead in my tracks and it has the effect of making my mother jerk forward, forcing Vanessa to do the same.

I don't even notice that I've stopped walking until Vanessa announces that I've just caused her to lose a shoe. Leaning forward, I examine the salads that the waiters have set down onto Table Twelve, certain that there's some kind of a mistake. It's got to be a mistake. There is no way in hell that these are the salads that we are supposed to be eating today at my bridal shower. Because what's sitting on top of the incredibly high salads that the waiters are serving is something that I'm absolutely sure can't be there.

Lobster.

This must be a misunderstanding. There is simply no possible way that the Solomons could be this passive-aggressive. The man I am about to marry cannot possibly be born from the loins of a woman who, in the face of a holy war over serving lobster at my wedding, has instead chosen to serve it at the bridal shower she's throwing for me.

And then my mother gets in on the action. She doesn't say a word, but I can see in her plastered-on smile that she is having the same thought process that I am having at this very moment.

"Oh, my God," Vanessa says and then covers her mouth when she realizes that she actually said it. Luckily, none of the guests at Table Twelve overhear her.

"Let's not make a scene, girls," my mother says quietly, "we're too good for that. This is the party that they planned, and this is what they chose to do. We don't agree with it, but let's not stoop to their level and make a scene."

Would not making a scene exclude crying? Because I can feel the tears beginning to form behind my eyes and I have to take a deep breath to keep them at bay. I turn to look at my mother and can practically see the smoke coming out of her ears.

"It looks delicious, doesn't it?" Joan says, coming up behind us, on her way to our table. "You said that you don't keep kosher normally, so Edward made the suggestion that a little bit of lobster today might be nice! Wasn't that a great idea?"

My mother and I don't say a word. We simply both look up, expressionless, and stare at Joan.

"Well, I, for one, don't eat lobster," Vanessa says, and I wonder if Joan is going to ask her if she keeps kosher.

"You don't?" Joan says, "Well, that's okay, we'll just tell the waiter. There's a substitution—salmon—for anyone who doesn't want lobster. Do you like salmon?"

Vanessa looks at me and I look back at her. Vanessa, unable to come up with a response, shrugs her shoulders in response to the salmon.

Across the room, I see my Great-Aunt Devorah get up from her table and walk out of the restaurant.

This is all Jack's fault. This is all Jack's fault.

My mother, Vanessa and I all order the salmon substitution, on principle alone, while the Solomons all gobble up their salads, oohing and aahing about how delicious they are, and *are your salads good, too?* My mother will later tell me that the fact that the Solomon girls all order their salads without the dressing on the side, with the dressing plopped right on top like a big fat blob, says a lot about their character. I don't really know what she means, but I will later just nod in agreement since I'm so angry about the lobster. Solidarity. Nothing like a mutual enemy to get a team to come together.

This is all Jack's fault.

We don't open any presents since Joan says that there are simply too many guests, so the whole shower is over in about two and a half hours, which Joan says is the perfect amount of time for a bridal shower.

I wonder aloud how on earth Jack and I will get all of our gifts home, and then, as if on cue, Jack, his father and all three of the brothers-in-law come in to help us out.

As per the usual, the brothers-in-law are all in uniform: pastel Loro Piana cable sweaters? Check. Pressed khaki pants? Check. Black Gucci loafers? Check. I don't even try to figure out who's who. I don't care who's who. I only care that Jack, the man I am going to marry, is walking right toward me.

In that instant, I just know that everything will be all right. Jack will fix everything.

Jack walks toward me, running his fingers through his shaggy brown hair, and I can't help but smile. The stress of the day just fades away and I forget about everything—about how tired I am, about how stressed I am at work, even about the lobster. Jack walks toward me, holding a bouquet of flowers that I recognize as being the same flowers we'll be using for our table arrangements at the wedding, and it all just fades away. It's just Jack and me in that room.

As he gets closer, I stand up to give him a hug and a big kiss. Everyone starts clapping for us as we kiss and I feel like the main character in a romantic comedy. He's Richard Gere and I'm Julia Roberts in *Pretty Woman*. No, wait, actually, she played a prostitute in that movie so I'm not Julia Roberts. Okay, he's Tom Hanks and I'm Meg Ryan in *You've Got Mail*. No, Tom successfully destroyed Meg's business in that movie—we're Hanks and Ryan in *Sleepless in Seattle*. No, wait, in *Sleepless in Seattle,* Tom Hanks had a kid and if it turns out that Jack has some love child stashed away somewhere, that would not be good. What kind of a cute romantic comedy would that be?

Wait—I've got it! He's George Peppard and I'm Audrey Hepburn! I can finally have my *Breakfast at Tiffany's* fantasy now. Yes, that's it. And, anyway, she was really more of a "party girl" than Pretty Woman prostitute, so that's okay. And she had such cute outfits in that movie.

Okay, so that's it. We stand there, in the middle of the bridal shower, kissing, and I'm Holly Golightly (sans the $50 for the powder room) and he's Paul Varjack (sans the whole kept-man thing) and I've decided to give the cat a name and we're kissing in the rain. Or, we're kissing at Mega, but you get the general point I'm trying to make. Then, he gives me the flowers and I tilt them toward me to take a sniff. We're going to have lilies at the wedding—my favorite—and I just love the delicious scent they give off.

Only, when I tilt the flowers back, I see something strange inside of the wrapping. And it's not the baby's breath. No, there's something blue in there that does not belong. And it's not a little something from Tiffany and Co. I look up at Jack and he's giving me a smirk, just staring at me. Waiting for something.

I put my hand inside the bouquet and take out the blue thing. It's the blue back of a discovery request, with the familiar Gilson, Hecht and Trattner listed as the attorneys who drafted it.

Jack is serving me with a set of Interrogatories. At my own bridal shower. I look up at Jack and he smiles at me.

"Gotcha, counselor," he says.

Am I the only one who is starting to think that this isn't very funny anymore?

19

"Can we move the appointment to this weekend?" I ask my mother.

"Again?" my mother says, "you want to move *another* wedding dress appointment?"

"I just have so much work to do," I say, looking around my office at the boxes of documents that are piled high, one on top of the other.

"You *always* have so much work to do, BB," my mother says, "it's time for a break."

"I'll take a break as soon as I'm done with these Interrogatories," I say, getting ready to hang up the phone. I had to skip our last wedding dress appointment since I had to meet with Monique to get the information I'd need to complete the Interrogatories, so I know that my mother is nearing her breaking point.

"That's what you said about the document requests," my mother says, "You said we could shop once you were done with those. But, now the wedding date is approaching quickly. Having a dress custom made is already out the door, I've accepted that, but at the rate we're going, we're not even going to have time for alterations for something off the rack."

"We'll find something," I say, doing my work as I speak to her. "We always do."

"Finding the perfect wedding dress isn't like running to Saks to pick up a little black dress. You saw how long it took us to find Monique."

Why does she always have to bring up the Monique thing? It drives me nuts the way she makes out like I've chosen my work over my relationship just because I took on Monique's case. When she knows that I'm just working hard to try to prove myself at work. Simple as that. Why does she have to infuse meaning into it? Why does she have to make it mean more than what it actually is?

I promise to make the appointment we have scheduled for tomorrow night and this seems to allay my mother for the moment. We hang up and I turn back to my computer screen. The words all seem to blur together, and I find it hard to focus my eyes. I pick up the Interrogatories Jack served on me and try to make notes on them, but they, too, seem to have words and letters scrambled across the page.

After I finish drafting my responses, I should draft my own set of Interrogatories to serve on Jack. That'll show him. As it is, I'll be in the office all night working on how to answer *his* set of Interrogatories. Drafting a quick set of my own wouldn't keep me here much longer. Once you're totally sleep-deprived, does an extra hour lost really matter that much, anyway?

Jack taught me how to draft Interrogatories; I should be able to do them in my sleep. First, you have to figure out what information you need in order to prove your case. Well, that one's easy for me—I need to know why Monique's husband is being such a jerk. I need to figure out why, in the face of a simple business matter, he has turned this into a contentious litigation. And more importantly, why has this attitude rubbed off on my fiancé and turned *him* into such a jerk?

These questions may not be appropriate for the Interrogatories. Perhaps I should just focus on answering the Interrogatories that Jack has asked me.

Interrogatory 1: State the grounds for dissolving this business partnership.

Haven't I told Jack that before? That sort of thing would have been in my Initial Complaint. As I click through my documents on my computer, though, I can't seem to find the original document. The file names all blur together and I feel my eyes beginning to close against my will.

I'm more tired than I realized. If I could just put my head down for one tiny little minute, I bet I'd feel much better.

A cat nap. That's what I need. I just need one of those twenty-minute naps that totally revitalize and rejuvenate you. Then, I can get back to my work.

Leaning back in my ergonomically correct chair, I slowly close my eyes and take a deep breath in, deep breath out. Yes, a little sleep. This is just what I need.

I get back to my apartment and the clock on the microwave oven blinks 2:45 a.m. Too tired to hang my coat and work bag up in the closet, I take them off and just let them fall where they will in the foyer. As I walk into the apartment, I realize that an enormous red silk screen is smack dab in the middle of my living room. I know I haven't been home much lately, but it's just so unlike Jack to just start redecorating the place without me. And, anyway, it's blocking my path into the bedroom.

I walk over to the screen and try to move it, but it's stuck in place. Turning around backward and putting all of my weight into it, I lean against the screen and try to push. I give it a few good heaves and hos, but it's no use. The thing simply won't budge.

I call out for Jack to help me. The silk that covers the screen is extremely fine and I know that he should be able to hear me through its smooth fibers. But, he doesn't hear me. Instead, I hear him. I hear voices, low and dim, giggling together, laughing together and then I don't hear anything at all.

"Jack," I cry out, "are you there?"

No response. More giggling from the bedroom. I turn around again and put my full weight onto the silk screen. I push and I push and the screen doesn't move at all. It doesn't move an inch.

"Jack," I say, trying to sound composed, "what is going on over there? Help me, I'm stuck!"

But he doesn't come. Instead, I hear more rustling from the bedroom and then a voice.

"Oh, Jack," I hear and I can barely make out whose voice it is. I march back into the kitchen and open the drawer. Rifling around, I finally find what I need—I grab the scissors and quickly make my way back to the gigantic silk screen. I consider, for a brief second, cutting the screen slowly and carefully, only making a hole big enough for me to walk through, but then reconsider in an instant and just stab the fabric quickly. It takes a few stabs before it rips, but when it does, the entire thing opens up for me. It opens wide, like the petals of a rose awakening in the spring, and I walk through the hole toward the bedroom.

As I make my way down the hallway, I hear the voices again. I try to move quickly, but my feet feel like they are lead. The faster I try to move, the slower I seem to walk. Everything around me gets blurry and dark, and I struggle to bring things back into focus. The hallway stretches out before me, seemingly getting longer with each and every step that I take.

"Jack," I hear the voice say again, and I rack my brain to

figure out who it is. I finally get closer to the bedroom door and I reach out to grab the doorknob. In an instant, I realize whose voice it is that I've been hearing: Miranda Foxley's.

"Jack!" I call out, reaching for the doorknob, but the more I try to reach for it, the further away it seems to get from my grasp.

"Jack!" I cry, "Jack!" Everything becomes so dark and blurry, I can't even see the doorknob anymore. I float backward, further and further away from my apartment, and suddenly, I feel my head jerk upwards.

I wake up with a start and realize that I was just sleeping. It was only a dream. More like a nightmare, actually, but the important thing is that it wasn't actually happening to me. I was only sleeping.

As I stretch out the crink in my neck from sleeping in my chair, I realize that I've slept for forty-five minutes and I need to get back to answering Jack's Interrogatories immediately if I have any chance at all of getting home before the sun rises and tonight actually becomes tomorrow. And it's so late that I can forget any chance I had of drafting my own set of Interrogatories.

But then, I look at my computer screen. Seems that I've already started drafting my Interrogatories. Funny, because I don't recall writing anything at all.

But, my computer screen tells an entirely different story:

IN THE UNITED STATES DISTRICT COURT
SOUTHERN DISTRICT OF NEW YORK

In the matter of:

The dissolution of
partnership of — Index No. 54930285-NY

Monique Couture, Inc.

STATE OF NEW YORK
COUNTY OF NEW YORK

INTERROGATORIES

1. State the grounds for your inability to stand up to your father.
2. State the grounds, if different than your response to Interrogatory No. 1, for your inability to stand up to your family as a whole.
3. Explain the nature of your relationship to Miranda Foxley.
4. List each of the reasons you love Brooke Miller.
5. You still love Brooke Miller, don't you?

20

"This sort of thing really doesn't come under the umbrella of what a bride should do for her wedding videographer," I say through the double-thick, bullet-proof glass.

"I didn't want to call my regular guy," Jay says, from the other side of the glass, "and the way I see it, you owe me a solid."

Great. Now I owe one to a mobster. According to Wikipedia, "soldiers" are low-level players in the mafia family. To get to be a soldier, you have to "prove" yourself as an associate to the family first. [Insert dramatic music as you ponder the question: "What exactly does one *do* to prove oneself to a mafia family?"] I really wish I wasn't an obsessive lawyer who just *had* to look that one up.

"But, you're not a paparazzo," I say, holding the phone about an inch away from my ear, for fear of catching something here at the Manhattan Detention Center.

Jay shrugs.

"So, what exactly were you doing rifling through Monique deVouvray and Jean Luc Renault's garbage?" I ask. I'm calm and cool and collected when I ask him this—I say a silent *thank you* to the gods above that I'd told Monique to start shredding all of her documents on the off chance that paparazzi would start going through her trash. Otherwise, this situation would have been stressful in many, many ways. More so than the obvious, I mean.

"It's public property," he says into the telephone.

"Actually," I say, "it's not. That's why you got arrested. Monique and Jean Luc own the property their townhouse is situated on, which includes the alley you were skulking around. That's why they had you arrested for trespassing."

"I wasn't skulking," Jay says. "Anyway, all they really had in their garbage was chantilly lace and thick silk."

"Ooh," I say, "you should keep that. It's really expensive."

"So, can you get me out of here?" he asks, looking around.

"First, I have a few questions I'd like to ask you," I say. I fail to mention here that I can absolutely get him out of here. Right this minute, I might add. When I got to the Manhattan Detention Center, I met the prosecutor who's holding him—an old friend of mine from law school who said she'd take care of this for me. Which is good, since I really just want to get Jay out and go—taking him on as an actual client would be a conflict of interest with my other, more important, more law-abiding client, Monique. So, I thank my lucky stars that the prosecutor is someone I know.

Do I have to invite another old law school friend to my wedding now? Under Jack's strict orders, I've been trying very hard not to befriend anyone new, since I'd like to keep my wedding to a modest count of just under six hundred people.

"Whaddya wanna know?" Jay asks, looking around the visitor's center.

"Well, it's just that," I start out. All of my stammering must have caught Jay's attention—or annoyed him at the very least—because he turns to me and fixes his eyes on mine. I realize that it's the first time that we've actually made eye contact and I don't really like it. I divert my eyes downward.

"Did you get anything on Miranda Foxley?" I blurt out.

"She is one fun girl," he says, leaning back in his chair. The phone cord barely extends as he flips his head back with a smile.

"What's that supposed to mean?" I ask, trying not to look judgmental. Or jealous.

"She likes to indulge in a little activity known as the afternoon delight," Jay says, rubbing his hands together.

Afternoon delight? What's afternoon delight? Is that some sort of drug I haven't heard of yet? Is that what all the kids are doing these days? Just when I figure out the difference between E and Special K, now there's some other drug I need to worry about my future children getting peer-pressured into taking?!?

"She does drugs?" I say, sotto voce, leaning in to the double-thick glass. I'm hoping that by whispering, the guards who monitor the conversations in this room won't notice that we are blatantly talking about drugs.

"Haven't seen her do drugs yet," he says, "but you never know what's going on during those afternoon delights."

"What?" I ask, "I don't get it."

Jay laughs and leans back toward me. "Sky rockets in flight..." he sings.

"Most people don't really feel like a sing-a-long when they're being held as a guest of the state at the Manhattan Detention Center," I say, looking around to the other lawyers all gathered on my side of the glass. No other lawyer seems to be getting a serenade like I am.

"Gonna find my baby," he sings, low and sultry into the phone, leaning closer into the glass as he does so, "gonna hold her tight..."

This is getting to be inappropriate. Surely in just a minute, he'll make a play for the glass and try to escape with me. I'll have to call the guards who will then call my emergency contact who is my fiancé, Jack. How am I going to explain how I got here? Well, let's see: I'm planning our perfect wedding, honey, but along the way, I decided to have the wedding videographer spy on you for me, so I had to hire a friend of a friend of a friend of a friend of my father's, who just so happens to be a made man, who thinks I owe him a solid, who is now in jail, who is now inexplicably serenading me. Which really happens to brides-to-be more often than you'd think.

As Jay gets to the part in his song about rubbing sticks and stones together, my cell phone begins to vibrate. I've got it set to vibrate since you're not allowed to bring cell phones into a detention center and I used Jack's little inside pocket trick to sneak it in. I excuse myself to run to the ladies' room for a minute, and answer the phone.

"Where are you?" my mother says. "You sound like you're in a mental institution or something. Why is there an echo?"

"Long story," I whisper into the phone. "My wedding videographer got arrested and I'm bailing him out."

"You have time to bail your wedding videographer out of jail, but you don't have time to come wedding dress shopping with me?" she asks.

I have no response to this.

A few minutes later, I come back to the glass partition and Jay is busy laughing and joking with his fellow inmates.

"I'm back," I say, "sorry about that."

"No problem," he says, "we were all just talking about how much we could use an afternoon delight right now."

"Do you really think you and your fellow inmates should be talking about drugs while you're in the slammer?" I whisper into the phone.

"This ain't the slammer, lady," Jay says, "this is a detention center."

"Whatever," I say, "the point is—"

"An afternoon delight is sex in the middle of the afternoon," Jay says. "It has nothing to do with drugs. Unless, of course, you're into that sort of thing."

"Which I'm *not,*" I quickly say, looking around to the guards, so that if any of them have overheard the conversation, they'll be able to see how innocent and law-abiding I look.

"Perhaps your friend Miranda is," he says, leaning into the glass. "Every afternoon at around three, a town car is waiting for her outside of the Gilson, Hecht offices. She hops in and goes up to the Upper East Side—a dingy little walk-up on 91st Street between 1st and York."

"To do what?" I say, riveted by Jay's tale of the seedy underbelly of the city.

"Play chess," he says, as I stare back at him with my mouth hanging open. "What do you think she's doing?"

"I don't know!" I say. If he thinks that I'm the sort of woman who would know what people are doing when they go to dingy little walk-ups on the Upper East Side in broad daylight, then I need to seriously reconsider my entire wardrobe. Possibly my makeup, too.

"Lots of men who work in the city keep little apartments uptown so that they can sneak out of work during the day and meet up with their girlfriends."

"They do?" I ask and Jay shakes his head knowingly. "*Married* men?"

"Grow up, Brooke," Jay mutters back into the phone. "Just grow up."

"Who was she meeting?" I ask.

"I didn't get the chance to find out yet," he says.

"Thank God my father always worked on Long Island," I say under my breath.

"Your father's the best," Jay says, breaking into a smile. "I love that man's chops."

"I'm partial to the sirloin," I say, "but his chops are quite good." Jay nods his head in agreement.

How confused are the guards who are monitoring our conversation right now?

"By the way," Jay says, "I never asked you. Where's your honeymoon?"

"I don't know yet," I say, "but we're thinking Hawaii. Why?"

"If you make it Mexico," he says, looking around at the other inmates to make sure no one is listening, "I could make it worth your while."

"Um, what?" I say. And then, so as not to appear rude, I add: "No, thank you."

"Won't you want some honeymoon video footage?" he asks, gesturing with his hands. "I've got some errands to run down there and I could do both at once."

How dare this man invoke my honeymoon! Doesn't he know that the honeymoon is the most sacred part of the entire wedding? Screw the ceremony—the honeymoon is where couples have their true religious experience! And he wants to besmirch it with his mob errands? This I cannot abide.

"I have a right mind to leave you in here for a while to stew in your own juices," I say, pursing my lips, "and think about what you've done wrong."

"Okay, okay," he says, "honeymoon's off the table. But are

you actually trying to *threaten* me?" He's leaning in and looking me dead in the eye as he says the word *threaten*.

Oh, God. Oh, God, Oh, God, Oh, God. I am going to sleep with the fishes. I am going to wake up with a sawed-off horse head in my bed.

Do not piss off the mobster. Do. Not. Piss. Off. The. Mobster.

"No," I say, using the same soothing voice I'd use with colicky babies or rabid animals. "Why on earth would I ever do that?"

"Look, do you want me to shoot you or not?"

"Please don't shoot me," I quickly say, eyes darting around for the prison guards. I know that this is only a detention center, but where are those guards when you need them? This is just like one of those mob films where the regular everyday person is just going about his or her day, ends up in a mix-up involving the mob, and then they come after her and her entire family. I'm too young to die!

"Shoot your *wedding video,*" he says.

"I knew that," I quickly say.

"Then get me out of here *now.*" He points his finger on the table for emphasis.

"Guard!" I say, "Mr. Conte is ready to go."

Just asking…

WHAT former model is so serious about her garbage that she will throw anyone who comes within ten feet of it into the Manhattan Detention Center? This is one celebrity you do not want to piss off—even though her customers think that she is as delicate as a piece of lace, this former "it" girl doesn't think twice about throwing a paparazzo who gets too close to her or her couture right into jail. Even a pap with known connections to the mob.

Column Five would never assume, but just *what* was in her garbage that got her tulle into such a bunch?

21

Many a bachelorette party has been thrown at Mangia e Bevi. (And I should know, since I've been to quite a few of them.) It's a tiny Italian restaurant in Hell's Kitchen where, on any given night, you can find a gaggle of girls celebrating someone's impending nuptials by dancing on chairs (which, at Mangia e Bevi, is strongly encouraged) and drinking their drinks through penis shaped straws.

In the winter of 2002, it was Tandy O'Donoghue's bachelorette party. The bride-to-be danced on a table, while wearing a hot-pink boa, to "You're the One That I Want" from the *Grease* soundtrack, with her maid of honor, Jen Moss, lip-synching the Danny lines to her Sandy. She refused to wear the veil with tiny penises hanging from its every inch (she insisted that they were no match for her groom-to-be's), but gleefully drank from a penis-shaped water bottle (which she insisted was more "true to size") and indulged in the penis-shaped cupcakes that were served for dessert (by that time, she was too drunk to form an opinion either way about the cupcakes). Tandy got herself into quite a bit of trouble when she accidentally drunk-dialed the Best Man on her way home that night.

In the summer of 2004, it was Eileen Massey's turn. She and her entire bridal party showed up in tiaras and bedroom slippers and danced on their chairs to "Come on Eileen." The girls that were there still talk about the scandalous dance that Eileen's maid of honor did with a huge blow-up penis (similar to the big Bozo blow-up dolls that were popular circa 1979), right in front of Eileen's fourteen-year-old stepsister. Eileen's stepmother was in attendance that evening, too, and Eileen spent most of the evening refusing to eat anything but salad, for fear of not fitting into her wedding dress and, perhaps more importantly, her stepmonster's watchful eye.

In the fall of 2006, Emily Carlson was the one we all came out to toast. She and her bridesmaids went crazy and decided to have a co-ed bachelorette party. The men all parked themselves at the bar to watch a baseball playoff game, while the girls stayed at the table and danced on their chairs to "I Want Your Sex." Only the groom-to-be joined the actual party and played along with the evening's festivities, even drinking his banana daiquiri out of a penis-shaped straw. That simple act of boldness earned him an impromptu lap dance from all of the bridesmaids, which quickly brought out the "angry drunk" in the bride. She decided that the best course of action would be to drag the groom-to-be out of the party and into the bathroom to have sex. (This is also the story of why we don't use the first bathroom on the right at Mangia e Bevi.) Said groom-to-be came out of the closet three weeks before the wedding.

This year, it's my turn, and Vanessa has the entire place rented out for the night since the guest list is so huge. The super-top-secret plan that's supposed to be a surprise is this: first, we start out with appetizers. Trays of bruschetta, stuffed mushrooms and fried calamari will be passed around as the guests enter and get comfortable. The restaurant brought in trays of mini hot dogs especially for this occasion, too, since my mother insisted that you simply could not have a girls' night out without them. Bottles of white and red wine will already be set out on the tables and to get mixed drinks, you'll simply have to go to the bar.

For the main course, you'll grab a seat wherever you like (take that, sisters Solomon!) and start out with a plate of salad, topped with fresh tomatoes and even fresher mozzarella (dressing on the side, of course). You'll then eat either chicken marsala, vegetable lasagna or veal scallopine. I've already decided on the chicken marsala.

Next, Vanessa and my mom will announce with clever little smirks that it's time for dessert, only they'll say the word *dessert* as if they're saying something really naughty, like *ménage a trois,* or, in my mother's case, *paying full retail price.* The waiters will roll out an enormous four-foot-tall cake that all of the guests will ooh and aah over. A very tasteful male stripper will jump out of the cake and dance around with us.

Is it any wonder my father's seven aunts have not been invited to the party?

Then, we will all get up on our chairs and dance to "You're the One That I Want," "Come on Eileen" and "I Want Your Sex." Vanessa's also requested that they cue up my favorite eighties song, "We Don't Have to Take Our Clothes Off."

There will be no penis-shaped straws.

Just when everyone thinks that the party is over and it's time to go home, Mangia e Bevi will dim the lights and the bachelorette party will turn into a co-ed after-hours party, with all of the guys coming in as a surprise. Vanessa, with a lot of help from Jack, had to orchestrate an entirely different e-vite for the boyfriends, husbands and assorted male friends, and then swear each and every one of them to secrecy. I think that the signing of actual legal affidavits may have been involved.

I know all of this because I helped my mother and Vanessa plan said festivities. We've all been fast friends since the lobster incident at the bridal shower and had to band together in order to take control of the bachelorette party. Without our intervention, my mother informed us, the bachelorette party would turn into a Hitler Youth Rally—and, as my mother informed Vanessa, it wasn't just the Jews that they were rallying against—Hitler was none too fond of black people, either.

Vanessa had to make up some very clever story about

how I was traumatized at a bachelorette party that I once attended (by the penis-shaped straws, no doubt) and how I now had to help plan the party with Vanessa and my mother, and *only* with Vanessa and my mother. Vanessa said that it wasn't easy to get the sisters Solomon to back off at first, but then I reminded her of her sacred vow as a maid of honor, and she did what had to be done to make sure that she, my mom and I maintained control of my bachelorette party.

"So, how did it go today?" I ask Vanessa as we sip our Diet Cokes through penis-shaped straws.

"Fine," she says, "it was totally fine. Wear this."

I allow her to place a Hawaiian lei on my neck and she puts one around her neck, too. These are not your typical brightly colored plastic leis that you'd find at a party store. No, these are seriously fancy Hawaiian leis, made out of beautiful silk flowers, keyed into the color scheme of my flowers for the wedding. "I wanted to come with you."

"I know," she says, "but Marcus was there and I just didn't want anyone else there. You know?"

"Of course," I say, "I just want you to know that you've got tons of support through every step of this thing."

"Well, that was the last step," she says, tipping her lemon into her Diet Coke with the penis-shaped straw.

"So, is it final?" I ask, taking the straw out of my drink and placing it onto the nearest table.

"Yup," she says, sipping the rest of her Diet Coke down, "I'm officially divorced. Let's go get something stronger from the bar."

"Was it okay being there with him?" I ask as we walk over to the bar. "Did he make a scene or anything?"

"No," she says as she motions for the bartender to pour us shots of Southern Comfort. "He did look ridiculously hot, though."

"Marcus *is* ridiculously hot," I say, as the bartender pours us our shots. For some reason, the shot glasses at Mangia e Bevi seem to be twice the size of a normal shot glass. Vanessa counts down from three and we down our shots at the same time.

"I know," she says. "It's weird. After you're with someone for so long, you kind of forget about what they look like. Good or bad, I guess. You just get used to them and the way they look. I haven't seen Marcus in so long that I think I forgot how *freaking* hot he is."

I turn around from the bar and see a waiter helping my mother hang a sign that reads: "Let's Get Lei'd!"

"What, so now you want him back?" I say with a laugh as I pour us each a white wine from the nearest table. Vanessa laughs without smiling.

"That looks perfect, Mimi," Vanessa yells out as she runs over to my mother. "Can we get it a touch higher?"

"This 'Let's Get Lei'd' theme is very clever," Jack's sister, Lisa, says as she walks over to me.

"Thanks," I say. "It was my mother's idea."

"She's adorable," Lisa says, looking over at my mom. "It must be so nice to be close to your mother like that."

"It is," I say, "although most of the time, I'm ready to kill her. But that comes with the territory. Are you close to Joan?"

"Where's Patricia?" Jack's sister Elizabeth asks as she walks over to us. As she stands side by side with Lisa, I recall that Lisa is the youngest of the three and Elizabeth is the one in the middle. Patricia is the oldest. *I actually remember who is who!* A waiter comes over with a plate of fried calamari and I grab a piece and dip it into marinara sauce to congratulate myself on being so darned smart.

"Probably off somewhere bossing someone around," Lisa says with a laugh and Elizabeth laughs, too. I give a tiny laugh. I'm not quite sure if I'm allowed to laugh at jokes that disparage one of the other sisters Solomon quite yet.

"How's Alan?" I say to Elizabeth and I marvel at how I just remembered which brother-in-law goes with which sister. The words just fell out of my mouth, and after I've said them, I realize that I definitely know who's who! Just as I'm about to ask Lisa how her husband, Aaron, is doing, Elizabeth answers my question.

"You'll see for yourself later," she says, grabbing a piece of bruschetta off the tray of a passing waiter. I decide not to take a piece so that my breath won't be garlicky later when Jack arrives and kisses me hello.

Who knows, we may even make some history of our own in the second bathroom on the left….

"Elizabeth!" Lisa hisses. "Ix-nay on the urprise-say."

"I know about the surprise," I say. "My mother's not

good with secrets. I look forward to seeing Aaron later. I haven't really had a chance to talk to him much."

"Most people think that all of our husbands are interchangeable, so don't worry," Elizabeth says and she and Lisa laugh at the joke.

I join in on the laughter and for a second I wonder if I've underestimated the Solomon sisters. I've sort of bunched them all together, and maybe I've made a real mistake in not making an effort to get to know each and every one of them separately. Their husbands, too.

"Seriously, though," Elizabeth says, "I've got to go and find Patricia before she starts some sort of trouble."

"She just doesn't want old Patricia to have any fun, now does she?" Lisa says, pouring herself a glass of wine from the nearest table as Elizabeth goes off in search of Patricia.

"You work in midtown, right?" I say to Lisa.

"Yes," Lisa says, taking a sip of her wine, "I'm on Third Avenue, too, just a few blocks down from your office."

"How about we go to lunch this week?" I say, as she pours a little more wine into my glass, too.

"I'd like that, Brooke," she says. "I'd really like that."

"We just got lei'd!" I hear in a thick Polish accent.

Now, there is only one person in the world that I know with such a thick Polish accent, and the other is her sister, Devorah. But there is simply no way in hell that my mother thought it prudent to include my eighty-two-year-old grandmother and her eighty-nine-year-old sister to this bacchanal. Surely she realized that such novelty items as a penis-shaped straw and a stripper jumping out of a cake would be lost on two elderly eastern European women.

Lisa and I both turn around. Sure enough, it's the thick Polish accent of my father's mother and her sister, Devorah.

At this moment in time, I am extremely grateful that most of my great aunts live out of state.

In my shock and awe at the arrival of my grandmother and Aunt Devorah, it barely registers that Miranda Foxley seems to have come into Mangia e Bevi, too. Out of the corner of my eye, I see her place her lei on top of her head, like a crown on her blaze of fire-red hair. She begins dancing to the music as she walks in and greets everyone with a big fake Southern-fried smile on her face.

Not like I'm jealous of her or anything.

"Now, there's something you don't see every day," Lisa says, eyes still glued on my grandmother and Aunt Devorah, adjusting their leis and accosting the waiter with the pigs in blankets.

I rush over to my mother: "Have you lost your mind?"

"What?" she says, fluffing out the silk flowers on her lei. Needless to say, she's got her lei of choice for the evening color-coordinated with her outfit.

I don't respond. I merely bob my head in the general direction of my grandmother and Aunt Devorah.

"You don't know your grandmother and aunt like I do," she says, "You see them as old women. I happen to know that they are going to have more fun than anyone here tonight."

"There is something wrong with you," I say and my mother laughs.

"Time for appetizers, BB," my mother says. "Let's start sitting everybody down."

My mother rushes over to the bar, and the bartender hands her a microphone. She announces that it's time to begin our appetizers and the assorted party guests begin finding their chairs. I see her order a drink from the bartender and then leave the bar with three champagne cocktails.

"Where are we sitting?" Vanessa says. "I tried to commandeer the table in the middle but Jack's sisters are there now."

"Let's sit with Jack's sisters," I say, and Vanessa stares back at me. "We're going to try something different tonight."

"We're pretending we're mature?" Vanessa asks, "I'm so impressed." We walk over to the table where Jack's sisters are all seated, every other seat, just waiting for Vanessa and me to fill the gaps. As we pass by my mother's table, I see my mother handing my grandmother and Aunt Devorah each a champagne cocktail. They all clink their glasses together—I could swear I hear one of them make a toast that involves the word *finally!*—and then take a sip.

In the opposite corner of the dining room, Jack's mother, Joan, is holding court at a table with her friends.

"I Want Your Sex" comes over the sound speakers just as Vanessa and I get to our table, and guests immediately start jumping up on chairs.

"We didn't even get a bite to eat yet!" I protest to Vanessa as we sit down in our seats.

"If you can't beat 'em," Vanessa says and hops up on her chair.

"I'm on a wedding diet anyway," Lisa says, and jumps up on her chair.

I begin eating my tomatoes and mozzarella—it is simply too early to start dancing on chairs. And, I'm going to have to put something in my stomach if I'm going to continue drinking like I have been tonight.

"Brooke!" I hear a voice with a thick Polish accent call out to me, "Get up on your chair!"

I turn around and see my grandmother and my Aunt Devorah up on their chairs. All of the waiters and guests around them are going crazy as they shake their artificial hips in time to George Michael. This is probably the first time, in the history of Mangia e Bevi, that orthopedic shoes have rocked the chairs.

I grab my camera, only to have a waiter take it from my hands.

"Please allow me," he says. "Which one is your grandmother?" I point at my grandma and then drag my chair over to where she and Aunt Devorah are dancing on their chairs. I jump up onto my chair and they put their arms around me. We all laugh and dance and somewhere in the middle of all of this, I see the camera flash go off.

22

"You said we were going halfsies," Vanessa whines as I eat my chicken marsala. Little does she know, somewhere in the middle of lip-synching "You're the One That I Want" with her, I decided that I was too hungry to share.

"We're still going halfsies," I say, "I'm just eating more than my half of the chicken marsala."

"Well, stop eating," she says, "I'd like to try some. The veggie lasagna's great." And with that, she takes the plate I'm eating from and swaps it with her own.

"If it's so great," I say, "then, why are you trying to swap with me?"

"Because you need the pasta to absorb all of the alcohol that you're drinking," she says and she's got a point. I grab a piece of Italian bread from the center of the table.

"At your own bachelorette party," Lisa says, over the loud music playing in the background, "you're supposed to drink too much!"

"Not as much as you drank at yours, though," Patricia says. "I practically had to carry you home from the Culture Club."

I catch Lisa and Elizabeth smirking at each other. Then Lisa winks at me and I try not to laugh.

"You did not," Lisa says, pouring herself another glass of wine for emphasis.

"Yeah," Elizabeth joins in. "I was the one who had to carry her home."

"I got too drunk at my bachelorette party, too," Vanessa says, fingering her ring finger with her thumb.

"Which is exactly what you're supposed to do," Lisa says. "Right?"

"Right," Vanessa says, and then audibly sighs. "Would you please excuse me from the table for a minute?"

I know where this is going. I've run this drill once or twice before. Vanessa never cries, but when she does, it's always a doozy. After eight years of friendship, I know that when Vanessa excuses herself from the table randomly—especially when there's some very delicious chicken marsala in front of her, no less—she's upset about something and is running off to be miserable in private.

Vanessa's been putting on a brave face today, all day, but there's just no way that she can actually be okay with her divorce being final. I knew it. So, that leads me to the undeniable conclusion that she is now running off to the bathroom to cry about the fact that her marriage is officially over in the eyes of the State of New York. Hopefully, she isn't too upset to remember not to use the first bathroom on the right. I jump up from my seat to run after her.

Only it's not that easy to run through a crowd when you're the guest of honor at a party.

"This is so much fun, Brooke!"

"Vanessa and your mom did such a great job, Brooke!"

"Excuse me, miss, can we have another bottle of wine? Oh, wait, that's you, Brooke!"

I reach over to the bar to grab a bottle of wine for the table who mistook me for a waitress and my mother is back on the microphone.

"And now, ladies," she says, "get ready, because it is time for *des-sert!*"

And with that, the waiters all begin to wheel out the huge four-foot-high cake. The top of the cake suddenly explodes and a male stripper pops out. Even though I knew it was coming, I'm still somehow totally surprised.

"Brooke Miller, where are you?" he says. I just stand steady, barely moving an inch, like a deer in the woods, hoping that if I don't move, he won't be able to see me.

"She's right here!" one of my so-called friends screams out.

"Then, let's dance!" he says and jumps over to me and grabs my hands to dance. My only saving grace here is that I know that Vanessa and my mom gave him very specific instructions to keep it PG-13. As we dance together, he begins peeling layer after layer of clothing off himself and I can't help but think that the stripper at the bachelor party vs. the stripper at the bachelorette party serve two entirely different purposes.

The stripper at the bachelor party is like the groom's last hurrah, his last night of something crazy. All of the men at the bachelor party are totally turned on by the strippers, and it makes most of the men wish they were still single. The stripper at the bachelorette party is the exact opposite—most of the women are totally overwhelmed by the stripper and his sweaty body and it has the effect of driving the bride-to-be directly into her groom-to-be's arms.

Which is what I'm thinking at this very minute. All I can really think about is how long I'll have to dance with this sweaty half-naked man before I can run to the bathroom to check on Vanessa.

The elder stateswomen of my family do not seem to be having the same thought process as me. I guess when you've been through natural childbirth a few times, you're not going to let a little thing like sweat keep you from dancing with a half naked man. They have circled us, and after the first song is over, I leave the male stripper dancing with my mother, grandmother and Aunt Devorah as I rush toward the bathrooms.

The bathrooms at Mangia e Bevi are tiny—they're clearly only meant for one occupant at a time—and Vanessa's in the second one on the left, which, conveniently enough, doesn't have a lock. I fling the door open and jump up onto the sink. I have to tuck my legs as close as I can to the base of the sink just so that we can both fit inside. Vanessa's seated on top of the toilet with her head in her hands and her elbows on her knees. I'm thankful that the toilets at Mangia e Bevi have lids that you can close before sitting down for Vanessa's sake, but I really wish I'd used some paper towels to dry off the sink before I sat down on it.

"Go back to your party!" Vanessa says, picking her head up from her hands, "I don't want to ruin your bachelorette party!"

"You're not ruining anything," I say. "This party wouldn't even have happened if it wasn't for you."

"Yes," Vanessa says, "but now I'm ruining it. Please just go back to the party. I promise, I feel better already."

"You're my best friend," I say. "If you want to cry—even in the middle of my bachelorette party—we'll cry. But, you haven't ruined a thing."

"I've ruined everything," she says, head in her hands.

"No, you haven't," I say, grabbing her shoulder, hoping she'll look up at me.

"My marriage is over, Brooke," she says, "and it's all my fault. It's all over. It's gone. So, don't tell me I haven't ruined anything. I *did* ruin everything."

"No, you didn't, Vanessa," I say, grabbing one of her hands and holding onto it. "You did what you thought the best possible thing was at the time. There's nothing wrong with that. You did what you thought was right."

"Except that now I'm divorced," she says, shoulders quietly shaking, "And Marcus will never speak to me again."

"Isn't that what you wanted?" I ask and Vanessa immediately begins to cry even harder. "I'm sorry! Was that the wrong thing to say? I thought that this was what you wanted? Are you reconsidering?"

"Yes," she says, looking up at me. "No. Maybe. I don't know. What if I am?"

"Then you should talk to Marcus," I say, grabbing some toilet paper off the roll and handing it to her to blot her eyes. "Maybe he feels the same way."

"He doesn't," she says, as she quietly blows her nose. "When we were at our lawyers' offices today, he asked me if I was sure. He asked me if I was a hundred percent sure, and I said 'yes.'"

"So?" I say. "You're allowed to change your mind, aren't you?"

"Not with Marcus. When I said that I was sure, he said that we were done, final, finished, and that I could never come back. That he would never speak to me again."

"Come here," I say, jumping down from the sink. I pull Vanessa up from the toilet seat and give her a big hug. "It's okay," I say, stroking her hair.

Vanessa takes a deep breath in and out and I keep holding her tight. I've been with her through other nights crying over Marcus, and I know that after the deep breaths, she'll start to feel better. We hold each other tight and I stroke her hair.

"I love you, Vanessa," I say, and, as I say it, I feel her hug me back.

"I love you, too," she says, and I feel someone's eyes on us. I look up and see that someone's opened the door to the bathroom by accident.

My future mother-in-law.

"Hi, girls," Jack's mother, Joan, says.

"Hi," we say in unison, our faces still pressed cheek to cheek, arms still intertwined. I have a feeling that I should let Vanessa go, that my future mother-in-law is probably wondering exactly what it is that I'm doing with my maid of honor cooped up in the bathroom with her, embracing her, on the night of my bachelorette party, but the bathroom is so cramped that there's actually no way for me to break away from the hug.

"This probably looks odd," I say.

"It actually reminds me of my own bachelorette party," she says, and I have no idea if she's joking or serious. Since there's no room for Vanessa and I to turn and face each other and make the requisite "I'm confused, are you?" face, we sort of hop out of the bathroom together and drop our arms. Joan walks into the bathroom without another word.

"Let's do more shots," Vanessa says, grabbing my hand.

Vanessa and I walk out to the bar and plant ourselves down on two stools. I melt into my bar stool, feeling like I'll never get back up. Vanessa is already halfway slouched over the bar, and dangling her feet from the bar stool like a little girl whose chair is too high for her. The bartender pulls out two oversized shot glasses without our even having to say a thing, and fills them with shots of Southern Comfort.

"Do I look so bad that he actually knew that I wanted hard alcohol?" Vanessa asks, holding her head up with her arm.

"No," I say, "you look gorgeous. He's probably just

getting you drunk so that he can take advantage of you later. Now drink!"

"Three, two, one," Vanessa calls out and we down our shots. We both bring our shot glasses back down onto the bar with a slam.

"Ready for another?" the bartender asks, waving the bottle around in front of our faces.

"Yes, please," Vanessa says, sticking her glass out. I hold onto my glass as I try to figure out if I'm too drunk to have another shot.

"He's cute," Vanessa whispers, pointing to the bartender.

The bartender overhears her and winks at her. I can't help but laugh. Thinking other guys are cute—the first step in the healing process of a breakup. Vanessa just may be all right, after all.

"Well, I am fixin' to get me a drink!" Miranda says as she sidles up to the bar.

"Just as long as she's not fixin' to steal my man from me," I say to Vanessa. Vanessa laughs quietly into her shot glass.

"Brooke, you're so funny," Miranda says, turning around to me. I'm surprised that she's answered me, since I thought I'd whispered that to Vanessa, but whenever you're drinking, you tend to think you're whispering when you're actually screaming, so I let it slide. "As if Jack isn't head-over-heels crazy for you, bless his heart! You are one lucky gal."

"I'm very lucky," I say, and I wonder if I'm beginning to slur my words.

"And I just think it's so cute how y'all are flirting with

each other by serving each other legal documents," she says, picking up her drink from the bar and taking a sip. "It is just too sweet."

"Well," I say, downing another shot of Southern Comfort, "it was funny at the beginning." Miranda smiles at me and takes a sip of her drink. Then, lowering my voice to a whisper: "Truth be told, it's kind of getting a little annoying now."

After I've said it, I suddenly realize how drunk I'm getting. Why on earth was I confiding in the one person here who I dislike and distrust the most? I motion for the bartender and order myself a glass of ice water. Vanessa frowns at me and orders herself another shot.

"I'm sorry to hear you say that, Brooke," Miranda says, "I had no idea. I never would have suggested to Jack that he serve you with Interrogatories at your bridal shower if I'd known that you didn't think it was funny anymore."

Stop the presses. Stop. The. Presses.

Miranda told Jack to serve me with Interrogatories at my bridal shower? That was all her idea? I'm not sure which I'm more upset about—the fact that Miranda suggested it, or that Jack actually followed through with the idea that she suggested.

I grab at the cocktail napkin that's underneath my ice water and tear it into two pieces. And then into four.

"That was your idea?" I ask, trying to articulate my words, an act that is becoming increasingly more difficult with each passing second.

"Yes," Miranda says, laughing, "we didn't even really have anything to ask you—I mean, it's a simple business transaction, right? But Jack and I thought it would be funny, so we served you. He didn't think you'd actually take them seriously. We were shocked when we got your responses."

Jack and I. She just said *Jack and I.* As if they're a team or something. Or friends.

Or more. I tear the napkin into eight pieces.

"Jack and I?" I say, eyes narrowing. Her face begins to blur as I squint my eyes until I can't really see her at all.

"Yeah," she says. "I'm his junior associate, right? Now that you're gone, I'm the junior associate working on all of his cases with him."

I tear the napkin pieces again and again, until they can't be torn in half anymore.

"Oh, I'm sure you're working it," Vanessa says, laughing from the bottom of her throat. She leans into me and puts her chin on my shoulder so that we are both staring directly at Miranda.

"What?" Miranda says. "Am I missing something here? Is there some joke I'm not in on?"

"Oh, so now you think I'm a joke?" I ask and I can feel Vanessa nodding, her chin bumping into my shoulder.

"What are y'all talking about?" Miranda asks, laughing nervously.

"Are you sleeping with him?" I say, eyes narrowing into tiny slits.

"With who?" Miranda asks.

"Wow," Vanessa says quietly, falling back onto her own bar stool. "She's sleeping with so many of them she can't even keep track."

"Jack!" I yell at Miranda. "Whaddya mean *who?* Don't play coy *now.* It's a bit too late for that, don't you think?"

"What?" she says, still laughing. "What on earth are you talking about, Brooke? Vanessa, what's she talking about?"

"How dare you come here," I say.

"You're kidding, right?" Miranda says, "Vanessa, would you please talk some sense into your friend here? Brooke, I would never—"

"Please don't give me 'I would never,'" I say and I am suddenly sure that I am, in fact, slurring my words. But I don't care. This needs to be said. "We all know what you would and would not do. And the 'would' category, as the entire legal community of New York City knows, definitely includes sleeping with partners. Married ones, preferably."

"My word," Miranda says, her voice barely a whisper. "I can see where I'm not wanted. I thought that we were becoming friends. But, I guess not, now that I know how you really feel about me. I'll just be going."

"Good idea," I say, trying to articulate each word.

"Way to lay the smack down, Brooke," Vanessa says, as Miranda rushes off. "I don't like her, either."

"You can't use that expression if you're over the age of twelve," I tell her, and slurp down more of my ice water.

"Twenty-two," she says. "The cut-off age for ridiculous expressions is twenty-two."

We stumble off of our bar stools and back to our table, where the sisters Solomon have made sure that we each had a slice of bachelorette party cake waiting for us.

"I got you a cup of coffee, Brooke," Patricia says, "how do you take it?"

"You're no fun," Lisa says, clearly on her way to having a lot of fun herself. "If the girl wants to get drunk at her own bachelorette party, that's her prerogative!"

In slow motion, I see Patricia shoot a dirty glare in Lisa's direction.

"The boys are going to be here any minute," my mother says, appearing out of nowhere over my shoulder, "and you have eyeliner running down your face." She dabs a napkin into my water and blots my face. I close my eyes as she puts makeup on it. She rubs concealer all over my face a bit too roughly, but I'm too drunk and tired to protest. Once she's done with me, she starts in on Vanessa, who has begun hugging anyone in arm's reach to tell them that they are her best friend.

Minutes later, the clock strikes midnight. On cue, the lights dim and the men start coming in. First, I see my father, who walks directly to my mother to give her a kiss and then I see a few of my friends' boyfriends, fiancés and husbands walk in, not to mention a few gay best friends. Finally, I see Jack walk in with his father.

"Jackie," I say, as Jack comes over to me and gives me a kiss, "consider yourself lei'd." I take my lei off and put it around his neck and he kisses me again.

"Counselor, consider yourself served," he says, handing me a legal document. I can feel the alcohol coursing through my veins.

"Are you kidding me?" I say, scanning the document. It's a subpoena for witnesses that Jack wants to depose. Even through my drunken haze, I can still tell that it's a lot of witnesses.

"Kind of," he says, laughing and adjusting the lei.

"It's not funny," I say. "It's not funny at all." I'm somewhat aware that my party guests are beginning to look at me.

"Well, it's meant to be a big joke," he says, "so why don't you try behaving unethically and we'll see if I want to withdraw my subpoena."

"That sounds dirty," Vanessa says, laughing, from across the table. *"Withdraw my subpoena."*

Jack laughs.

"You think that I'm a joke or something?" I say. "Is that why you and Miranda have been playing your little games with me? Playing jokes *on* me?"

"Well, to be fair," he whispers, leaning into me, "we never really thought you'd take us seriously."

"Oh, I take things seriously," I say, "In fact, I'm *very* serious when I say that you've been playing dirty all along. You know that I have limited resources, and yet you've been inundating me with work."

"Brooke," he says, looking around at all of our party guests who are now beginning to stare. But I don't care. I'm saying what needs to be said. What *should have* been said a while ago.

"It's probably because you're having an affair with Miranda and you just want to spend extra time with her," I say.

"We've all had too much to drink, Jack," Lisa whispers to Jack, gently taking my arm. "Sweetie, why don't we go to the bathroom for a minute and get you some water? Let's just try to have some fun, okay?"

"Fun?" I yell at Lisa. "This is not fun. Litigating this case has not been fun. Planning this wedding has not been fun. In fact, Jack probably learned how to play dirty by being a part of *your* family, since your family has been steamrolling over mine the entire time that we've been planning this thing."

"No, we haven't," Lisa says quietly. And then to Jack: "Jack, would you please tell her that we haven't?"

"Lobster!" I yell at her. "You served lobster at my freaking bridal shower!"

"What's she talking about? What's wrong with lobster?" Lisa asks Jack. "Brooke, what are you talking about?"

"You know what, Brooke?" Jack says, grabbing my arms away from Lisa. "You don't even seem to *want* to get married, so I don't know what you're so upset about."

"Excuse me?" I say, trying to release my arms from Jack's grasp, but he's holding on too tightly.

"You don't even have a wedding dress and the wedding is a month away!" he says. "What does that say about how much you want to get married to me?"

"No," I say, "I think it's *you* who doesn't want to get married, since you've given me no time to *look* for a wedding dress. I would have gone shopping for a wedding dress, but you kept inundating me with work!"

"We didn't actually think you were actually going to do it!" he says, laughing like a mad professor.

"See?" I say, looking over to Vanessa. "There's that *we*

again." Vanessa nods back at me, her eyes beginning to involuntarily close. I feel mine beginning to shut, too.

"Since when did you ever choose work over your real, actual life?" he says, running his hand through his shaggy brown hair. "When? Name one instance in the entire five years we were working together."

"I don't even know who you are anymore," I say to Jack. "And it's quite clear that you have no idea who I am, either."

Everyone's staring at me and the room begins to spin. Vanessa and my mother rush to my side, a show of support, and I try to fight back the tears that are threatening to explode from my eyes. I turn to my father, whose face has gone completely pale.

"Daddy, would you please take me home?"

23

I wake up the next morning in my old room at my parents' house. The room I grew up in from the time I was born straight through to high school and college. My toes practically touch the tip of my twin-size bed and I nearly knock over the glass of water my mother left for me the night before on my bedside table as I stretch my arms out.

"Knock, knock," my mother says quietly as she opens the door to my bedroom. She's holding a tray with coffee, a buttered sesame bagel and a bottle of Advil. The perfect South-Shore-of-Long-Island hangover cure. "Can I come in?"

"Of course," I say, even though she's already halfway across my room. "Morning."

"I thought you could use some of this stuff," she says. I sit up in my bed and she sets the tray down next to me and perches herself at the end of the bed by my feet. I'm instantly reminded of all of those sick days when I was growing up and how my mother would prepare a tray with everything I needed to feel better—ginger ale, toast with strawberry preserves, tea with honey—and would then sit on my bed with me until I felt better.

"Thank you," I say, picking up the bagel and taking a bite. It's just the right amount of soft and sweet and the butter melts in my mouth. I wash it down with a greedy sip of coffee and think that this is the best bagel I've ever eaten in my life.

"A buttered bagel always does the trick for me," my mother says, "and we have to get you back, good as new, before we send you back into the city."

"I'm not going back into the city," I say, with my mouth full of bagel. My mother furrows her brow and regards me. I take a huge gulp of coffee and rearticulate, "I'm not going back into the city."

"I heard you the first time," my mother says, "But I don't understand. Don't you want to go back home and make up with Jack?"

"No," I say, taking another huge gulp of coffee.

"Well, you don't have to go back tonight," my mother says, laughing. "You can stay out here and take the train to the city in the morning. Then you can go back to your apartment after work."

"I'm not going back," I say, polishing off the first half of the bagel in two bites.

"What do you mean, you're not going back?" she says,

laughing. "Eventually you have to go back to your apartment. It's your home. Your home with Jack."

"I'm not going back," I say, looking down at the tray.

"Brooke, you're not going to give up your whole life over one fight," my mother says. "Be reasonable here. Now, I know that you are hungover and not thinking properly, but—"

"That's the thing, Mom," I say, "I *am* thinking properly now. The problem was that I wasn't before. But now I am. I was just ignoring all of the things that were wrong, all the things that were bothering me."

"Those are silly things," she says, "none of it was real. What *is* real is the fact that you and Jack love each other. Once you're feeling better, you'll see."

"What about how his family has been treating us?" I say.

"There's always an adjustment period when the families meet," she says. "Do you think that my family and your father's all just magically loved each other at first? No, they didn't. We had our problems, too. But, you work at it. And look at how close we all are now."

"What about the fact that Jack never stood up for us?" I ask.

My mother gets up from the edge of my bed and walks to my window. She looks out at our backyard, at the huge pine that is in the center of it, and exhales deeply.

"I don't know," my mother says, and doesn't turn around to face me as she does. "I just don't know."

"Well," I say, getting up to join my mother at the windowsill, "neither do I."

★ ★ ★

I don't get back out of bed until six o'clock that evening, when the smell of New Hunan Taste fills the house all the way up to my bedroom.

"You want an egg roll or a spring roll, BB?" my dad asks me as I pad downstairs, still in my pajamas. My dad is in sweatpants and my mother is in a fancy teal-colored yoga suit that I know for a fact she bought at Saks.

"Egg roll," I say as my mother pours me a Diet Coke. "I'll get the ice."

I walk to the freezer and grab a few cubes of ice. As I go back to the table, I'm suddenly very cognizant of the fact that my parents are smiling manically at me, sort of the way you'd imagine that the family of a mental patient would treat that person. *Everything's just fine, honey.*

"I'm fine," I say, looking at them.

"We know that," they say in unison.

"Boneless spare ribs?" my father asks, reaching across the table to pass them to me. Now, I know that my father is a kosher butcher, but his deepest darkest family secret is that one of his most guilty pleasures in life is the boneless spare ribs at New Hunan Taste. Which is why he normally hoards them all to himself.

"You're offering me boneless spare ribs?" I say, my expression blank.

"You can have anything you want, BB," my mother says. "Right, Barry?"

"Anything you want, BB," my father says, still pushing the

boneless spareribs on me. I decide to test him. I take the tin and systematically take out all of the well-done pieces. My father and I both love the well-done pieces, and I watch him as he watches me pick them out. The smile remains plastered on his face and as I look between he and my mother, I realize that they must both be very good poker players.

"You don't have to treat me like a mental patient," I say. Their expressions don't change at all; in fact, they barely move at all. They are like those animals in the woods who, upon being attacked, try to freeze themselves so that the crazy attack animal leaves them alone.

"We're not, honey," my mother says. "It's just that you hardly ever come home and we're so happy to have you, aren't we Barry?"

"So happy," he says, still smiling. "Mu shoo?"

I take the mu shoo, but make a big show of how happy and decidedly *not* insane I am as I pour the hoisin sauce onto a pancake. It continues like this for the rest of dinner—we all smile at each other incessantly and use really good table manners and don't chew with our mouths open at all. The perfect little Stepford family. That is, if the Stepford wives were mah-jongg-playing petite Jewish women.

Finally, the torture is over and it's time for fortune cookies.

"What does yours say, Barry?" my mother asks my father, giggling. They had one of their first dates together over Chinese food, so fortune cookies always make my mom especially giddy.

" 'A smile is your personal welcome mat,' " my father announces, flashing his pearly whites. "How about you, Mimi?"

"That one is perfect for you! Mine says: 'Don't worry about money,'" she says, squinting, since she needs reading glasses but refuses ever to wear them in front of my father. "'The best things in life are free.' Hmm. Obviously these people have never been to Saks. What does yours say, BB?"

"'You would make a great lawyer,'" I say, tucking my fortune under my plate, along with my napkin.

"Really?" my mother says, "maybe there really *is* something to these fortune cookies!"

"That's not what it says," my father says, eyes burning into me as if he can read my mind. "What does it really say, BB?"

How is it that my father always knows when I'm lying? Even when I was a little girl, he always just knew.

Growing up, my mother's most prized possession in the world was a cameo that belonged to her grandmother. Alabaster white and a shade of delicate pink set in gold, it was the most beautiful thing my thirteen-year-old eyes had ever seen. I desperately wanted to wear it to my junior high school dance—certain that it would make my crush, Danny, immediately fall in love with me on the spot. My mother flatly refused. I was dumbfounded—how could she say no? Didn't she know how important this dance was to me? I made an unsuccessful plea to my father. He explained to me that it was the only thing my mother had left of her grandmother and that it had huge sentimental value. It couldn't be replaced. I told him that it wouldn't need to be replaced, since I would only be borrowing it for one evening—mere hours, really, if you thought about it—but, he remained unconvinced.

My first losing oral argument.

In my heart of hearts, I just knew that if my mother knew how unbelievably important it was for me to wear her cameo, she would have said yes. So firm was my belief that, on the night of the dance, I took it. While she was downstairs in the kitchen, I walked into her room, stealthily as a cat, and went to her jewelry box. A wooden box painted an antique gold, I opened it, slowly, quietly, revealing its insides encased in a rich red velvet, as if it were a buried treasure. I ran my fingers over the soft fabric. My mother, from out of nowhere, appeared behind me and looked over my shoulders, making me jump. I tried not to look guilty.

"I bet we can find you something special in there," she said and picked out a pair of pearl earrings for me. "Those will be beautiful," she said, holding them out for me to try on. "They were a Sweet Sixteen present for me from my Aunt Florence."

I smiled and she beamed back at me. As she admired the earrings in my ears, I slowly put my hand behind me, into the jewelry box, and took the cameo.

I never even made it into the dance that night. My girlfriends and I ran into Danny and his friends on our way in, and decided that we were all way too cool for a junior high school dance. We instead ended up in Danny's basement, drinking wine coolers. Come to think of it, the majority of my junior high and high school memories took place in that very basement, Danny's parents never being home. Within minutes of the wine coolers being passed around, games of

Spin the Bottle and Seven Minutes in Heaven began. I can barely remember the details of the evening, though—my only memory being that it was the night that Danny asked me to be his girlfriend. I floated home at the end of the night and walked in the front door just before my curfew.

"Have you seen your mother's cameo?" my father asked me as I walked in. His eyes burned into me and I could barely meet his eyes.

"No, why?" I answered, my hand instinctively flying to my chest. The cameo was not there.

"It's missing and your mother is really upset," he said, looking at me calmly. "If it doesn't turn up, she'll be devastated."

"Guess I should have let you wear it tonight, sweetheart," my mother said, walking out of the kitchen in her bathrobe. "At least then I'd know where it was."

My father's eyes stayed glued upon me as I ran up the stairs quickly. I flew into my room and checked everything I was wearing, shaking my coat and my sweater out, praying that I'd hear a thump on the carpet. The cameo was nowhere to be found. I could hear my parents talking in their bedroom. My father was trying to calm my mother down, but she was inconsolable. It was the first time I'd ever heard my mother cry.

I prayed the whole night through. I don't even remember ever having gone to sleep. I prayed and prayed with every fiber of my being that I would wake up in the morning and I would find the cameo. I told God that if I found the cameo the next morning, I would never lie to my father again.

The next morning, my prayers were answered—I woke

up from the previous day's horrors as if it were only a bad dream. Danny brought the cameo back, having found it on the floor of the closet in his basement. My mother was thrilled, but my dad wanting to know how the cameo ended up there of all places brought on a whole host of other problems.

I never lied to my father ever again.

"What does your fortune *really* say, BB?" my father asks, eyes still on me.

"It says: 'Every exit is an entrance to a new experience.'"

I look down at the fortune and take a big bite of the cookie. My eyes don't come up to meet those of my parents. Leave it to this seemingly innocuous fortune cookie to make the whole evening explode into a discussion about Jack and me and how I'm ruining my life by not rushing back to him immediately.

When I finally do look up, I see my mother and father looking at each other. Then, in an instant, my mother's up clearing the table and my father's washing the dishes in the sink.

"Do you have these under control, honey?" my mother asks my father once she's done clearing the table. "My show's coming on."

"Yes, Mimi," my father says, giving my mother a tiny peck on the lips before she flits off. "It's all under control."

"Let me help you with those, Daddy," I say, joining my father at the sink.

"I've got it," my father says with a smile. "Why don't you go and watch TV with Mom?"

"But I want to," I say, and he regards me, passing me the yellow plastic gloves.

"You rinse off and I'll load the dishwasher," he says, "deal?"

"Deal," I say, and turn the water all the way to as hot as it goes.

"So, do you want to talk about it?" my father asks, waiting for the first dish to load into the dishwasher. The steam begins to rise up from the sink.

"There's really nothing to talk about," I say, passing him an appetizer plate. "It's over. It's done."

"Do you really want it to be over, BB? Do you want it to be done?" he says, "I thought that you loved Jack?"

I scrub at a particularly sticky spot of hoison sauce.

"I do," I say, "it's just that I don't even know him any more."

I pass the dish to my father, only partially clean, and move on to the glasses.

"I don't think that that's really true," my father says, and as I turn to face him, a glass slips out of my hands and crashes into the sink, breaking into pieces.

"Oh, my God," I say, turning back to the sink and picking up the pieces with my rubber gloves.

"It's okay, BB," my father says, his voice low and soft, "it's okay."

"I'm so sorry," I say, and I begin to cry.

"You don't have to be sorry," my father says, turning me to him so that he can hug me. My face melts into his chest and I begin to cry even harder. He puts his hand on my head and tells me that everything's going to be okay.

Minutes later, my father's put up a pot of tea and we're seated at the kitchen counter, having left the rest of the dishes piled up in the sink.

"It's just that we've been friends for years," I say, still crying as I speak. "But now all of these things are happening that make me question who he really is."

"But he wasn't running around with that Miranda woman you accused him of cheating with," my father says. The teapot begins to scream and my father goes to pick it up.

"It's not just that," I say as my father pours the boiling-hot water into my mug, "It's other things, too. Like when we went to Tiffany's to register, and like how he litigated against me. It's like I've been seeing this whole other Jack. A Jack I don't know at all. A Jack I don't want to know."

"That reminds me of something," my father says, setting the teapot back down on the stove. "There was this *Twilight Zone* episode that I used to love. I think it was called 'Button, Button.' A salesman comes to this couple's home and leaves them with a machine that has a big red button on top. He tells them that if they press the button, they'll get a million dollars, but, once the button is pressed, someone in the world—someone who they don't know—will die. The couple argues about it all night. They could really use the money, but the thought of killing someone, even someone they don't know, is just too much to bear.

"Finally, they go to bed, but the wife wakes up in the middle of the night and can't stand it any more. She presses the button. The next morning, she wakes up to find that her husband has died in his sleep. When the salesman returns to give her the money, the woman is furious. She screams at him: 'I thought you said that someone we *didn't know* would die?' And the salesman responds: 'Do you think that you really knew your husband?'"

"That's not how it ended!" my mother yells at us as she comes walking into the kitchen. "And why are there still dishes in my sink?"

"That *is* how it ended," my father says, "and we're just taking a break."

"Why do you need a break from cleaning dishes for three people?" she says, walking to the sink and rinsing off the remaining dishes and piling them into the dishwasher. "And anyway, that's not how the story ended."

"How did it end?" I ask. I'm still unsettled by the ending to the story that my father just offered, and am, therefore, willing to take any challenging interpretation of the story.

"It ended with the guy saying: 'Now, I will take the box and give it to another couple. A couple who does not know *you*.'"

"I think you're mixing up the short story by Richard Matheson," my father says. "That's how the short story ended, but not the *Twilight Zone* episode."

"Well, I think that *you're* the one who's all mixed up," my mother says, "what the hell kind of story are you telling her anyway? Don't you *ever* want her to get married?"

As my parents bicker in the kitchen where I spent most

of my young life, I realize that I want what they have—the kind of relationship that they have. That sort of comfortable, natural relationship where you can bicker and argue and still know that you'd never go to bed mad at each other.

I had that with Jack. But what kind of a relationship can you have with a man you don't even know?

But that's what I want. That's the kind of relationship I've waited my whole life for. The comfort, the love, the silly flirtatious bickering after over thirty years together. They'll probably go back to bed tonight and have sex.

Ew.

But the relationship. That's what I want for myself. I thought that that was the kind of relationship I had with Jack, but it turns out that I just didn't know him at all. My father seems to think that you never really know the person you're with, but I don't believe that. More importantly, I don't want that for myself. I want to know, when I walk down the aisle, every inch and fiber of the man I'm going to marry. I thought I did. But, I just don't anymore.

I look down at the table and grab at the paper napkin under my mug. I tear it into two, and then four.

"Why do you do that?" my mother asks, finally laying off my father for a moment and directing her energy at me.

I shrug in response since I have no idea what she's talking about. I tear the paper napkin into eight.

"That thing with your hands," she says. "Whenever you get nervous or upset, you grab at the closest paper product and just begin to tear it into pieces. Why do you do that?"

"It's just a bad habit, I guess," I say. "It's just like when you start picking at your fingernails or when Dad's face gets beet-red. Just something I do."

"You do tend to do that when you get nervous, don't you?" my mother says.

"Do what?" I ask.

"Tear things apart."

24

"Usually when you break up with someone, you move in with me," Vanessa says. We're on the fifth floor of Saks, searching for suitable "date" clothing (read: slutty) for Vanessa. "Should I be offended?"

"I seem to recall that when I stay with you," I say, picking up a Nanette Lepore camisole for Vanessa to try on, "I have to train for the New York City marathon with you, and I really think that at this point, I've been through enough torture."

"It's good for you," Vanessa says, grabbing every Marc Jacobs camisole in her size, and piling it onto her arms, "running helps clear your head."

A salesperson comes by and asks us if we want to start a dressing room. We pile the clothes into her arms, and then get started on the Cynthia Steffe collection.

"I broke my ankle last time I went running with you," I remind Vanessa.

"It was just a sprain," she says, barely looking up from the green sundress she's checking the price on.

"I'm not running with you," I say loudly over the racks to her, being sure to mouth the words clearly, so that there's no confusion, even though she's not even looking at me.

"Well, you have to get out of your parents' house," she says, turning back to face me. "If you want, you can move in with me and I won't make you run."

"I think I'll just stay where I am," I say, as we head back to the dressing rooms. "I'm kind of liking staying with my parents, actually."

"Even with Mimi?" Vanessa says, turning to me and raising an eyebrow.

"Even with Mimi," I say, surprising myself as I say it. Normally there's a threshold on the amount of time I can actually spend with my mother, but this past week, she's been uncharacteristically well-behaved.

"Suit yourself," Vanessa says, walking into a fitting room. Then, as she shuts the door: "So, I'm dating this new man."

"What?" I say, trying to open the dressing room door, but Vanessa's got it locked already. So I say into the door: "Tell me all about him! Wait, this isn't the guy who was so short that he only came up to your boobs?"

Vanessa opens the dressing room door and comes out in a Theory wrap dress that fits her slender figure perfectly. She does a quick spin in the three-way mirror and casually says: "No, it's not boob-level guy. It's another guy."

"Not the one who told you that it was unconscionable to wear such expensive shoes when children are starving to death in Africa?"

"No, not him, either," Vanessa says, looking down at her Chanel four-inch-heel spectator pumps without realizing it. "It's another guy. But, I think that maybe this one I'll keep to myself."

I furrow my brow. "We don't keep anything to ourselves," I remind Vanessa.

"True," she says, "but, just this once, okay?"

"Okay," I say, trying to conceal the fact that she's piqued my interest. I'll have to take her for high tea at the Saks restaurant next. Their scones would make anyone spill their guts.

"Thanks for that," she says, as she retreats to her fitting room. "I really appreciate it. So, have you spoken to Jack yet?"

"No," I say, "Why would I talk to Jack? There's really nothing to talk about."

"Of course there is," Vanessa says, walking out of the fitting room in a Nanette Lepore top that is so low-cut, her navel practically shows. "There's tons to talk about."

"Only buy that top if you are planning to give this new man of yours a coronary," I say, as Vanessa turns from side to side to inspect the top.

"Really? I'll take that as a 'yes,'" Vanessa says, smiling, and turns around to go back to her fitting room. "When are you going to see him?"

"See who?" I ask.

"What do you mean, who?" she asks. "Jack."

"I'm not going to see Jack," I say.

"Well, don't you have to at least see him to give back his grandmother's engagement ring?" she asks, as she walks out in a Marc Jacobs dress that looks a bit too big on her.

I look back at her blankly.

"You can't possibly keep it," she says, turning around so that I can zip her up. "Are you thinking about keeping it?"

"Actually, according to the laws of the state of New York," I say, sitting back down, "I don't have to give back the ring. Since Jack gave it to me as a gift in contemplation of marriage, and then effectively broke off our engagement, I get to keep the ring."

"It was his grandmother's ring," she says, spinning around to look at me. "The ring that the man's grandfather came home from the Second World War with and then gave to the man's grandmother. It is a family heirloom. You can't possibly be serious."

"I'm just saying that in the eyes of the law, I'm well within my rights to keep it. That ring was a gift with a promise attached to it. A promise that he in turn, couldn't deliver on."

"I don't remember that from law school," Vanessa says, "in fact, I recall just the opposite. I'm pretty sure that, legally, you have to give the ring back."

"No," I say, shaking my head, "I don't think so."

"What grade did you get in first-year Property?" she asks, as she walks back to her dressing room.

"An A-, thank you very much," I call out to her.

"Well, I got an A," she yells back at me, "so, I'm right."

"Professor Silverman didn't test the law of engagement rings on the final," I say, "so that really doesn't prove a thing."

"Your argument's got a big flaw, anyway, Brooke," Vanessa says, walking out of the dressing room in her own clothing, holding a big pile of clothes. "*You* called off the engagement."

"No," I say, as Vanessa and I make our way to the cash register, "I maintain that *he* called it off by acting in such a way that I had no other option but to call off the engagement. *But for* his behavior, we would still be engaged. Thus, it stands to reason that he forced me to call it off. So, in the eyes of the law, it would totally be considered his fault."

"If that's the sort of logic you're using in your Monique case," she says, piling her clothes onto the counter so that we can check out, "you're definitely going to lose."

"The way he acted in Tiffany's—" I begin, only to be cut off by Vanessa.

"You're breaking off your engagement because you don't like the way he used a zappy gun?"

"No," I say, "you know that that's not it at all. Registering at Tiffany's was just the beginning of the end. It was the first time that I realized that I didn't really know him at all.

It snowballed from there—next came the way he litigated against me—"

"That's because you two never should have been opposing each other in court in the first place," Vanessa says, handing over her credit card to the cashier.

"The way his family treated mine," I say.

"You're marrying Jack," she says, turning to face me, "not his family. If I'd judged Marcus by *his* family, we'd have never made it down the aisle. You've met his sister. What was it that you called her?"

"Now whose argument is flawed?" I say, turning to face her, too. "You divorced Marcus."

"But still," she says.

"But still nothing," I say. "I think your argument proves my point. Maybe you *should* judge a guy by his family. I remember what I called Marcus's sister that time I met her. But, I'm a lady, so I refuse to repeat it."

"You know, Brooke," Vanessa says, "people get very stressed when it comes to planning weddings and stuff. I'm sure that Jack's family isn't nearly as bad in reality as they were in the course of planning this wedding. I'm sure they were just as stressed about all of this as you. Let's just assume that what we saw wasn't actually the real them. I'm sure that if you just explained to Jack how you really feel, he'd save the day and fix everything for you. Just like he always does."

"Well, it's too late for that now," I say, grabbing one of Vanessa's shopping bags while she grabs the other one and the garment bag, "so let's go get a bite to eat in the café. I'm thinking scones?"

I will be finding out who Vanessa's mystery man is, no matter how many scones it takes.

When I walk in the door from work the following evening at 11:00 p.m., my mother's still up, boxing up engagement and wedding presents to ship back to their respective senders. She's in a pale-pink robe that I bought for her for Mother's Day last year. She always wears pretty robes and nightgowns to sleep—something about advice her great-aunt gave her as a newlywed about "always keeping the magic alive"—so that's been my go-to present for her for as long as I can recall.

"Late day, huh?" she says, looking up from her bubble wrap. "Want something to eat?"

"I grabbed a slice of pizza at the office," I say, throwing my work bag down in the foyer and taking off my jacket.

"Reminds me of when you worked at Gilson, Hecht," my mother says.

"Please don't even *mention* the name of that law firm to me," I say, slipping my shoes off and sitting down next to her in the living room.

"It's just that you seem to be working just as hard now as when you left the firm," she says, putting down the industrial roll of tape she'd been using. "See, I didn't mention the name."

"Thank you," I say, and grab the roll of tape to help her seal up a box from Crate and Barrel. "I'm on a very high-profile case. You know that."

"You've told me that," she says, passing me a black Sharpie to use to write the address on the box, "I know how important the case is. For God's sake, you sacrificed your wedding dress for it."

"I didn't sacrifice anything for it," I say, looking up and trying to meet her eye.

My mother slowly looks up from the box she's packing and regards me.

"I didn't," I say.

"Okay," she says, going back to her box. "It's just that I thought that the reason you left your old firm to go to a smaller firm was so that you wouldn't have to work quite as many hours. So that you could have more of a life."

"I do have a life," I say.

"Okay," she says with that smile again. It's that same smile she's been using since I've been home. I want to scream: "It really *is* okay!" but I know that screaming like that will not prove my point. It will prove hers.

I just know her too well. And being here, back at home, reminds me of everything I forgot about my parents. Well, I didn't forget, it's just the things that I stopped noticing since I moved out. Like how my mother dons these adorable nightshirt and robe sets and doesn't take her makeup off until the second before she jumps into bed. Or like how my father calls out "Honey, I'm home!" when he walks in the door at night, or really any time he enters a room in the house.

It reminds me of things that I've forgotten about myself,

too. Who I used to be. Who I used to think I'd grow up to be. How I thought my life would turn out.

After boxing up a few more presents, my mother and I retreat upstairs where I plop down onto my bed without even taking off my work clothes. I look around my room—up at my bulletin board, untouched since the day I graduated high school, with my varsity letter from cheerleading and various snapshots from Senior Weekend, into my closet, with my prom dress and assorted bridesmaid dresses from throughout the years, and my bookshelf, with my books from law school piled high.

Back when I lived in this room, I thought that I had it all figured out. I'd go to college, go to law school and then meet and marry the man of my dreams. Soon thereafter, my 2.4 children would follow. When I thought all of these things, I suppose I was a child myself. I had no idea all of the heartbreak and hard work real life would bring. How hard it would be to have a life and make a life for yourself.

I took for granted that I could just have a happy life and live happily ever after. Happily ever after never included being over thirty and moving back in with your parents.

I turn onto my side and begin to quietly cry. I try to keep it down, since I don't want my parents to worry, so I turn my face toward my pillow.

As I look at my bedside table, I see the messages set neatly next to my phone, the way they have been every evening since I've been here. I get the same messages every night: Jack called (7:05 p.m.), Jack called (7:49 p.m.), Jack stopped by to see you (8:40 p.m.), Jack called (9:55 p.m.). They are almost the same as the ones I get at work every day, which my assistant drops on my desk without looking up to meet my eye: Jack stopped by (9:27 a.m.), Jack called (11:45 a.m.), Jack called (2:15 p.m.), Jack called (4:01 p.m.), Jack stopped by (5:55 p.m.).

I pick up this evening's messages and look at them for a moment before throwing them into the trash.

25

"Oops, she did it again!" Esther sings to me as she comes sailing into my office.

"Did what?" I say, barely looking up from my research on dissolution of partnership. "Who?"

"Miranda!" Esther says, clearly enjoying the delivery of this news way too much.

"What did she do?" I ask, barely able to choke the words out.

"What does she always do?" Esther says.

But, I don't have to ask because I already know what Miranda always does.

Sleep with partners. That's what Miranda does.

I just hope that she hasn't slept with *my* partner.

"Who was it?" I say, just as the phone begins to ring.

"Come to my office when you're off," Esther whispers, and then disappears before I even have a chance to tell her that I'll let the call go to voice-mail.

I don't pick the phone up anyway, and instead choose to just stare at my computer screen blankly. Out of habit, I go onto the Internet and pull up the Gilson, Hecht Web site. First, as I always do, I type in Vanessa's name, as if that's the real reason I'm there. From there, it's just a few clicks over to the S section of the "Our Attorneys" page and I'm at Jack's profile.

I remember the day he got the picture taken for the Web site. Even though the Gilson, Hecht attorneys get photographs taken every year for the firm Web site, this was the first year he'd be getting his done as a partner. We obsessed the whole week before over what Jack should wear in his photo. Should he wear his navy single-breasted suit, so as to denote "serious junior partner on the fast track to becoming an equity partner?" Or, should he instead go simply with a shirt and a tie, so as to denote "serious junior partner who's just too busy working hard to worry about dressing up all fancy for a silly firm photo?" In the end, we'd decided on the navy suit, since his shaggy brown hair was always mussed, denoting the "too busy working hard to worry about my appearance" thing all on its own. He wore a pink Chanel tie that I'd bought for him as a gift when he made partner. I put my finger up to the computer screen just as my intercom begins to buzz.

"Excuse me," my assistant says over my intercom, "Monique deVouvray is on the line for you."

"Thank you," I say, and pick up my phone to speak to Monique.

"We had plans to discuss settlement," Monique says in her thick French accent. "Am I calling at the right time?"

"Yes, of course," I say, minimizing my computer screen so that I can focus solely on Monique. "What were your thoughts?"

After speaking with Monique for almost an hour, I can barely wait to call Vanessa. At least three different times during my phone call to Monique, I was tempted to e-mail Vanessa to ask her about Miranda. In the end, I decided to wait until my phone conference was over to call her, in case she had bad news to share. Bad news is one thing, but getting bad news over e-mail would just be too much to bear.

"Break it to me gently," I say to Vanessa, practically closing my eyes to prepare for the news. I had to have Vanessa's assistant pull her out of a meeting with a new client in order to speak with her, but I simply couldn't wait another second to hear about what happened with Miranda.

"Break what to you?" Vanessa says back quickly, sounding strangely like a kid caught with her hand in the cookie jar. She was clearly glad to have been sprung from her meeting. "What did you hear?"

"Miranda," I whisper into my phone. I consider closing my door for a second, but then remember that since no one at SGR ever closes their door, it will actually attract more attention if it's closed. I whisper: "Please tell me it's not Jack. *Please* tell me that she didn't sleep with Jack."

"I thought you said that you don't even care about Jack anymore," Vanessa says.

"I don't," I say back a little too quickly.

"Haven't your parents been canceling deposits all over town?" she asks. "First the Pierre, then Maximo Floral—"

Why is Vanessa torturing me like this? On the one hand, I'm probably in the clear, since she wouldn't be goading me if she was about to tell me some horrible news. On the other hand, she just got divorced and maybe now she's taking her bitterness and angriness out on me.

But, she didn't sound bitter or angry. She actually sounded rather playful, which is odd, seeing as usually Vanessa doesn't do playful. Maybe this new guy she's seeing is making her soft. (I never did find out who it was that day at Saks—I blame this on the fact that the café was only selling blueberry scones that day and was sold out of the chocolate chip. If they'd had chocolate chip, I would've been set.)

"Just tell me, already!" I say. It comes out sounding a bit crosser than I had intended.

"You're stealing his grandmother's ring," Vanessa says, "Can't you at least let the man have a few kicks with a junior associate?"

"Oh, my God," I say, practically dropping the phone into my lap. "So, then, it's true. Jack slept with Miranda."

"Of course it's not true!" Vanessa says. "Are you insane? Why on earth would Jack sleep with Miranda? A delicate

Southern belle? You know his tastes skew more toward neurotic Jewish girls from Long Island."

"Do you find this funny?" I say, taking a sip of water from a bottle at the end of my desk.

"Actually," she says, "I do. I cannot believe you called me out of a meeting for this."

"It was an emergency," I say.

"It really would be much easier to help get you and Jack back together if you were living in my apartment like last time."

"What on earth are you talking about?" I say. "I'm not getting back together with Jack."

"And you said that you'd never get together with Jack in the first place," she says, "but, you did. And then when you guys had that fight and didn't speak for three weeks, you said you'd never talk to him again. But, you did. And then you moved in with him. And then you got engaged to him."

"But last time was different because *I* was the one who'd screwed things up. This time, it wasn't me, it was Jack."

"Is that what your emergency was?" she asks. "To tell me all that stuff? Because all that stuff, I already knew."

"No," I say. "The scandal with Miranda is the emergency."

"Oh, yeah," she says, "Well, Miranda is, in fact, in yet another scandal with a partner. But it's not Jack. She got caught in a compromising position in the fourteenth-floor men's room with the head of the bankruptcy department."

"Will Peters?" I say.

"Yup."

"Ew."

"Yup," she says. "Classy. She could at least have done it in one of the bathrooms on a reception floor. Those are marble. Much nicer."

"Ew," I say, "you just gave me a really disgusting visual."

Vanessa laughs. "So, can you please get back together with Jack now?"

"No, Vanessa," I say, "I'm not getting back together with Jack."

"Why not?" Vanessa asks, "that whole Miranda obsession was completely in your head."

"I know, Vanessa. I know that. But that wasn't the real problem, anyway," I say. "The problem is that Jack isn't the man that I thought he was."

"Yes, he is, Brooke," Vanessa says. "He is."

"No, he's not," I say. "And I would expect you of all people to understand where I'm coming from. It's the same thing with you and Marcus. Isn't that what happened? You found out that he wasn't the man you thought he was?"

"I guess so," she says, her voice a notch softer than before.

"That's exactly what happened," I say. "But, now it seems like you've found someone even better, right?"

"Actually, yes," Vanessa says. I can hear her voice begin to lighten at the mere mention of her mystery man.

"So," I say slowly, as if approaching a tiny puppy that I don't want to scare away, "do I get to hear about him?"

"You know, if you were this tenacious in the courtroom—" Vanessa begins.

"Please?" I say, still treading lightly. I've almost got her,

I can tell. "Hearing about your mystery man will totally cheer me up."

"Okay, okay," she says, laughing on the other end of the phone.

"Is he as handsome as—" I begin, before catching myself from finishing the thought. I shouldn't be comparing Vanessa's new man to Marcus. For one, most men couldn't possibly compete with Marcus, but also, I don't want thoughts of her ex to cast a pall on the new love she's got brewing. "I mean, what I meant to say was, is he handsome?"

"Yes," she says, "he's as handsome as Marcus. Even more so, actually. In fact, he's just like Marcus. Only much, much better."

"Oh," I say, unsure of what to say next. If her mystery man knew that she was comparing him to her ex, he would be very unhappy. I puzzle over how to tell that to Vanessa. More importantly, I need to remind her to be careful in bed—nothing would quash her new love affair faster than calling out her ex's name in the heat of passion.

Not like I know about that from past experience or anything.

"It's like he's got everything that Marcus had that I fell in love with, but he's also got so much more."

"Just be careful," I say. And then, as a self-conscious afterthought: "Just don't call him Marcus!"

"I'm fine," she says, "this time I actually think I know what I'm doing."

We hang up and I can't help but smile. I'm so thrilled for Vanessa. She deserves some happiness after all that she's gone through lately. Going through a divorce while your best friend is planning her wedding can't be easy. I truly am happy that she's figured things out and knows what she's doing.

I just wish that I did, too.

26

Canceling your own wedding has got to be one of the most humiliating and humbling experiences a girl can ever have. It's pure torture telling your friends and family the news, trying to explain what happened, and that's all before you've even thought about having to return all of the presents. Then, you're faced with the worst part of it all—having to call each and every one of the vendors and losing your deposit as you cancel the most important day of your life. Even when your mother and father do most of the actual canceling for you, it's still pretty awful.

The process began for me with my mother stoically packing up all of my engagement and wedding presents, one by one, and then shipping them back to their respective senders with a kind note. Next, my father called the Pierre

Hotel to tell them that the whole thing was off. It pained my father to call the Pierre to cancel his little girl's wedding. It truly killed him to give up on the plan for my wedding day—a day he and my mother had dreamed about since the day I was born. And even more so to actually lose the twenty percent deposit he'd put down on the whole thing. When he made the call, he had that expression on his face that he reserves only for impromptu visits from the health department, tax audits or a particularly bad New York Jets game loss. Actually, I'm not really sure what he was more upset about: losing the deposit money itself, or that he was unable to "chisel them" down to a smaller amount the way he'd bragged to my mother and me that he could.

Most of the wedding vendors have been nothing short of kind and understanding. I'm sure I'm not the first person in the world to have had second thoughts and cancel her wedding—they've been through this before. Most of the people we spoke to were absolutely professional and appropriate. For example, when my mother called Maximo the florist to call off the wedding, he told her, in his charming Spanish (or definitely Italian) accent, that she needn't worry—a woman as enchanting as her daughter was sure to find another man immediately. In fact, he explained (or, she *thinks* he explained—this was over the phone and his accent is really very thick) that while he had to keep the deposit money as per the contract, he would use the deposit money for my next wedding, which undoubtedly would be coming up very soon. My hairdresser, Starleen, after bursting into hysterical tears when I told her the news and then composing herself because she "wanted to be strong" for me, was very supportive of my decision to cancel the wedding and agreed not to keep the deposit. And that's not just because I hadn't actually *given* her a deposit yet. She truly meant it from the bottom of her heart. And even Savannah Moore, the bandleader (who, it bears mentioning, I didn't want to use in the first place), refunded all of the deposit money to my father, saying that she wouldn't feel right keeping it, since she had a wait list in place for our wedding date and would definitely be rebooking a different party for the night. Probably within the hour.

Yes, all of the vendors we'd used had been a pleasure to deal with, even in the darkest hours of my life. Or my parents' lives, as the case may be. They made this very difficult time for me and my family easier, and the transition from bride-to-be back to single girl as painless as they could.

But not Jay Conte. Not my wedding videographer to the mob. You'd think that after you bail a guy out of jail—well, technically a detention center, but close enough—you'd have formed a bond with him. But, no. Even after your father calls him to explain to him that your wedding is off, he will still track you down like the rat that you are in your place of business.

"Brooke," my assistant says over the intercom. "Your wedding videographer is here to see you." I can hear her faintly giggling in the background.

My wedding *what?* Did she not get the memo that my

wedding was off? Clearly, I no longer have a wedding *anything* anymore. Jay Conte, of all people, should not be here at my office. As I try to articulate this to my assistant, I hear more giggling over the line.

Oh, God, I think. *What on earth is going on out there?* Has he threatened her life? Has he threatened *my* life? Is he already trying to kill her or something? But then I hear more giggling. This is worse than I could have imagined. There's a lot of giggling going on out there. Is my assistant—dare I say it—*flirting* with him?

Oh, God. This is the first thing they teach you in the movies. Do not flirt with the mobster. Do. Not. Flirt with the Mobster! Have we learned nothing from *Scarface?*

"Uh," I babble into the intercom, "who?"

"Me," Jay says, materializing in my doorway. "I brought you flowers, but your assistant loved them, so I gave them to her."

"You brought me flowers?" I ask.

Oh, no! Is he hitting on *me?* Has he come here to ask me out? I should have seen this one coming—I guess he was secretly *thrilled* when he heard the news that Jack and I split up and ran down here as quickly as he could to profess his love for me! I had a feeling that I'd seen him trailing me when I went to Monique's brownstone for meetings. Vanessa said I was crazy, but I knew that I was right! Damn it—why am I so darned irresistible?

"Yes, flowers. Roses, actually. Because I knew you'd be in mourning," he says, taking his fedora off and holding it across his chest, as if he was about to recite the National

Anthem. Or the pledge of allegiance. "For the death of your relationship."

Whaaa?

"Well, thanks," I say, "I guess. But, really, that was unnecessary."

"Good," he says. "Because your assistant out there really is quite a looker."

"She's my secretary," I say, sitting down behind my desk. Jay takes that as a cue to sit down in one of my visitor's chairs.

"So, I spoke to your father," he says. "I really am sorry about what happened with you and Joe."

"Jack," I say.

"Yeah," he says, "Jack. What did I say?"

"It's not important," I say. I lean back in my chair as I puzzle over how to ask him why he's actually here if the wedding is off.

"Well, there's another reason for my visit here today," Jay says, taking a toothpick out of his jacket pocket and sticking it into his mouth. He moves it to one side of his mouth with his tongue, where it sits for the whole time he's talking. "I know that you've called your nuptials off, but we have a contract."

How come when Jay says the word *contract* the *on your life* part sounds like it's implied?

"Yes," I say, sitting up straight in my chair as I shift it back to the regular seated position, "I understand. You keep the deposit money. Didn't you speak with my father about this?"

"Yes," he says, toothpick still firmly placed in the side of his mouth. "I did speak to your father. But you do realize that you can't just cancel on me, don't you? That's not how it works."

Oh, God. I have a mobster in my office and he's pissed at me for canceling on him. Any minute he's going to tell me: "Say hel-lo to my little friend...." And I'm too young to die!

"Can I get you two some coffee?" my assistant says into the intercom. Ah, saved by the bell. Or assistant, as the case may be. "That was so rude of me not to ask earlier."

"I'd love some, sweetheart," Jay says. "Black."

Now, I suppose that I don't have to tell you here that if any attorney ever used the term *sweetheart* on his or her assistant, that attorney and that attorney's law firm would immediately be slapped with a million-dollar lawsuit for sexual harassment. They give us lectures and workshops about this sort of thing constantly, so I really know what I'm talking about. But using such unpolitically-correct terms of affection apparently works for Jay, since my assistant giggles and says: "Coming right up!"

"Brooke?" she asks. "Anything for you?"

"May I please have a glass of water?" I say, barely choking out the words. *And a cigarette,* I think. Now, I know that I don't smoke, but since that's what they give prisoners before they get executed, I figure that now's as good of a time as any to get started.

"So, our contract," Jay says. *On your life...*

"You know what?" I say, using my best negotiation techniques. "Why don't we do this—how about you just keep the full amount of the contract? I'll get you a check tomorrow."

Jay shakes his head "no."

"Bank check?" I offer. More head-shaking. "Certified check?"

Jay shakes his head "no" again and flicks the little toothpick over to the other side of his mouth.

"I'll get you cash," I say. "How's cash?"

"You know, this really isn't all about the money," Jay says. I will later find out that my dad actually already paid him in full. Cold hard cash. "The damage here extends well beyond the amount of the contract."

There's that contract again. *On my life.*

"It does?" I ask. I'm terrified to have him tell me what this actually *is* about, and why the damage well exceeds the amount of the contract, but I figure the sooner I find out, the sooner I can get him out of my office. Or the sooner they take me out of my office in a body bag. Either way, mission accomplished.

"But the way I figure it," he says, "there's a way for you and I to make things right."

"There is?" I ask. Do I really want to hear more?

"I want the exclusive deets on your girl Monique and her idiot husband Jean Luc," he says, leaning back in his chair. My visitor chairs are really not meant to be leaned back in. All I can think is, *if he breaks the chair's legs and falls down, RUN!*

"Jean Luc's not an idiot," I say, even though I've never actually met him.

"I don't really care whether he is or isn't one. What I care about is getting an exclusive on any dirt," Jay says, as my assistant comes back in with Jay's coffee and my water. We both thank her simultaneously and she gives another gratuitous giggle before exiting my office.

"There's no dirt," I tell Jay as soon as the coast is clear. "There's nothing to get. And anyway, I thought you weren't a pap?"

"I'm not a pap," he says, "those guys are disgusting. *I* am an artist. But a guy's gotta eat. If the pictures I take and the stories I tell just so happen to get printed somewhere, and *I just so happen* to get paid for it, well, then, that's that. But, I'm no pap. Paps are the scum of the earth, as far as I'm concerned."

Okay, taking pictures and getting the inside scoop on celebs and then accepting money for them. Um, so then, doesn't that mean he's a pap? I'm so confused.

"There's nothing for me to get for you," I say.

"I can get you outfitted with a tiny little camera that she wouldn't even see," he says. "I know how much you love the world of surveillance."

"I do not want to be outfitted with a camera," I say. "And that was not surveillance we were doing. That was background footage of the groom!"

"Whatever, hon. We could put it into a pair of earrings for you," he says. "You like earrings, don't you? Tell you what, you think about it."

"I don't have to think about it because there's nothing to find out. The pictures wouldn't be anything more exciting than the inside of any bridal salon. Muslins, fabrics, dresses. A bridal magazine or two. That's it."

"Do you ever see Jean Luc?" he asks.

"No," I say. "Why would he be there? I'm there for a wedding dress. I try on muslins and Monique fits them. He's never around for that."

"He's never around?" Jay asks, leaning forward in his chair.

"That's not what I meant," I say, leaning back in my own chair. "He just isn't at the bridal studio."

"I see."

"There's nothing to see!" I say, and then take a sip of my water.

"Well, when there is," he says, "you keep me in mind. And I'll keep you in mind."

Now, I know I should just let him leave my office at this point. It doesn't really matter what he thinks he's going to keep me in mind for. It doesn't. Nothing more could be gained by continuing this conversation. The goal was to settle my business with the mobster and then get said mobster out of my office. My assistant would have to be on her own once he got out there. So, even though it seemed like he was close to leaving my office, I inexplicably ask: "Keep me in mind for what?"

"Well, I'm saying that you can just owe me," he says, and then shrugs. "I could use a lawyer on retainer. My usual guy's been giving me trouble lately."

"Um, no, thank you," I say.

A lawyer for the mob? Somehow I just know that when my parents sent me to law school, this was not what they had in mind. And at any rate, who really remembers the lawyer in *The Godfather?* I think I'd actually rather be Jimmy

Caan, if anything. Not that I want to be on retainer for a mobster in any capacity. And more importantly, does this mean that Jay's been promoted from soldier? I didn't hear anything about that from my father. Is there, like, a Facebook for the Five Families you can look stuff like this up on?

"Why wouldn't you want to be my lawyer?" he asks. "I can introduce you to friends. Drum up some business."

Great, I can just see it now in my law school's alumni newsletter:

Brooke Miller—promoted to *consigliere* of a prominent New York City crime family. Next year, she's hoping to make underboss. We've got our fingers crossed for you, Brooke!

"I don't—" I say, only to be interrupted by Jay.

"And I'll be your photographer on retainer," he says. Visions of beautiful Kennedy-like portraits of me and my family for the rest of my life fill my head.... Only, I'm not going to have family any time soon, since I just called off my wedding. "So, we've got a deal?"

"No. No deal."

"Great," he says. "I'll be in touch, then. And you do the same."

"There's nothing to be in touch about," I say. "I don't need any pictures and I certainly won't have any dirt on Monique and Jean Luc."

"Just keep your ear to the ground," he says, standing up and putting his fedora back on his head. "You never know what might happen. Your life can change in an instant. You know who told me that?"

"Who?"

"Mr. John Gotti."

Why did I even bother to ask?

27

"So, counselors," Judge Martin says, leaning back in his big leather chair, "are we ready to settle?"

"My client is not, your honor," I say, and Jack says the same. We're both in Judge Martin's chambers for our final discovery conference—the last conference before the trial is set to begin—and it's taking all of my energy to not look at Jack. Even Miranda Foxley isn't there to break up the tension, having been unceremoniously shipped over the George Washington Bridge to a massive document production in a warehouse in Parsippany after she was discovered with the head of the bankruptcy department. Gilson, Hecht is notoriously scandal-averse, and to hear Vanessa tell it, they had Miranda out of her office and knee-deep in documents for a most unglamorous client, Toilet-Cleen, before word of the scandal had even reached the seventeenth-floor real estate department. They didn't want to fire her, since the only thing worse than a public scandal was a sexual harassment lawsuit, so instead, they sent her to the one place where even Column Five wouldn't deign to go—New Jersey.

"You know these cases don't go to trial," Judge Martin says, rubbing his forehead with his hand. "So, what are we doing here?"

"My client misjudged the way her husband would treat her in this matter," I say, clearing my throat. "She thought that they'd be able to handle this small business matter amicably."

"My client never thought his wife would let a simple misunderstanding spin out of control like this," Jack says. I can feel his eyes burning into me, but I refuse to turn and face him. One look at those baby blues might just melt me, and I want to stay strong.

"My client is very serious about her business, Your Honor," I say, as Judge Martin strokes his chin and regards me. "She is very serious about business."

"That's become increasingly clear to me," Jack says. "I mean, to my client."

"My client didn't want it to come to this either, but she's learning things about her husband that she really didn't know."

"Such as?" Judge Martin asks.

"He wasn't able to stand up for her in the way that she needed him to. I mean, stand up for the company, of course. So, she really thinks it's best that they dissolve their partnership now, before they get hurt even more. The shareholders, I mean."

"I still think that we can come to some sort of agreement here, though," Judge Martin says. "Isn't there some way we can meet in the middle?"

"I'm sorry, Your Honor," I say, shaking my head, "it's just too late for that."

"I'm very sorry to hear that, sweetheart," Judge Martin says, looking at me as if I were his own daughter.

"I am, too, Brooke," Jack says, and I can see out of the corner of my eye that he's about to try to grab my hand. Not knowing what else to do to stop him from taking my hand, I lean to the side and begin fishing in my briefcase for my day planner.

"Then, we set a date," Judge Martin says, looking at Jack.

Set a date. Judge Martin wants Jack and I to set a date. Sure, it's for a trial, but I can't help but think about how those words had such different meaning to us just months ago. When Jack and I first set a date, it was the beginning of our lives together. Now, we're setting a date to end it, once and for all.

Jack doesn't say a word. I can see him staring straight ahead at Judge Martin out of the corner of my eye.

"I'm going to schedule this for one day," Judge Martin says, "this shouldn't take more than one day, should it?"

"No," Jack and I say in unison.

"One day should be perfectly sufficient," I then add.

Judge Martin picks up his calendar, the large red leather book that sits on the edge of his desk, and flips through it.

"Next week's out, since we've got the Federal Bar Council luncheon," he says. He pauses for a moment and looks up at us. "Honoring Judge Solomon. I assume you'll both be there?"

Jack nods—of course he'll be at a Federal Bar Council luncheon honoring his own father—but I'm already formulating ways to get out of it, so I do a sort of yes/no nod to stay noncommittal.

"Then we'll do the week after next," Judge Martin says, flipping through the book's massive pages until he hits a Tuesday. "The week after next on Tuesday. I never like to start a trial on a Monday."

"That's fine," I say.

"Thank you, Judge," Jack says.

Jack and I stand to shake Judge Martin's hand and then leave chambers together. It kills me that he holds the door open for me as we walk out. I thank him so quietly, it's practically under my breath, and I walk briskly toward the elevators.

"So, there's no hope of settlement?" Jack asks, after he pushes the button for the elevator and stands next to me.

"No, Jackie, I'm sorry," I say, looking down at my feet.

"We really need to settle this." He gently grabs my arm.

The elevator doors open with a slight *ping* and I release my arm from his grip and walk in. Other lawyers are already inside, all facing front, and I get in and do the same.

"You don't answer my calls," Jack says, "and you're never there when I come by."

"I'm busy, Jack."

"We need to talk," Jack whispers to me.

"There's nothing to talk about." I'm whispering, too.

"Yes, there is."

"Anything you want to say to me," I turn to him, "you could have said in Judge Martin's chambers."

"It's not about the case—" as the elevator doors open to the lobby and I rush to get out "—it's about us," Jack says, walking quickly to catch up to me.

"Still nothing to discuss, Jackie," I stop dead in my tracks.

"I made a mistake. But you've made mistakes, too, before, you know. And I've always forgiven you."

"It's not just one mistake, Jack," I say. "We don't even know each other. I don't know you. And I can't marry a man I don't know."

"What are you talking about? Of course you know me. We've known each other for six years. How can you say you don't know me?"

"No, Jack," I say, shaking my head. "No. The way you litigated against me, the way you let your family treat mine… I don't know you at all."

"Of course you know me." He takes my hand and holds it gently. "Let me give you a ride back to your office so that we can talk."

"I've got a car waiting outside to take me back to the office," I say, releasing my hand from his grasp. "There is one thing I wanted to give you, though. That I thought you'd want back."

I take his grandmother's engagement ring from out of my purse and place it in his hand. I can't even bring my eyes up to meet his as I rush off to the town car idling outside the courthouse.

Life imitates art in the southern district of New York

By Shawn Morgan (AP)

The court papers may still be sealed, but sources now reveal that former model Monique deVouvray is divorcing from her husband of thirty-three years, businessman Jean Luc Renault. And the feeling is catching: during the course of litigating the divorce of deVouvray and Renault, Manhattan lawyers Brooke Miller and Jack Solomon, who were engaged to be married at the time that the court papers were filed, have called off their *own* engagement and subsequent wedding at the Pierre Hotel in Manhattan.

Solomon is the son of Circuit Court judge Edward Solomon, who sits on the Third Circuit, and socialite Joan Solomon, chair of the Friends of the Metropolitan Museum of Art Summertime Bash Committee, and board member of the American Cancer Society Spring Gala. Miller is the daughter of kosher butcher Marty Miller and homemaker Miriam "Mimi" Miller, chair of the Temple Beth Shalom Bowl for Life! annual fundraiser.

28

"Noah wants to see you in his office," my assistant announces, and my hands freeze on my keyboard. I can't type another word of the memo I'm working on because I know what's about to happen. Usually when Noah wants to see you, he just picks up his phone and calls you directly. When Noah calls your assistant to summon you, you can rest assured that you are in pretty big trouble.

"So," my assistant says as I sail by her, "what can you tell me about that wedding videographer of yours?"

"Nothing," I say, furrowing my brow to show my disapproval of the mere mention of him. "You should probably stay away from him."

"Is he single?" she asks, twirling a stray curl around her index finger.

I consider telling her the truth—that I really have no idea whether or not Jay is single. But then I realize that I've just told a twenty-two-year old girl to "stay away" from a guy she's got her eye on, and in doing so, I've just about ensured that she'll go after him. Full guns blazing. So, in an effort to protect my assistant's life, I tell her that Jay's married. I just hope, for her own personal safety, that she doesn't have the same view on married men as Miranda Foxley.

As I rush down the hall to Noah's office, I take a quick stop into the ladies' room to make sure I'm presentable. Standing in front of the bathroom mirror, straightening my skirt and smoothing back my hair, I can't help but remember how nervous I was during my first week at SGR. I was acutely aware of the fact that I'd never worked anywhere but Gilson, Hecht before, so starting work at SGR was a whole new world for me. I was used to Gilson, Hecht's mammoth offices—encompassing 17 floors of their building at 425 Park Avenue—and was getting adjusted to life at a firm that only had one floor of offices. I was just beginning to find my way around, figuring out where the mail room was, the file room, and, of course, the bathrooms. Which wasn't as easy as you may think when you're used to an office with the same exact floor plan on all seventeen floors.

I remember the day, even, that it happened—it was a Thursday. On my way to the ladies' room, I bumped into Manny, the head of the file room. As he saw me walking toward the bathroom, he called out "Wrong one!" I had no idea what he was talking about—maybe this was some cool new street slang that I hadn't heard of? So, I did what any tragically un-hip person would do—I called back "Wrong one!" and smiled. I may have even given him the thumbs-up, too, I can't really recall. I slipped into the ladies' room and checked myself out in the mirror, proud that I was beginning to fit in at my new office. I smiled at my reflection and then retreated to use the bathroom. Only, when I turned around, I saw a row of urinals. *Funny,* I thought, *the ladies' room has urinals?* And then it hit me—wrong one. As in, wrong bathroom. Not the ladies' room. I rushed out, only to find Manny waiting outside for me. We laughed hysterically and it became our inside joke. Any time I'd get nervous like I was that first week at SGR, Manny and I would call out to each other, "Wrong one!"

As I give my front teeth one final check for lipstick and smooth down the front of my skirt, I silently tell myself "Wrong one." Without Manny there to laugh with me, though, it doesn't have the desired effect.

"You wanted to see me?" I ask Noah, standing in his doorway. By not walking in and not committing myself fully to the idea of walking into his office, I'm secretly hoping that this will all be a misunderstanding, that he doesn't really want to see me, but I know that that's not the case. I know what this is about.

"Have a seat," Noah says, and I walk into his office and sit down on one of his visitors' chairs. "I noticed you've got a personal day for next Wednesday."

"Yes," I say, "I have some things that I need to tend to, so I figured I'd just take the day."

"Take Tuesday then," Noah says, staring me down.

"I can't," I say, looking out his window. "I need to take Wednesday."

"Thursday?"

"Noah, I can't—"

"Brooke," Noah says.

"I've made up my mind," I tell Noah. "I'm not going to the Federal Bar Council luncheon."

"You have to go. The firm bought a table. Everyone's going."

Noah's office is one of the corner offices—all three of the named partners have them—and its enormous windows overlook Third Avenue. I glance down at the nameplate that sits at the end of his desk which announces his full name in bold letters set in gold: Noah Fisher Goldberg, and then look back up at him.

"I can't go to this luncheon," I say, "they're honoring Jack's father. I just can't do it."

"Brooke—" Noah begins to answer.

"You can't honestly expect me to go," I say, interrupting his train of thought. "After all that's happened."

"There are going to be over a thousand lawyers there, and anyone who is anyone in the New York legal community will be there. Of course I expect you to go."

"Noah—" I begin to say, but this time, he's the one who cuts me off.

"You won't even *see* Jack there."

"He's giving the keynote address," I say, pointing for effect to the invitation that's tacked onto Noah's bulletin board. It's a gorgeous invitation—ivory with brown lettering on heavy cardstock:

Please join us
as the Federal Bar Council
honors one of its most esteemed members,
the Honorable Edward Solomon,
Circuit Court Judge for the
United States Court of Appeals for The Third
Circuit

Keynote address to be presented by
Jack Solomon, Esq.

12 noon
The Waldorf-Astoria Hotel

"Can you just trust me on this one?" Noah asks. "You didn't think that you could take the lead on the Monique case, but I pushed you and you did, and now look at how well that's going. You're doing a great job, and Monique absolutely loves you. You've earned this firm a client for life."

"That's exactly what I'm talking about," I say. "I'm finally choosing life over work and I'm not going to go to this thing simply to please you. I'm sorry, but I'm done. You can fire me if you want, but I need to do what's right for me right now."

"Life over work? I didn't think that was a choice I ever forced you to make."

"I worked around the clock on the Monique litigation and it ruined my relationship. I'm not sacrificing my life for this firm any more. It's time for me to have a life."

"But that's what I'm trying to say to you, Brooke," he says, getting up from his chair and coming around his desk to sit on one of the visitor chairs beside me. When I was at Gilson, Hecht, any time a partner came out from around his desk to sit next to me on a visitors' chair, I always got an immediate sense of panic. My fight-or-flight instinct would kick in and I'd find myself perched on the edge of my seat, ready to make a quick getaway at a moment's notice.

But sitting next to Noah is different. As I look into his enormous, brown, puppy-dog eyes, I can see that he really does care for me. He is giving me honest-to-goodness advice, as if I were his little sister. We're talking friend to friend, not partner to associate.

"Listen to me, Brooke. Go to this luncheon. If you miss it, you'll never get back together with Jack, and the fact is that you guys belong together."

"No," I say, looking down at my hands, "that's just it. We don't belong together. Not by a long shot."

"Yes," he says, "you do. And everyone around you can see it. Half of the reason I hired you was because Dani Lewis over at Gilson, Hecht told me about the two of you at dinner one night. She said that you guys were in love and that firm policy would make one of you leave Gilson, Hecht. I actually wanted Jack to come, but Dani Lewis wouldn't even hear of me recruiting him, and since we're old friends from law school, I didn't even try. So we interviewed you and Rosalyn fell in love with you the minute you walked through the door. It was just a bonus that you happened to be a great lawyer, too."

"What on earth are you talking about?" I say.

"You should be with Jack," he says, "everyone knows it. I just don't know why you don't."

Column Five

You didn't hear it from us...

ARE Monique deVouvray and Jean Luc Renault headed for a reconciliation?

Insiders say that Renault's moved back into their shared Upper East Side brownstone and things are better than ever for the glamorous couple.

But if things are so perfect with the two, then why have they fired their entire house staff of twenty-two?

29

What do you call a ballroom filled with thousands of lawyers and judges?

A: The Federal Bar Council Luncheon honoring the Honorable Edward Solomon.

B: My worst nightmare.

C: [Insert your own cheesy lawyer joke here.]

Enormous signs announcing the Federal Bar Council Luncheon point us toward the Grand Ballroom of the Waldorf-Astoria, where Noah is forcing me to eat lunch today against my will. You can spare me the free salad and piece of catering-hall salmon. I, myself, have never wanted to work through a lunch before so badly in my life.

I walk in the door, flanked on either side by Noah and Rosalyn, both of whom are sworn not to leave my side the entire luncheon. Inside of two minutes there, Noah spots an in-house attorney from Healthy Foods and darts away with a pocket full of business cards to network.

"I'm much tougher than Noah," Rosalyn tells me. "You really only need me to protect you."

I give Rosalyn a smile and she holds my hand as we find our firm's table—Table Thirty-six. Rosalyn and I sit down and order iced teas just as Vanessa walks over to us.

"I'm at Table Thirty-seven!" she announces to Rosalyn and me, "how funny!"

And you thought I wouldn't see anyone from Gilson, Hecht.

I shoot a look of horror in Vanessa's direction, and she assures me that even though Gilson, Hecht bought ten tables, all of which are scattered about the room, it doesn't matter anyway, since Jack is seated on the dais with his father.

A half hour later, the salads are set on the table and the program begins. Noah sits down and mouths the words *I'm sorry* to me from across the table, but I pretend to be far too engrossed in my seven grain roll to take notice.

Jack's father's law clerk gives a stirring introduction—full of the equal parts fear and ego that you'd expect from a Third Circuit law clerk—and then Jack takes the microphone.

"Thank you all for being here," he begins and launches into his introduction. He looks around the room until he finds my table. Our eyes meet and Jack loses his train of thought for a moment. I wonder if anyone's noticed, but then Rosalyn gently grabs my hand under the table and I realize that everyone's staring at me.

"Ah, where was I?" he says. "Yes, with my father's father. That's right. Isaac Solomon was one of eight children born to his parents. He was the first of all of his siblings to come to America from Poland. He and my grandmother were only eighteen years old when they arrived at Ellis Island. He worked his fingers to the bone just so that he could afford to bring the rest of his family to this country. And because of that, there was never any money for my father when he was growing up.

"Seeing all of the struggles his own parents faced in being immigrants coming to America, my father decided, sometime in elementary school—was it elementary school, Dad? Is that how this story goes?—that he wanted to be a lawyer, so that no one could ever take advantage of him in the way that people had taken advantage of his own immigrant parents.

"My father's mother worked as a housekeeper to a wealthy family who helped get my father a full scholarship to Andover, and from there it was easy for him to get a full scholarship to Harvard. From Harvard undergrad, it was then on to Harvard Law, where he met Judge Martin, and together, they were the only two Jews in their class at Harvard. Imagine that."

Huge peals of laughter come from the more Jewish law firms, while the more white-shoe law firms smile tightly.

As Jack goes into his father's career path from large law firm to United States Attorney's office to the bench, I take a sip of my iced tea and then place my cold hand on my forehead.

"We can leave when he's done speaking," Rosalyn whispers to me. "The second the crowd starts to applaud, let's you and I sneak out the back."

"Thank you," I whisper back. I look up and see Noah staring at the two of us sternly.

"Shhh," he hisses, finger over his lips.

"He's an amazing attorney, and an even better judge, and I know that that's why everyone in this room respects him. He's my father, and I love him," Jack says, to a round of roaring applause. The judges on the dais all begin shaking Judge Solomon's hand and patting him on the back.

"I think I've had enough," I whisper to Rosalyn and we both get up quietly and walk out of the room. I don't even look at Noah—I know he would disapprove of my leaving, so there's no sense in turning around to see his disappointed face.

"Wanna go get a drink?" Rosalyn asks me as we leave the ballroom. "I think you could use a drink."

"I think I'd actually just like to go home," I say, feeling suddenly totally exhausted. "I'm ready to go home. If you think that would be okay, that is."

"Of course," she says and we walk out of the hotel. "I'm going to go back to the office for a bit. Let's go get cabs." We get on the taxi line and in seconds, two taxis pull up to the curb to let off passengers, as if on cue. Rosalyn and I say our goodbyes as we open the doors to our respective cabs. A woman wearing a large scarf wrapped around her head and enormous Chanel sunglasses that hide half of her face comes out of the cab that's in front of me, and I realize that it's

Monique, wearing the same get-up she was in that day I saw her at the divorce attorney's office.

"Monique?" I say, "is that you?" I'm not sure who's more surprised to see the other at the Waldorf in the middle of the day—her or me.

"Brooke," Monique says, "what are you doing here in the middle of a workday?"

"The Federal Bar Council luncheon is today," I say and hope that she doesn't think that I was playing hooky from work on a day that the newspapers announced that she was getting a divorce from her husband. "But, I'm on top of it, you don't have to worry."

"On top of what?" Monique asks me, eyes darting around furtively.

"Let's go inside," I say, realizing that she's checking the area for paparazzi and that I should probably be doing the same. When I got to work this morning, the place was swarming with media. Reporters immediately recognized me from the first *New York Post* article the second I stepped out of my taxicab and stuck microphones and cameras in my face as they asked me about the status of the Monique/Jean Luc divorce. I managed to eke out a tiny "No comment" as I pushed my way through the crowd to my office building, where the doorman grabbed my arm and pulled me into the building, like a lifeguard helping a little kid out of the adult pool.

Monique and I walk back into the Waldorf with our heads bowed slightly and make a beeline to the bar just off the side of the grand entranceway of the Waldorf-Astoria.

"The divorce rumors," I say, as I walk into the bar with Monique. We take the table in the corner, and I seat Monique facing the wall so that she's not easily visible to any reporters who might come in. "I was going to call you later to let you know that we are on top of it, and we are going to take care of it."

"Oh," she says, shrugging, and motioning for a waiter to come and take our order. "I saw that in today's *Post.* Would you like a drink?"

"But the story," I say. "How can you be so calm at a time like this?"

"I'm just so relieved that the dissolution of partnership didn't become public," she says, as she orders champagne for the two of us. I consider interrupting her and ordering something other than champagne, but then reconsider. Somehow it seems only natural to be drinking champagne if you're at the bar at the Waldorf-Astoria hotel in the middle of the day. "Brooke, if word had gotten out about the dissolution of partnership, that could adversely affect the company's stock. And the stock of our shareholders."

"The dissolution of partnership? I thought you'd be more concerned about your impending divorce going public."

"Divorce?" Monique says to me, taking off her sunglasses, "How silly. Jean Luc and I are not getting divorced, so there's no gossip to get."

"I saw you at Robin Kaplan's office," I say, my voice almost a whisper. "A divorce attorney's office." For a moment, I begin to panic as I think that maybe she was only there because she was designing a wedding dress for Robin, but then I look at her whole Brigitte Bardot get-up that she was sporting that day and again today and think that there's no way I could be misinterpreting what is going on.

"Oh, Brooke. That was just an impulsive French woman trying to spread her wings and see how she felt," Monique says, laughing for full effect. "I wasn't ever *really* going to divorce Jean Luc. I love him, I want to be married to him, that's the reason I want to dissolve our business partnership."

"Then what about the Lowell? Wasn't he really staying there?"

"Ah, yes," she says, looking down. "He was. But now he's back at home, where he belongs. And I'm meeting him here today for a little romantic rendezvous."

"I don't understand," I say as the waitress comes back with our glasses of champagne.

"After all these years, the one thing that I've learned about marriage is that you must keep your work life and your personal life separate. Combining the two can be a lethal combination. Especially in the case of Jean Luc and me. But we still love each other. Nothing ever changed that. And sometimes a couple needs time apart from each other. Nothing wrong with that."

"Then why is he fighting us to the death?" I ask, shaking my head side to side involuntarily.

"Men and their egos," she says, laughing, taking a sip of her champagne. "You know that, don't you? If you don't, you should probably figure it out before you get married."

"Well, that's not going to be a problem," I say, looking down into my champagne, "Since I'm not getting married now."

"But why?" she asks, look of shock registering on her face.

Without even thinking, I begin to cry and recount the whole messy story to Monique. Any time I try to stop crying, in an effort to start acting professional, the tears flow ever harder. Monique doesn't seem to notice that she's my client, not my therapist, as she listens with rapt attention, pausing for only a moment when she fishes out an embroidered antique handkerchief and passes it to me, putting her hand on my shoulder as she does so.

I've never cried in front of a client before and I pray to God that Noah doesn't find out about my waterworks being on display here today. Which could be tricky, being that he's in a ballroom just down the hall from us.

"I'm so embarrassed," I say, dabbing the corners of my eyes with Monique's hankie. "Please forgive me."

Monique stands up, motions for me to do the same, and then wraps her arms around me.

"It will be okay, my dear," she says, "it will be okay."

I regain my composure in time to thank her and hand her back her hanky. It's crisp linen edges are soaked through and through and it practically sticks to my hand. "On second thought, why don't I get this dry cleaned before returning it to you?"

"It is okay," she says, with a kind smile, "don't worry about it."

"Thank you," I say, as we sit back down at our table.

"It took me a long time, too," she says, "so don't be sorry, don't be embarrassed. It is okay."

"Took you a long time for what?" I ask, sniffling slightly, but my tears beginning to subside.

"To figure things out," she says, taking a slow sip of her champagne.

"To figure what out?" I ask, taking a gulp of mine.

"What's important and what's not."

"With all due respect, Monique," I say, "I think I know what's important. That's exactly what I've been saying—Jack isn't the man I thought he was, and I'm just cutting our losses now before anyone gets even more hurt."

"But, Brooke," she says, taking my hand from across the table, "that is what I mean. You are talking about this as if it is a business transaction. As if you thought you did your due diligence on a company you wanted to buy, and now that there are some things with the company that you don't like, so you want to cancel the deal."

"Not things I didn't like," I correct. "Things I didn't even know."

"That would be a solid argument if we were talking business," Monique says, "but we're not talking about business. We're talking about love."

Without even asking, Monique hands me another antique handkerchief about thirty seconds before I'm about to need one again.

30

I walk out of the bar with Monique and back into the hotel lobby to see her off to her romantic rendezvous with her husband. She hugs me goodbye and I give her a big hug back. In the distance, I can hear the tell-tale click of a paparazzo close by, ruining our moment. I hope that Monique doesn't hear it too, and can just go off and have the fabulous reconciliation with her husband that she deserves.

"Do you hear what I hear?" Monique asks me, furrowing her brow. Vanessa and I had wondered, back when we first met Monique, whether or not she'd had Botox injected, but now, with her brow wrinkled like a question mark, I'm sure that she has not.

"Hear what?" I ask, thinking that if we can just ignore them, maybe they'll go away. Okay, well, the paparazzi probably won't go away, but maybe she can just ignore them and go about her afternoon.

"Watch this," Monique says, a determined look on her face.

And with that, Monique marches right over to the enormous white column that the photographer is hiding behind, and pulls him out into the open by his ear, like a schoolmarm disciplining a misbehaving pupil. My mouth drops to the floor as I see that the lone photog is none other than my wedding videographer, Jay Conte. Well, former wedding videographer, but you know what I mean.

"What on earth are you doing here?" I demand, rushing over to them.

"My job," he says. "Just like I've been trying to tell your client here. I'm just doing my job."

"Is your job ruining people's lives?" I say. "Please, Jay, just go."

"Brooke," Monique asks, "you actually know this man?"

"Long story," I say, my face turning three different shades of red, "But yes."

"Ladies," Jay says, "I'll go—"

"No," Monique interrupts him, "don't go. In fact, please feel free to report that I was here. You even have my full permission to take a picture of me walking to the elevator. Let's clear things up here and now—Jean Luc and I are here together. We are back together and everything is fine again. We are meeting up to spend some time alone this afternoon in the bridal suite—yes—the bridal suite, and I don't expect you'll see us leaving the suite until tomorrow morning at the earliest. So, there you go. There is your precious gossip. I know that you would rather run blind items about relationships falling apart, but now you have your story. I am sneaking around in a hotel to spend time alone with my husband. I hope you are now satisfied."

As Monique walks away from Jay and me, I can see a spring in her step. She practically dances her way to the elevators, pulling the scarf off her head as she does. Jay doesn't take a single shot of her.

"So, I've had a tiny little matter come up that I was meaning to call you about. Do you have some time to talk now?" Jay asks, putting a toothpick into his mouth, and I roll my eyes.

"What do you think?" I say through clenched teeth.

"No problem," he says, "I'll just swing by the office tomorrow." He scurries off before I have a chance to get in another word and leaves me alone in the foyer.

Standing outside the bar, between the front door of the hotel and the ballroom where the Federal Bar Council is still being held, I'm torn as to what I should do. Monique's words mean so much to me, her actions even more, but I'm just not sure if I'm ready to walk back into that ballroom yet. As I make my decision, turning to walk out of the hotel, I hear someone calling my name. In an instant, I realize that I left without saying good-bye to Vanessa, and that it must be her, coming to check on me.

But things are never really that easy, are they? Instead, I spin around to find Miranda Foxley chasing after me. I immediately turn back around and start walking even faster to the exit.

"Brooke," she calls out. "Wait! Please just wait for one second."

She catches up to me and I turn to face her: "You are the last person in the world that I want to see right now, so please just leave me alone."

"Brooke, I understand that you don't like me," Miranda says. "But you really should hear Jack's closing statements."

"You know what, Miranda?" I say, "I think I've heard enough."

"Look, I know that you and Vanessa think I'm a horrible person. And, I guess that in many ways that I am. But I don't mean to be. I don't set out to do the things that I do. The truth is, you just can't help who you fall in love with."

"Please," I say, "*you're* going to try to lecture *me* on love now? Give me a break."

"I know," she says, "I know. I've got a crappy track record, an even worse reputation, and I deserve everything that everyone says behind my back. I've made more mistakes in my life than I care to admit, but.... Look, you can't tell me that you don't know, just as much as I do, that you can't help who you fall in love with. I know that you do—I can see it in your face right now. You want to hate Jack right now, maybe you even *do* hate Jack right now, but you're still in love with him. You still love him. And he still loves you.

"I thought it was bad when we were in discovery and he couldn't stop talking about how amazing you were and how much fun you used to have when you worked together, but now it's even worse. He mopes around the office like a sad puppy and all he really wants is to talk to you. To talk things out."

"Is everything here okay?" Vanessa says, rushing out of the ballroom and over to me. "I've been e-mailing you for the last hour to make sure you got home okay, and I didn't hear back. I was just about to hop on the Long Island Rail Road to start the search party with Mimi." And then to Miranda: "You can go. I've got it from here."

"Okay," Miranda says, "but, Brooke, please hear what Jack has to say."

Vanessa grabs me and hugs me tight.

"Do you want me to take you home?" she asks me.

"You know what?" I say, "maybe Miranda's right."

"Not possible," Vanessa says.

"True," I answer, smiling. "But still, let's hear what Jack has to say."

"Fine, but I'm coming to sit at your table," Vanessa says, grabbing my hand, and we walk back to the ballroom together.

"Oh, my God," I gasp, "is *Noah* your mystery man?"

"He's *married,*" Vanessa says. "What do you think, I'm pulling a Miranda?"

"Is that our new term for cheating?" I ask.

"It's our new term for making a move on a married man," she says. "Yes. Think of it as the new Miranda warning—you do *not* have the right to hit on a married man. Anything you do with said married man *can* and *will* be used against you by every other woman you know."

"You know what? I kind of feel sorry for her."

"I feel worse for the wives of the men she's messed around with," Vanessa says. Said like a wife who's been betrayed. I feel a tug of sadness for Vanessa and all she's been through.

"Oh, honey. Me, too. I feel terrible for the wives. What she did, what she *does,* is awful. I mean, I'm not saying that what she did was in any way excusable, I'm just saying that I feel sorry for her. It's like she just can't help but fall in love with the wrong guy."

"Are you trying to say that *you* fell for the wrong guy, too?" Vanessa asks, as we approach the ballroom.

"You know what? I don't think so, but I guess we're going to find out right now."

The double doors to the ballroom open with a swoosh and the people at the few tables nearest to the doors turn around to look at us as we quietly make our way to the SGR table. I sit back down in my seat and Vanessa takes Rosalyn's seat. Noah looks at me from across the table and smiles. He mouths the words *I'm glad you came back.*

I mouth back the words, *"Me, too."*

Judge Solomon's law clerk announces that Jack is going to be giving the closing statements, and the crowd applauds as Jack takes the mike once again.

"Thank you all for coming today to honor the Honorable Edward Solomon. My father. The man we all love and respect, and by being here today, you've truly honored him. Thank you for that." The crowd all stands to applaud. Then, as everyone begins to take their seats again, Jack turns to his father: "Dad, you've made me the lawyer I am today. The *man* I am today. You've taught me how to fight to the death in a courtroom, and I've litigated against the toughest adversaries in the jurisdiction without flinching because of it. But the one person I could never go against is you. I always thought that having respect for you meant never standing up to you, but I was wrong. Now, I think that having respect for you would actually be to show you that I've become the man you've always taught me to be. To be strong, to take responsibility for things. To stand up for what I believe in." Jack says, to a round of roaring applause. The judges on the dais all begin shaking Judge Solomon's hand and patting him on the back. The Judge's law clerk begins to get up from his seat, thinking that Jack is done speaking, but Jack doesn't move a muscle. He stays firmly planted at the mic. He runs his hand through his shaggy brown hair and takes a deep breath.

"Dad, I love and respect you, but I don't want lobster at my wedding if Brooke doesn't want it. And, Dad, if you want lobster, then that's fine, but then you won't be at my wedding, and I'll have to respect that, just as you'll have to respect my decision here today. Because I love Brooke Miller and I'm going to do anything in the world to get her back. I let my fear get in the way of the best thing that ever happened to me, and I'm correcting that mistake here and now. Being afraid cost me the most important thing in my life and I'm going to get it back. I'm going to get it back right now."

And with that, Jack jumps off of the dais and begins walking straight toward my table. Everyone stops and stares as he makes his way through the massive ballroom, straight through to my table.

I get up from my seat and walk toward him.

Finally! My real, live *Breakfast at Tiffany's* moment! You know, without the whole $50-for-the-powder-room and kept-man thing, though.

What? Wouldn't you want your *Breakfast at Tiffany's* moment to be cleaned up a bit, too?

"I want to settle," I say as we meet in the middle of the ballroom, both gasping for air.

"Being with me is settling?" Jack says. He runs his fingers through his shaggy brown hair and I can tell that he's not sure whether he should put his arms around me. "I thought that my speech wasn't half bad."

"No," I say, "Not settle on *you*. Settle with you. Our case. I want to settle our case. And then I want to marry you."

"Whatever you say, counselor," Jack says as he leans in to kiss me. And we kiss and we kiss and we kiss. And we don't care that Jack's dad is there, watching us with his mouth down on the floor. And we don't care that we're standing in a room full of judges and lawyers. We kiss and it's like the rest of the world has ceased to exist.

I'm vaguely aware that as we stand there kissing, some people in the crowd begin to clap. Soon, it becomes a roaring applause and I detach myself from Jack's face long enough to look out and see everyone standing up and applauding for us.

I turn around to see Jack's father standing and applauding

for us, too. He then grabs the mike and says: "Jack, I'm very proud of you. I'm proud of the man you have become. So, if you and Brooke don't want lobster at your wedding, then I don't want it, either. And Brooke, if I've done anything to offend you and your family over the last few months—well, it sounds like I've done a lot to offend you and your family over the last few months—I truly am sorry. I hope that you all will see fit to forgive me.

"I really am happy that Jack's found a woman like you, and my family would be lucky to have you as a daughter-in-law. Beauty and brains, that's our Brooke!"

"Of course we forgive you, Judge Solomon," I call out, hoping that it's loud enough for him to hear.

"Why don't you try calling me Dad?" Judge Solomon says, and the crowd begins to applaud again.

I am *so not* calling that man Dad anytime soon.

"Now, I think that I've got a conflict of interest here," Jack's father says. "So, who's going to marry these two for me?"

A voice booms from the back of the ballroom. Large and commanding, it's a voice that doesn't need the assistance of a microphone. I turn around and see a familiar face: Judge Martin, walking toward us, yelling, "I will!"

You didn't hear it from us...

WHAT former model turned fashion designer was seen canoodling with an unidentified brunette at a midtown hotel for an afternoon rendezvous? Onlookers say they stopped in for a drink and tearfully declared their love for each other before embracing out in the open, just before sneaking off to a room.

Could this be why her husband moved out of their Upper East Side brownstone a few months ago?

31

We're all squashed into Judge Martin's chambers for an impromptu wedding ceremony the following week. After having swept me off my feet the week before, Jack informed me that he refused to take another chance that I might get away from him, and insisted on marrying me as soon as humanly possible.

Which turned out to be the following Tuesday—the day we were supposed to go to trial.

We've turned the three rooms that make up Judge Martin's chambers into an ad hoc wedding hall, with his personal chamber being used for the ceremony, his law clerk's office being used as the bride's room, and his assistant's office in the middle, which connects the two, as a long, makeshift wedding aisle. Our immediate families and best friends are crushed into Judge Martin's chamber, standing room only, while they wait for me to make my entrance.

I'm out in the law clerk's office, just waiting to be called into the ceremony—not quite walking down the aisle, but more of walking down the hallway, if anything—and do one final check for my something old, something new, something borrowed and something blue.

My something old is Jack's grandmother's engagement ring, which I took immediate repossession of from his coat pocket the second we left the Waldorf-Astoria.

Oh, please. As if the diamond ring wouldn't be the first thing on your mind the second you got the guy back.

My something new is a custom-made wedding gown made lovingly stitch by stitch by Monique. Apparently, when I took on her case and then told her that I couldn't buy her dress since it would be a conflict of interest, she decided right then and there that she would make it anyway and give it to me as a wedding gift. She kept throwing me off the scent by fitting me for fake muslins whenever I came to meet with her at her brownstone, but she ended up making me the exact dress that she sketched for me that first day in her studio. Good thing Jack and I ended up back together since I seriously doubt that you can resell one-of-a-kind couture. Especially one-of-a-kind couture that's a size ten.

My something borrowed is the pair of ruby earrings that Vanessa decided to buy from Moishe that day we went wedding ring shopping. They look absolutely perfect, especially since I've got my hair tied up loosely and they peek out from the waves falling down from the top of my head. These earrings also satisfy my grandmother and Aunt Devorah to no end, both of whom insisted that I wear at least *something* red, so as to ward off the evil eye which would undoubtedly be following me on my wedding day.

My something blue is the baby-blue garter that my mother wore at her own wedding. And as a special wedding gift to me, she didn't even say a word about the fact that the fit was a bit snug, to say the least.

Vanessa has been taking her maid of honor duties very seriously, and in addition to having *the* Vera Wang whip up gorgeous navy bridesmaids' dresses for her and Jack's sisters at the last minute (another favor courtesy of her mother), she also insisted that, as maid of honor, she be allowed to plan the reception. So, we'll be heading over to her mother's downtown art gallery after the ceremony for the reception. ("She lives for this stuff and would actually be offended if you *didn't* have it there.")

She also (as part of her duties, of course) did me the favor of posting bail for my wedding videographer, *yet again* (yes, that's two federal arraignments in the course of one engagement, for those of you who are keeping count), since I felt that it wouldn't help relax me to have to go down to the Manhattan Detention Center *yet again* just days before my wedding. Unfortunately for Vanessa, these charges were much more serious than the last—something about filming someone's honeymoon down in Mexico and sticking some contraband into his camera case—so, Vanessa actually ended up referring the case to one of our friends from law school who practices criminal law. But on a lighter note, now my mobster wedding videographer owes Vanessa "a solid," should she ever choose to cash it in. She was none too pleased about the whole situation, solid or no solid, to be sure, but she did it with a smile since she's such a good maid of honor.

(Note to self: Must look into whether or not the solid I owe Jay can be traded for the solid that Jay now owes Vanessa. There really should be somewhere to look this sort of stuff up on the Internet.)

"You ready to go, BB?" my father asks me as Judge Martin's assistant buzzes us on the law clerk's intercom to let us know that it's time to come into the judge's chamber.

"For God's sake, Barry," my mother says, "why are you asking her that? Do you want to give her *another* chance to run away?" And then to me: "We're going."

"Let's go," I say, and then we do.

Jack breaks the glass with his foot and we are officially husband and wife.

"You may now kiss the bride," Judge Martin says and Jack takes me into his arms and kisses me. I can feel a camera flash go off as we kiss and I have a feeling that this will be one of those perfect photos that you keep framed in your house forever and ever. And then it becomes a family heirloom and eventually your kids all fight over who will get to keep it since they all chipped in equally for that really really *really* expensive sterling silver picture frame from

Tiffany's for your thirtieth wedding anniversary and then they all start laughing about that funny story when Mom and Dad fought and almost broke up while registering at Tiffany's and then they all forget what they were even fighting about in the first place. You know, a picture like that.

Sorry. I just get a little worked up at weddings.

But we kiss and we smile and then, there being no aisle for Jack and I to then walk down, we simply spin around into the arms of our families and friends.

With all that we went through with the planning of our big formal wedding, we never once considered what it was that *we* actually wanted as a couple. Did we want the traditional Long Island temple wedding that my parents dreamed of, with our friends and family close, and God, undoubtedly, that much closer? Or did we want the fabulous, splashy Manhattan hotel wedding, with a fancy wedding planner, designer food and guest list that read like a Manhattan phone book?

As I look around Judge Martin's chambers, with his various diplomas and certificates on the wall (papered and painted circa 1979), institutional carpeting and run-down leather couch and visitors' chairs, I can't help but think that what I got was the most perfect wedding in the world.

"You're married!" Vanessa calls out, grabbing me for a hug. "I can't believe it!"

For so long, it was Vanessa who was the married one, and

me as the crazy single friend, and I'm just so happy that she's got someone new in her life to share this day with her. I just couldn't be as happy as I am today if I thought Vanessa felt lonely or sad.

"So when is this mystery man of yours going to show his face?" I whisper into her ear.

"He's actually meeting us after the ceremony at my mom's art gallery," Vanessa says. Her face is glowing as she says it.

"Meeting your best friend and your parents at the same time?" I ask. "You are truly one brave woman."

"I have a feeling that it'll be okay," she says, looking down.

Judge Martin's intercom goes off and his assistant announces that our cars are here, ready to take us to Millie's gallery for the reception.

"Our chariots await!" my father calls out as we each file out of chambers.

There's something incredibly sexy and fun about being downtown at the federal courthouse—where I normally wear my most conservative suit—being all dressed up in my wedding dress instead. Sort of like that time I went to a friend's wedding in Chicago and we all went out at 3:00 a.m. after the wedding, still in our formal wear, to go and get authentic deep-dish pizza. Vanessa said that she felt that way, too, in her gorgeous custom-made bridesmaid dress.

When I told this to Jack, he suggested taking the subway downtown to make my fantasy complete. Instead of screaming at him *Have you lost your goddamned mind, you idiot, even suggesting such a thing? I don't even take the subway when I'm wearing fancy jeans, much less my wedding dress!* at the top of my lungs, I simply told him that I didn't need the subway to complete my fantasy, since my fantasy was complete by being married to him.

See how good I am at being a wife *already?*

32

It is an old Jewish custom, dating back to the time of Rebecca, that the bride and groom must go to a private room after the wedding ceremony and be alone for the first time. Since Jack and I were living together for almost a year before our wedding, we most certainly have had occasion to "be alone" together, but, nonetheless, my father made sure that, the second we got to the art gallery for the reception, we went back into Millie's office to have our time in the *Yichud*.

"We're finally married," Jack says, as he grabs me and gives me a kiss. It's not the sweet and innocent and totally family-appropriate type of kiss that he gave me in Judge Martin's chambers. This kiss is serious, earnest, burning—downright smoldering. It's a kiss that tells me everything I need to know about the type of life we are going to have together: Jack loves me and always will.

And I love Jack and always will.

We kiss shamelessly for God knows how long when finally one of us realizes that it might be bad form to spend the whole of your wedding making out with your new husband in your best friend's mother's art gallery office. It's actually Jack who says it, because I don't really see a problem with it.

"We're finally married," I say to Jack as I touch up my lip gloss in the reflection of Millie's huge floor-to-ceiling window. You'd think a former model like Millie would be vain enough to have a mirror somewhere in her office....

"You didn't think I'd let you get away from me again?" Jack says.

"I was hoping you wouldn't," I say, turning around to look at my new husband. "I was really hoping you wouldn't."

Jack and I finally walk out into the reception and I'm awestruck by how Millie's created such an ethereal space out of her art gallery. Sure, it's in a huge penthouse loft in Tribeca, with fourteen-foot ceilings and views looking out to the water that make you feel like you're in a movie. Sure, it's all exposed brick and original wood, framed perfectly by its many picture windows on each of the four walls. But, for the reception, she's taken out the huge eight-foot white walls, normally arranged like Stonehenge, on which the art is displayed, and has replaced them with tables dressed in crisp white linens with chairs dressed to match. She's got tiny little white lights strewn across the ceiling, making you feel like you're outside on a crisp summer's night.

I see Vanessa from across the floor with her father and the new guy she's dating. I'm shocked to see that this new guy is actually someone I know. The new guy is also someone who her father already knows. It's someone Vanessa knows, too. Very well, I might add.

Her husband. Well, ex-husband as the case may be, but the fact remains that Vanessa's here with Marcus. And they're holding hands and giggling like two children. Two children who are madly in love.

Jack and I walk over to the other happy couple of the evening and say hello.

"Congratulations," Marcus says to me. "May I kiss the bride?"

"Of course," I say.

As he leans over to kiss me I look over his shoulder at Vanessa. She just shrugs and laughs.

"May I kiss the bridesmaid?" Jack says and gives Vanessa a big hug.

"I'm the maid of honor!" Vanessa says.

"I beg your pardon," Jack says, "May I kiss the maid of honor?"

"Because I didn't do all this," Vanessa goes on, throwing her arms out wide so as to indicate that she's talking about the reception, "to *not* get top billing."

"Of course you get top billing," I say, just as a waiter

breezes by with a platter of mini hot dogs. Jack and I both grab one at the same time.

"These are my favorite," I say, dipping my mini hot dog into the mustard and then grabbing for a cocktail napkin. I have to do a double take when I look at the monogram—BSJ—for Brooke and Jack Solomon.

We are officially husband and wife.

"Mine too!" Jack says, dipping his mini hot dog into the mustard and then popping the whole thing into his mouth.

"I know," Vanessa says, smiling. "A good maid of honor does her research."

And she had. In fact, all of Jack's and my favorites were there: a potato bar in one corner, a caviar station in the other, tuna tartar and tiny vegetable dumplings being passed around by elegant waiters in pristine white jackets, and even a martini bar.

And then, of course, there's lots of kosher meat, lovingly supplied by my dad.

As Jack and I approach the prime rib carving station, I overhear my father trying to convince Jack's mother to taste a tiny piece of his meat.

I assure you, this conversation does not sound even *half* as dirty as I just made it out to be.

And, anyway, get your mind out of the gutter, you horn dog, I'm talking about my wedding day here, for God's sake!

"It's kosher," my father pleads. "It's blessed by a higher power."

"That's really not the issue, Barry," Joan says, eyeing a crudité platter nearby.

"Then what is the issue?" he asks, "I'd really love for you to love my meat."

Okay, yes, I admit, that last part does sound a bit off.

"I just like to watch my weight," Joan says, running her hands across her hips without even knowing it.

"It's your son's wedding," my father says, lowering his voice and talking to her like he's a high-school senior who's got a freshman girl in his car after curfew. "Live a little."

"It's not just that, Barry," she says. "I've had a lifetime struggle with my weight, and sticking to a vegetarian diet is really the only way I've found that helps me to keep the weight off."

"Is that what it is?" my father asks. "My Mimi eats my meat all the time and still stays thin as a rail. I can get you some really lean cuts that are low in fat, but will load you up with protein, so that you don't feel hungry when you're dieting."

After then assuring her that her figure is gorgeous anyway, my father promises to get Joan what he called his "Mimi cuts" that would help her to diet more effectively. I could have sworn that I later even heard my mom giving Joan some of her best diet tips.

Which is odd, seeing as she never really shares them with me.

The band begins to play and Jack puts his hand out for me to take. I can't help but recall that other time that Jack and I danced at a wedding—when we were at my ex-boyfriend's wedding and I was pretending that Jack was my Scottish fiancé so that I could keep my dignity ever-so-slightly intact.

(Long story.) It was at *that* wedding, on *that* dance floor, that I realized that Jack was the man of my dreams and that I wanted to spend the rest of my life with him.

We've had countless ups and downs since that night—too many even to think about—but we finally made it here. To the day of all days. Our wedding day. Where we're dancing as husband and wife, and I truly couldn't be happier.

Now, here, in the middle of Millie's art gallery, I look around the room and see friends and family. All of the people who mean the most to us in this world. My parents, Jack's parents, Jack's sisters and brothers-in-law and Vanessa… All here for us. To celebrate this day with us.

It may not be the Pierre Hotel in Manhattan and it may not be a temple on the South Shore of Long Island, but all in all, I couldn't have had a more perfect wedding if I'd actually planned it myself.

It is the happiest day of my life.

New York Times
Vows

Brooke Miller and Jack Solomon

Brooke Miller, 30 (some sources put the bride's age at 28, but a quick call to her undergraduate school confirmed her age as 30), daughter of Marty Miller and Miriam "Mimi" Miller of Long Island, New York, today married Jack Solomon, 36, son of the Honorable Edward Solomon and Joan Solomon. Ms. Miller, who could not decide as of the time of this printing whether or not she'd be keeping her maiden name, is an associate at the Manhattan law firm Smith, Goldberg, and Reede ("I'll probably be making partner, like, any second now," says the bride), and Mr. Solomon is a partner at the law firm Gilson, Hecht and Trattner, also based in Manhattan. Miller and Solomon first met when they worked together as associates at Gilson, Hecht and Trattner (although, as the bride explains, "Nothing inappropriate happened when we were working together at all! But it was, of course, so obvious that Jack was completely, madly, desperately in love with me!"). Miller later left the firm, after a stunning victory in the Healthy Foods false advertising case, to become an associate at SGR, and the two began their relationship. ("Please don't tell my 82-year-old grandmother that we were living in sin before we got married! She will literally die, and do you really want that blood on your hands?" the bride joked.) The wedding ceremony was held in the chambers of the Honorable Harold Martin, an old law-school crony of the groom's father. Judge Martin's chambers hold special meaning for the couple—it was during a case in his chambers that the couple temporarily broke up. "We all knew they'd be getting back together," Vanessa Taylor, Miller's maid of honor, explained. "It was just a matter of time until Brooke realized it herself." The reception was held at the art gallery of Taylor's mother—former model and sixties "it" girl Millie—and catered by the bride's father, owner of Miller Kosher Meats on the South Shore of Long Island. "Best chops on Long Island!" says the father of the bride, and in the humble opinion of this reporter, I can't help but agree.

Epilogue

"Oh, my God, Vanessa," I say, staring at her as she comes out of the fitting room, "you look so beautiful I think I'm going to cry!" And then, since I'm not the type to let a good occasion to turn on the waterworks pass, my eyes begin to tear up.

"Please don't cry," Vanessa says.

"You just look so beautiful," I say, dabbing at a tear.

We're at Monique's townhouse where Vanessa's trying on muslins for the wedding dress that Monique will be making Vanessa for her wedding to Marcus. (Her *second* wedding to Marcus, for those of you who are keeping count. And if you're my mother, yes, it's her second wedding to a doctor. And I haven't even married *one* doctor yet. Now, I know Marcus isn't a Jewish doctor, but still, in my mother's eyes, a doctor is a doctor is a doctor).

"I hate it," Vanessa's mother, Millie says, "take it off." And then, to Monique, "do you have anything with capped sleeves? It would hide how—how—skinny her arms are." She whispers the word *skinny* as if, though standing two feet away from her, Vanessa cannot hear her.

"I can hear you. And I'm not skinny," Vanessa counters, "I'm a runner."

"When we were models, we had curves." Millie says to Monique. And then, to Vanessa: "Maybe you should stop running a few months before the wedding. Just to let yourself fill out a little."

"I don't need to fill out," Vanessa says to no one in particular. I offer Vanessa the glass of champagne Monique served us when we walked in, but Vanessa shakes her head "no."

"Maybe Brooke can give you some tips," Millie says. "Honey, what do you do to keep your curves so nice and curvy?"

"I eat raw cookie dough straight from the roll when I'm upset." I offer, going for the rest of Vanessa's champagne, but Vanessa's got it before I do and downs the whole thing in one gulp.

"You know," Millie says, "when I got married, I was Yves Saint Laurent's muse."

I excuse myself to go to the ladies' room just as Vanessa is formulating an answer to her mother. Something about inheriting the brains of the family instead of the hips.

It's strange, but for the past month I haven't been able to kick this stomach flu that's been going around. Sure, since

I began taking the lead on cases at my law firm, I've been busier, but I don't think that I'm so run down as to be ill for a whole month. Or maybe it's the stress from becoming so incredibly important to the firm. Now that I'm running cases on my own, I'm sure I'll be making partner any day now. Surely that must be it.

"I was the same way when I was pregnant with Vanessa," Millie says as I walk out of the bathroom and back into the showroom.

"But, I'm not pregnant," I say, laughing. I subconsciously put my hand over my stomach. Sure, it's not as flat as it used to be, but in my new role as perfect little wife, I've been cooking for Jack and myself just about every night, and everyone knows when you cook a lot, you tend to taste everything.

Okay, okay, well, not so much as *cooking* every night as ordering in and then putting it onto paper plates. But I'm sure to put it onto very *fancy* paper plates, thank you very much! And I already told you that I'm becoming absolutely indispensable at my firm, so I really don't have much time to be home cooking all the time, so get off my back, would you?

And, anyway, my husband seems to think that I am a woman of many *other* talents, so there.

So, I certainly don't have any time to be barefoot and pregnant. Which I'm not. And I most certainly do not *look* pregnant, thank you very much! And even if I was, I wouldn't be barefoot. I'd be pregnant in, like, totally cute shoes.

"Yes," Millie says, "you should never tell anyone before your first trimester is up. But we can quietly look for a matron of honor dress that is expandable."

"I don't need an expandable dress," I say.

"She's not pregnant," Vanessa says, grabbing my hand and standing by my side.

"Do you think you and Jack will find out if it's a boy or a girl?" Monique asks, getting up from her sketch pad and joining in on the conversation.

"I'm not pregnant!" I say.

"Are you kidding?" Millie says to Monique. "She's clearly having a girl! Just look at her face."

They both lean in and examine my face as if they were scouts for Elite Model Management. Just what any normal woman wants: two gorgeous former models examining every square inch of her face at close range.

"What's wrong with my face?" I say, feeling my hand fly up to my face without even thinking about it.

"Well, you know what they say," Millie explains, "when you're having a girl, it steals your beauty."

"Okay, that's it," Vanessa says, thrusting her body, skinny arms and all, between Monique and Millie and me. "She's not pregnant. She's still beautiful, and more importantly, today's really all about *me.* So, please focus."

"I don't mean that you're not beautiful, Brooke," Millie says, to me, "it's just a saying. It's an old wives' tale that when you're having a girl, your nose gets wider."

My nose? Isn't it enough that society drives us crazy about

our weight? That we endlessly obsess about our thighs and our butts and our tummies? Now we have to worry about how wide our *noses* are?

Vanessa and I retreat to the fitting room to try on another muslin. As Vanessa steps into a strapless A-line with a fishtail, she whispers, "You'd better not be pregnant. You were supposed to wait for me to get pregnant!"

Yeah, right. As if I want to wait to be pregnant with a woman whose biggest problem in life is that she's just too darn skinny. (I can just see it now—Vanessa's mom: "Why isn't your tummy getting as big as Brooke's?" Vanessa: "Because we're only two months along." Me: "That's just the way my stomach looks naturally." I don't think so....)

"I just thought it would be fun to take one of those things, don't you?" I say, as I unpack the premade chicken parmesan that I picked up at Bernard's Market on Third.

"You thought it would be fun?" Jack asks, getting out the plates and silverware.

"Yes, Jackie, fun!" I say, laughing. Really, since getting married, sometimes Jack can be such a fuddy duddy!

"Remind me what's fun about taking a pregnancy test again?" Jack says, furrowing his brow.

"Well, I've never taken one, have you?" I ask. Jack regards me for a moment and I quickly explain: "I mean, a girlfriend of yours or anything."

"There was this time in high school," Jack says, "and then once in college. No, wait, twice in college—"

"You know what, forget it," I say, and make my retreat to the bathroom.

I shut the door and put the pregnancy kit down on the sink. I look up at myself in the mirror. Having a girl steals your beauty. How ridiculous!

"How can you possibly be pregnant?" Jack asks me as I come out of the bathroom. "Aren't you on the Pill?"

"Well, yes, Jackie," I say, "I am. And I take it every day."

"But…" Jack says. "I can tell there's a 'but' coming up."

"No 'buts,'" I say, "I mean, there *was* this one day a few months ago, though, when I popped a Pill out of the container and it went flying into the sink and then down the drain. So, I suppose that I did skip just that one day. But, that's okay, because I took it every other single solitary day that month, so I'm sure that it didn't really count. I'm sure there's residual Pillness left from all those other days that I took it, so I was covered."

"Um, no, Brooke," Jack says, running a hand through his shaggy brown hair, "I'm sure there's not. That's why you're supposed to take it every day."

"Well, I do take it every day," I say, looking off out the window. "Almost every day."

"Almost?" Jack asks, turning my head back to face him.

"No, every day!" I assure Jack. "Except that once. Most of the time, to be sure."

"Most of the time?"

"Is the time up yet?" I ask Jack.

“No,” he says, “three more minutes.”

We both sit and stare at the digital clock on the microwave oven.

“So,” Jack says, grabbing my hand but still staring at the microwave clock, “I guess this means I should start looking into the baby Manolo thing, huh?”

Acknowledgments

Thank you to Sherry and Bernard Janowitz, my parents, whose love and support means the world to me. A big thank you also goes out to my brother, Sammy, and sister-in-law, Stephanie. (And, heck, my nephew, Noah, too, whose cuteness undoubtedly inspired me.) I am so fortunate to have all of you in my life.

Thank you to Mollie Glick, my amazing agent. I am so lucky to have you—your constant support and guidance help me to become a better writer every day. You are a truly wonderful agent and have also become a great friend. Am I supposed to be having this much fun working with my agent?

A big thank you goes out to the fabulous team at Red Dress Ink. Thanks to Adam Wilson and Margaret Marbury for your endless support and inspiration. It was so sweet of you to invite Brooke to the party again! Thanks to Don Lucey and Megan Lorius for your fabulous PR skills. Your tireless efforts mean so much to me.

Special thanks goes to everyone at Mediabistro, especially Jessica Eule, who forces me to teach class after class on creative writing. And, of course, Mara Piazza for throwing the best book launch parties a girl could ask for.

Thank you to Grandma D for being one of my earliest readers and for letting me borrow your maiden name once again.

Many thanks to Shawn Hecht and JP Habib. Special thanks go to Selina McLemore, Danielle Schmelkin, Aunt Myrna, Robin and Jeff Kaplan, Jen and Scott Kaplan, Lauren Lindstrom, Cousin Melissa Kraut, Cousin Brandon Kraut, Jessica Shevitz Rauch, Greer Gilson Schneider, Esther Rhee, Donna Gerson, Tami Stark, Kim (Trattner) Kramer and all of my great relatives and friends who make my life so wonderful on a daily basis. Big thanks go out to everyone at Barnes and Noble in Chelsea and Philly, Books and Books in Florida, the JCC in Manhattan, Makor/92nd St. Y, the Cornell Club, Justine Reichman and Twilight at Vzones.com and the many book clubs who supported SCOT. It was so much fun to meet all of you!

And, of course, thanks to the Luxenberg family: Judy and David; Jen, Lee, Spencer, Oliver and Ruby; Stacey, Jon, Jordan and Ethan. I'm so excited to join your family on May 25th!

And last but not least, thank you to my honey, Doug Luxenberg. Who knew when we were walking the halls of Lawrence High School together that we'd end up here? I love you.

xoxo,

Brenda

Questions for Discussion

1. Brooke and Jack litigate the biggest cases of their respective careers against each other, and Monique and Jean Luc work in a business partnership with each other. Is it ever a good idea to mix business with pleasure? Have you ever had a relationship with someone you worked with?

2. Brooke begins to question whether or not Jack is really the man she thought he was. Do you ever really know the person you are in a relationship with? If so, how long does it take? Do you ever really know yourself?

3. Which would you rather: to finally find love after you've turned thirty and have had to endure bad date after bad date for years, like Brooke, or to have found love when you were eighteen, and then lose it and have to start all over again, like Vanessa?

4. When Brooke and Jack's families meet, they do not get along. This concerns Brooke, but Vanessa assures her

that you marry the man, not his family. Do you think that you marry just the man, or that you marry his family, too?

5. When Brooke and Jack go to look at flowers, Maximo gives them each a penny to throw into the pond and make a wish. What do you think that Brooke wished for? What about Jack?

6. Do you think that Brooke and Jack's marriage will last? Why or why not? What about Vanessa and Marcus? Monique and Jean Luc?

7. Miranda tells Brooke that you can't control who you fall in love with. Do you think that this is true? Have you ever fallen in love with someone who you shouldn't have?

8. If you were to make *Jack With a Twist* into a movie, who would you cast as all of the major characters?

9. This story is narrated by Brooke. How would it be different if it was told from Jack's point of view?